MISSING SUSAN

Also published in Large Print
from G.K. Hall by Sharyn McCrumb:

The Elizabeth MacPherson Novels
Sick Of Shadows
Lovely In Her Bones
Highland Laddie Gone
Paying The Piper
The Windsor Knot
Bimbos Of The Death Sun
If Ever I Return, Pretty Peggy-O

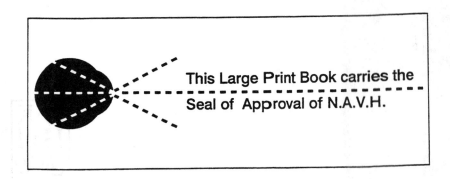

This Large Print Book carries the
Seal of Approval of N.A.V.H.

MISSING SUSAN

An Elizabeth MacPherson Mystery

SHARYN McCRUMB

G.K. Hall & Co.
Thorndike, Maine

Published in Large Print by arrangement with
Ballantine Books, a division of Random House, Inc.

G.K. Hall Large Print Book Series.

Printed on acid free paper in the United States of America.

Set in 18 pt. Plantin.

Library of Congress Cataloging-in-Publication Data

McCrumb, Sharyn, 1948–
    Missing Susan : an Elizabeth MacPherson mystery / Sharyn
McCrumb.
        p.   cm. — (G.K. Hall large print book series)
    ISBN 0-8161-5566-6 (pb)
    1. MacPherson, Elizabeth (Fictitious character)—Fiction.
2. Women detectives—Great Britain—Fiction. 3. Large type books.
I. Title.
[PS3563.C3527M57 1993]
813'.54—dc20   92-46703

For the ladies and Milton;
with thanks to Phyllis Brown,
of Grounds for Murder bookstore;
and especially for Martin Fido,
who knows where the bodies are buried.

SOME OF THE INFORMATION on true crime in this book is derived from *Murders After Midnight* and *The Murder Guide to London*, both by Martin Fido.

CHAPTER 1

"I love my work and want to start again."
Letter from Jack the Ripper
September 25, 1888

WHITECHAPEL

IN A DINGY and antiquated district of east London called Whitechapel, the shivering drabs huddled against a faded brick wall, thinking of Jack the Ripper. It was twilight, and a piercing March wind tore through Whitechapel Road, cutting into the bone-chilled mass of humanity camped outside the tube station (District and Metropolitan lines). In the dim circle of light, they clumped against the old building, seeking shelter, ignoring the wino collapsed in a nearby doorway, and talking in hushed tones about the infamous Ripper: the un-caught killer of five women in this dreary stretch of London's East End. The more knowledgeable ones speculated on the identity of the dreaded killer, debating whether they would have been clever

1

enough to elude his deadly grasp. Others wondered if they had been wise to brave the dangers of Whitechapel in the bitter chill of night. The rest, numbed by the gathering darkness, merely waited.

From the shelter of a nearby shop, cupping his last cigarette of the twilight hour, he watched them, sizing them up as a wolf might survey a flock of Dorset ewes. There were a good many of them tonight, despite the cold. They came every night, even when slags of rain turned the alleyways into a sodden blur. His eyes narrowed as he singled out the likely ones: the young, the vaguely pretty, or, if all else failed, the flashy ones on the make. After a few moments study, he could surmise which of them traveled alone, which were timid and eager to please, and which might be more trouble than he cared to have. Eliminating the latter from his reckoning and concentrating on the first two requisites, he decided that the group offered three or four possibilities. The choice would narrow down as the night wore on. He was ready now. He knew them as well as he cared to. They were always much the same in Whitechapel. Night after night, rain or hunter's moon: much the same.

He threw the smoldering remnant of the cigarette on the pavement, ground it out with his heel. His eyes never left them. Hurry, before the cold drives the weak ones back into the Underground. He drew one last anticipatory breath. Ready now. Move in for the kill.

Striding briskly toward the milling crowd, he raised one hand above his head and motioned for them to gather round. "Good evening, ladies and gentlemen!" he said in his heartiest stage voice. "Welcome to the Jack the Ripper tour. My name is Rowan Rover, and I am your guide for this evening. That will be three quid, please, everyone!"

A bewildered woman in a Penn State ski cap rummaged through her purse and held out a handful of coins. With Olympian dignity Rowan Rover indicated the proper currency and intoned, "That will be three of the little round bronze ones, madam. Yes, they are rather like your American quarters, aren't they?"

◆ ◆ ◆

JACK THE RIPPER, the Scourge of Whitechapel, killer of five aging prostitutes in the autumn of 1888, had been abstaining from

3

mayhem for one hundred and one years and four months, but his sinister presence was still felt in the east London thoroughfares between Houndsditch and Brick Lane. He was, in fact, a cottage industry, supporting—within his native borough—an inordinate number of tour guides, crime enthusiasts, T-shirt makers, and pub owners. Indeed, had a superannuated Ripper appeared on the old turf, brandishing his bloody knife and proclaiming his guilt, the local residents might have been impelled to call the police, but many would also have felt obliged to stand the old boy a round of drinks while awaiting the law's arrival.

Rowan Rover, tour guide and criminologist extraordinaire, owed much to Jack the Ripper. Not that he approved of butchering women, you understand—he himself was a ladykiller only in the metaphorical sense—but in an intellectual way, he had always been interested in tales of true crime, particularly in the enigmatic Jack. A century after the fact, the abomination of the Whitechapel slayings had dimmed to a nostalgic and scholarly absorption in criminology's greatest mystery. Besides, the public's morbid fascination with history's most famous serial killer had enabled a poor but clever Oxford alumnus to escape the thin gray line of academia (in Wisconsin, Guyana, and Sri Lanka) after years of teaching English lit to the unwashed, the unpromising, and the uninterested; and to return to his native England in untenured triumph.

Rowan Rover had thus escaped the wrath of two ex-wives (the third lived perilously close—in Glasgow—but you couldn't have everything), and he had put his upper-class English lecture voice and his teaching skills to more glamorous use: leading murder walks around London and giving seminars on English true crime. It was steady work: the Ripper tours drew a crowd in even the most inclement weather; and the exercise of a two-mile walk five nights a week had kept him as fit as a man half his age, despite his incessant smoking. It was not, however, an inordinately profitable way to earn a living, educating tourists at three pounds a head. Still, it provided him with a subsistence, an admiring audience to buy his book and to stand him drinks at the pubs he cleverly wove into each evening's walk, and an occasional one-night stand gleaned from the pack of sightseers. No danger of one of those tourist birds becoming Wife

Number Four; most of them were due to leave London only hours after their brief encounter, probably returning to husbands or lovers back home. Rowan Rover was always the first to agree with these birds that traveling did not actually count as part of one's real life.

It was an agreeable existence, all in all. Or it would have been, if he could have catered to his own pure and simple needs and left it at that. Unfortunately, as an older Oxonian, Oscar Wilde, had put it: "Life is rarely pure, and never simple." In Rowan Rover's case, the complications involved child support payments to Wife Number Three; hefty public school fees for Sebastian Melmoth Rover, his son by Wife Number One; and some expensive recaulking required by Rowan's boat, in order to keep afloat the residence that allowed him to live in London without paying the rates demanded by the city's demented estate agents. He lived in a cabin cruiser moored at St. Katharine's Dock, an abode roomy enough for one person, yet sufficiently cramped to discourage any woman from wanting to share it for more than a day or two. Now, though, thanks to a harsh winter in corrosive Thames water (which contained God knows what, these days), the boat needed repairs, or else Rowan might find himself sharing a locker with Davy Jones. And Sebastian's school fees were to be raised by ten percent beginning next term.

These debts looming on his personal horizon were of such magnitude that they didn't bear contemplation. It was useless to think that giving up the odd pack of cigarettes or setting aside his pub money would stem the tide of insolvency. Before the summer was out, Rowan Rover stood in actual danger of having to go out and secure a real job. Or at the very least, a teaching position. This prospect so profoundly depressed him that he resolved not to dwell on his financial situation if he could possibly help it. He had purchased a book called *Do It Yourself Boat Repair*, but its illegible technicality had only increased his despair. Life, he told himself, had been simpler in the Ripper's time, what with no income tax, and drinks to be had for a penny. Doubtless the Ripper would have agreed with him. In 1888 there had been no fingerprinting or DNA testing. Why, in those halcyon days a man could get away with murder.

THE TOUR BEGAN at the Whitechapel tube station, thus allowing tourists from all over the city a convenient means of transport to the starting point. It was also ideally situated for introducing a note of delicious dread at the onset of the tour. A few yards from the entrance to the Underground was a narrow alley leading to Durward Street; it had been called Bucks Row a century ago, when Polly Nicholls' mutilated body had been discovered there with her throat cut. The Whitechapel residents had petitioned to change the street's name a few weeks after the murder of Nicholls, the first of the Ripper's victims.

Rowan Rover made his introductory remarks where the group convened on Whitechapel Road, giving a general overview of the Ripper tale, for those tourists who had only a vague idea of the case.

"Isn't it a bit anachronistic to have us arrive by subway?" asked a Canadian professor.

Rowan Rover attempted to disguise his sneer as a cheery smile. "Actually, the Metropolitan Line of the Underground was completed in 1884," he said with the briskness of one to whom the question has become a commonplace. "That's four years before the murders occurred. Jack himself might have used the tube you just arrived on." *Unless you're daft enough to think he was the Duke of Clarence,* he finished silently.

Having thus intimidated the self-styled experts in the party, Rowan continued his spiel. "In the autumn of 1888, a killer who was to become known as Jack the Ripper killed five prostitutes. No, not seven"—he added with a nod to the waving hand at the back of the group—"we'll go into that later. That left approximately 79,995 common prostitutes still alive and busy in the East End of London at that time. It was a dreadful time and a dreadful place. Let me give you an idea of what it was like." He proceeded to paraphrase a few shocking anecdotes from Jack London's *Children of the Abyss,* touching on the thirty thousand homeless, the workhouses, and the living conditions of the nineteenth century poor. Rowan took pride in imparting social awareness in addition to the prurient thrills of the tour.

"There are those who contend that the Ripper was a social reformer," he told them. "At the time, George Bernard Shaw wrote a letter to the *Star* stating just that. Certainly the Ripper did more to focus attention on the East End than all the do-gooders in all the charities combined. The murders forced the authorities to pay attention to the appalling conditions in the slums, and some aspects of East End life actually improved as a result of the Ripper's work."

The staring crowd digested this thought in silence. Finally a woman said hesitantly, "Do you think . . ."

"That the Ripper was a zealot with a social conscience?" asked Rowan Rover. "No. That's complete rubbish. Move along now, please."

After discouraging more of the usual anticipatory questions about the identity of the Ripper, he led the group to the alley where the evening's sightseeing—and the murders—began.

"It was here that Jack the Ripper met his first victim: Mary Ann Nicholls. Polly, as she was known. She was nobody's idea of a beauty. Fortyish. Looked sixty. Sallow complexion, mouse-brown hair. Five teeth missing from a brawl with another prostitute. He led her away from the busy Whitechapel Road, and through this alley to

Buck's Row." Rowan Rover shepherded the group through the narrow passage.

He liked to linger in the squalid confinement of the brick-lined alley, urging his charges to get the feel of the East End as it once was, in all its unsavory glory. The ammonia stench from the encrusted walls usually warned the tourists to keep their distance, but in case they were too preoccupied to notice, he was always careful to admonish his flock not to touch the walls as they passed through. Less respectable pedestrians than themselves visited that alleyway for reasons that wouldn't bear thinking about, he told them, nodding toward another wino. After his warning, they proceeded single file, making narky comments about the local citizenry.

Still, he was glad for a bit of sordidness at the beginning of the tour, because the fact was that the dreadful slum of the Ripper era had almost completely disappeared. In place of the grimy clusters of tenements that had once harbored the East End poor, there were now newly erected brick office buildings, and wide well-lit streets, much to Rowan's regret. It didn't make his job any easier. After a couple of double Scotches at the Ten Bells, Rowan Rover had been heard to remark that if the White-chapel district had any interest in preserving the unique character of their infamous tourist attraction, they should tear down all those characterless modern office buildings and put up rotten, reeking tenements. That's what tourists wanted to see when they came to Whitechapel! Failing civic co-operation of such magnitude, Rowan had to darken the tour as best he could with dramatic descriptions of the bygone squalor, and by reciting, with BBC solemnity, graphic accounts of the Ripper's handiwork. He set the tone of the murder walk in the longish trek from Buck's Row to Hanbury Street, where the body of Annie Chapman had been discovered in the backyard of Number 29, one week after the Nicholls' murder. The death site is now occupied by Truman's Brewery, just opposite a nice tandoori restaurant.

By now Rowan Rover was beginning to size up his audience. There was the usual assortment of Americans, crime buffs, adventurous Londoners, and earnest Japanese tourists. He had recited the particulars of the Ripper tour so often that he could conduct it almost entirely on automatic pilot, so that while the group was hearing him say, "Annie Chapman's face was bruised and the tongue protruded from her mouth. She had also been disemboweled . . ." he was actually thinking: Three more minutes until we reach the Ten Bells. Must take care not to sit with that beefy woman who wants to talk about her sodding Duke of Clarence theory. The Welsh chap looks like he might stand me a drink, but what about the lovely blonde in the Burberry? She's been dogging my heels since we started. I could ask her back to the boat on the pretext of discussing . . .

A hand touched Rowan Rover's arm, startling him to full consciousness. He turned to see a tall, well-dressed American regarding him with an expression of quiet urgency. Rowan had mentally tagged him The Businessman, and wondered what had possessed him to come on a Ripper tour. He wasn't the usual type; at least, not without a teenager or a few tipsy colleagues in tow.

"Mr. Rover, I wonder if we could have a talk before the evening is over," the man said, in a voice one degree above a whisper.

Various scenarios flashed through Rowan's mind: the man was a publisher, soliciting a Ripper book; he was a journalist doing a Ripper article and wanted a contemporary slant; he had a boat of his own and his taste in companions differed markedly from Rowan's. A closer look at this solemn middle-aged gentleman convinced him that none of these theories was correct. *What the hell did he want?*

Rowan summoned a polite smile. "Why, certainly," he said. "The tour will conclude at a pub in Aldgate, and perhaps you'd care to stay on after that and chat." He regretted having to part with the idea of trying his luck with the blonde, but his curiosity had got the better of him. As long as the proposed conference was confined to the Aldgate pub, and the businessman provided the drinks.

The man smiled back. "That will be fine," he said. "I'll talk to you then."

After the Chapman death site, the tour took a half hour intermission so that the freezing tourists could rest their feet and thaw out. The scene of the rest stop was the Ten Bells Pub in Spitalfields, where Ripper victim Elizabeth (Long Liz) Stride was seen drinking on the night that she later turned up murdered in Berners Street. Rowan ushered his charges inside, explaining in a voice of careful neutrality that while

14

the pub had been called the Ten Bells at the time of the Ripper murders, its name had subsequently been changed, and it had until recently been called the Jack the Ripper Pub. A group of protesters had succeeded in forcing the resurrection of the original name on the grounds that a pub named after the Ripper encouraged violence against women.

"Too bad," said an American college boy. "It would have been awesome to get a picture of the pub sign. Maybe a T-shirt."

A British matron in tweeds gave him an icy glare. "How would you Yanks like a fast food restaurant named after Ted Bundy?" she demanded.

During intermission in the Ten Bells, Rowan Rover had a double Scotch with a contingent of Manchester sightseers, and the talk inevitably turned to Murderers I Have Known. Rowan, who hadn't known any, listened politely to the woman who lived two blocks from Myra Hindley and her friend, who claimed that the 1970s Yorkshire Ripper had gone to school with her second cousin Vivian.

"Have you ever met a real killer, Mr. Rover?" asked the woman in the Penn State ski cap.

The guide shook his head. "Modern murder doesn't interest me much," he said. "Especially not the mob sort of killing-for-hire. I prefer to study the nineteenth century cases, when crimes were committed in style—by amateurs. The old murder tales have atmosphere and the trappings of tragedy. Today it's all *News of the World* pathos. Besides, all these modern murderers of yours are failures, aren't they?"

The woman blinked. "Failures? What do you mean?"

Rowan smiled with Scotch-fueled mirth. "They got caught. I think that we'll never know who the truly interesting modern killers are. If they're really good, they won't be arrested. In fact, the best ones will make their killings look accidental so that we'll never know they murdered anyone at all."

Through his glass, as he drained it, he saw the American businessman give him a nod—and the barest of smiles.

◆ ◆ ◆

THE REST OF the tour was uneventful. In Whites Row the gaggle of tourists had stood between the children's wear shop and the multistory car park while Rowan Rover described the Ripper's last and most terrible

16

murder: the killing of Mary Ann Kelly in the no-longer existing Dorset Street. His voice rose and fell with ominous intonation as he detailed the horrors of the Kelly death scene. Forgotten were the modern buildings and the drone of distant traffic. The listeners stood spellbound, peering inside a phantom, firelit hovel on Dorset Street, crimson with the evidence of the Ripper's handiwork. Rowan Rover, who preferred not to let his attention dwell on the anatomical atrocity of the Kelly case, was on automatic pilot again. Next came the graffiti and the bloodstained apron stops, and then Mitre Square—not the last of the murders, but a geographically convenient place to end the tour, near the Aldgate tube station. Then would come the summing up, and the inevitable questions. Who was it, then? *Who was Jack the Ripper?*

Rowan Rover dutifully presented the evidence, patiently explaining why the group's favorite suspects were simply not on. ("Madam, the Duke of Clarence was in Scotland at the time of the murders. How do you suppose he managed the four-hundred-mile commute?") Occasionally, though, he longed to alleviate his own boredom by announcing, "Oscar Wilde was

17

Jack the Ripper! Let me tell you why!" Or Lewis Carroll. Or Ellen Terry. Anybody, really. He could trump up a case against practically anybody who was in London in 1888, and ninety percent of the tourists would depart convinced that whoever he chose was undoubtedly the murderer. But the habits of scholarship die hard; one does not lark about with one's chosen subject.

Every evening, Rowan resolved to denounce a new and improbable suspect, and every evening by the time he reached the final pub stop, he found himself telling the group the truth as best he knew it. He knew from experience that so many tourists were disappointed to have their pet theory dashed that he refrained from actually stating "This was the Ripper." Instead, he outlined the most sensible theories, gave the evidence for each, and left the group to draw their own conclusions. Those who wanted further enlightenment were encouraged to purchase copies of Rowan Rover's book *Murders in Whitechapel,* copies of which were kept for him in the Aldgate pub.

This time he dismissed the temptation to fabricate without a moment's consideration. The American businessman wanted to talk to him after the tour. He might be a movie producer planning a Ripper documentary. Surely such things paid well. Rowan Rover resolved to provide a memorable finale.

As he ended the tour, a drizzle of rain began to fall, making the streets glisten, and chilling the tourists past caring whether Montague John Druitt had an alibi or Sir William Gull a motive. Some of them trooped off to the tube station; the rest followed their guide to the pub, where they bought him drinks, purchased his book, and insisted on his autographing it, while they chattered happily about themselves and their reasons for taking the tour. Through all this, the American businessman sat quietly in the corner, drinking a Bloody Mary, and listening without apparent interest. Rowan Rover held court with his customary charm, wistfully eyeing the blonde, and wishing that he could afford a life of simple lust. After a quarter of an hour, and two more double Scotches, the last of the tour group said their goodnights, and, *London A-Z* street directory in hand, they made their way back toward civilization.

As the door closed behind the gaggle of

departing sightseers, the American businessman picked up his drink and sat down
beside Rowan Rover. "Interesting tour," he
said. "You do it quite well."

"Thank you," said Rowan, attempting a
modest smile. "I've often thought of doing
a lecture tour in the States. I'm quite an
authority on other nineteenth century
crimes as well, you know."

The man nodded. "So I'm told. I believe
you have been hired by British Heritage to
lead a three-week murder tour of the south
of England in September."

"Oh, are you interested in that?" asked
Rowan, cursing himself for giving up a
chance at the blonde. "Yes, I think it should
be rather amusing. First-rate accommodations, of course, and lovely country. I suppose there are a few places left on the tour.
I could tell you whom to contact, if you
like."

The man seemed not to have heard him.
He looked about to see if anyone was in earshot, but the other patrons of the pub
seemed preoccupied with their own conver-
sations. Thus reassured of the privacy of
their discussion, he said quietly, "Mr.
Rover, my name is Aaron Kosminski, and
I have a business proposition for you. It will

require some discretion on your part, though."

Rowan Rover endeavored to look as if the conversation was making sense to him. "Oh, yes?"

"I have done a bit of checking up on you, and I know that you might not be averse to making some quick money. Say, fifty thousand dollars?"

Rowan, who had guessed at the current dollar exchange rate and was multiplying furiously, nearly forgot to nod.

"I thought so," grunted the business-man. "With your ex-wives, your boat, and your paternal obligations, you seemed to be a good prospect for the job I have in mind. Also you're an expert on murder."

"You want me as a consultant for an American film?" guessed Rowan hopefully.

"No. Something much more important, Mr. Rover. My niece is going to be one of the people on your September murder tour. I want you to kill her."

CHAPTER 2

*"If you've got a nice fresh corpse,
fetch him out!"*
—Mark Twain,
Innocents Abroad

EDINBURGH

ELIZABETH MACPHERSON (now Mrs. Cameron Dawson and newly endowed with a Ph.D. that she would brandish at the slightest provocation) had reached that post-honeymoon stage of matrimony when a young woman's fancy lightly turns to thoughts of murder.

"What do you mean you'll be gone six weeks?" she demanded of her hitherto satisfactory husband.

"Well, it was something I agreed to in June before our rather"—Cameron coughed delicately—"*hasty* marriage was decided upon. It didn't seem sporting to back out on my hosts when they'd got it all settled. So, barring serious objections or obstacles from you—your imminent death from tuberculosis comes to mind—I said that I would go."

"That seems reasonable," Elizabeth agreed, remembering somewhat guiltily her insistence on advancing the wedding date so that she could attend the Queen's Edinburgh Garden Party. "But when you said you were going, did you mean alone?"

"Well, hardly that," said Cameron with that little laugh one gives to assure tigers that one is completely inedible. "There will be a whole boatload of other marine biologists, but since this tracking business is rather a specialty of mine, and because of that journal article I wrote, they very kindly asked me—"

"It won't work," said Elizabeth, setting aside the copy of British Heritage that had, till now, been claiming her attention. "You are hoping to burble on in this fashion for hours until I fall asleep or lose interest in the discussion entirely, aren't you?"

"Certainly not." Cameron glanced at his watch, then toward the television. "Although I should point out that *Spitting Image* comes on in ten minutes."

"You're sure they have no room for a deckhand, or fish cleaner, or something? Because I haven't anything to do just now—"

"I know," said Cameron. "But there's not a lot of space on the boat, and they've restricted the group to scientists. We'll even do our own cooking."

Elizabeth sighed. "Well, it was worth a try. This is what comes of having a two-career marriage. You have to go chasing sea lions all over the Atlantic, and I'm stuck at home cutting up dead bodies. Or I would be, if anyone would let me."

"People will get nervous if you go around saying things like that," Cameron told her. "Remember that Edinburgh was the home of those renowned body snatchers Burke and Hare."

"They were amateurs," said Elizabeth. "I am a forensic anthropologist. They could be self-employed. *I* can't. Still, I have applied to all the appropriate potential employers. I suppose something will turn up eventually."

There didn't seem to be a correct response to this, since Cameron knew very well the calamity that would require the services of a few extra specialists in corpse identification. He smiled encouragingly to show sympathy with his wife's professional frustration.

She sighed again. "So I'm to be stuck at

home like Penelope while my lord and master sails the high seas."

"Yes," said Cameron. "Although I hope to be back nine years and eleven months sooner than Ulysses. And you must admit that Edinburgh in September is an alluring place to be stuck in."

He looked around at the old-fashioned flat in Edinburgh's New Town (which was built by Robert Hutchinson in 1819). On short notice Cameron's brother Ian, with his real estate connections, had managed to find this dwelling for the newlyweds to sublet. It belonged to a retired barrister who was spending a year abroad. Elizabeth, who refused to live in anything that had been built after the Boer War, loved the high-ceilinged rooms, with their molded ceilings, and the fireplace she insisted was an Adam. She settled down happily amid the chintz and polished oak, and spent much of the early evening composing thank-you notes to those who sent belated wedding presents by sea mail. They were only just arriving, and Elizabeth was becoming a skilled diplomat, refraining from explaining the AC/DC electrical inconsistency to toaster givers, and managing not to write: "Thank you very much indeed for the set of carving knives. I have decided to use them only at home." Cameron assured her that his elderly cousin, a minister in Aberdeen, would find the letter most unfunny, so she settled for a more conventional bride's reply, leaving forensic anthropology out of it.

The only thorn in all this wedded bliss was that Elizabeth had not yet managed to find a job, and she was not keen on being the only housewife in the building with a doctorate in anthropology. She realized that a specialized subject such as hers made it more difficult to find employment than, say, a cocktail waitress, but she had not given up hope. Cameron, meanwhile, was back at his old job, happily communing with mammalian sea creatures, and using his free time to go sightseeing with his restless bride.

"You're right," she said, flipping idly through her magazine. "Edinburgh isn't a bad place to be stuck in at all. It's wonderful after the festival closes and all the bloody tourists go home, but after all, I've seen most of it. Especially"—she added with a mischievous smile—"Halfords." Cameron's fondness for auto parts stores was a family joke. "Anyway, why should I stay in Edinburgh? We don't even have any plants to water."

"I hadn't thought about it," said Cameron. "Where would you like to go?"

Elizabeth was examining the advertisements in the back of *British Heritage*. "Murder?" she said aloud.

Oh no, thought Cameron. *She's going to Ireland.*

She held the magazine closer to the light. "Listen to this: 'A murder mystery tour of the south of England. Why bother with old churches and rose gardens when the game is afoot, Watson? Visit all the sites dear to a crime-lover's heart: the scene of a king's murder in the New Forest! Daphne DuMaurier's Jamaica Inn, an ancient smugglers' haven! See the infamous Dartmoor Prison!' That sounds wonderful! Don't you think so?"

"Let's hear the one about the rose gardens," said Cameron.

Elizabeth made a face at him. "Only if you'll promise to go seal hunting in the Commonwealth Pool."

Cameron took the magazine and read the advertisement carefully. "It seems all right," he said with limited conviction. "Reputable company; interesting stops; de-

27

cent accommodations. I don't see what trouble you could get into." He sighed. "Though you always manage somehow."

"But this is a tour," Elizabeth reminded him. "It's like being on a leash."

"True. And you'll probably be traveling with two dozen blue-haired Boston matrons."

Elizabeth's eyes danced. "But I'll be visiting crime scenes!"

"A century after the fact. Perhaps it will be fun. Is Jack the Ripper on the agenda?" He studied the itinerary. "Yes, last thing, apparently. I'm beginning to wish I could go with you."

"I wish you could, too," said Elizabeth. "But I'll take lots of pictures. And if I find any really wonderful places, we can go together later." She held out her hand for the magazine. "Let me have it back so I can get the address. I'm going to send a deposit right away."

"So you don't mind my going off on the seal expedition?"

"What?" said Elizabeth, diligently copying the postal code. "No. Poor you. It will probably rain the entire time you're out there. Whereas I shall be on the English Riviera."

Cameron turned up the volume of the television to catch the beginning of *Spitting Image*. I suppose Jack the Ripper can't be all bad, he thought to himself. I have a feeling that he just saved *my* life.

CHAPTER 3

*"An Englishman thinks he is moral
when he is only uncomfortable."*
　　　　—George Bernard Shaw

THE THAMES

IN THE TINY sleeping quarters of the boat
Morvoren, beneath the sheet of polythene
that substituted for the missing part of the
coach roof, the captain was preparing to
abandon ship. His suitcase lay open on the
bunk, and various items of apparel were
strewn about on every flat surface, awaiting
consideration by their distracted owner,
who seemed inclined to fill up his case with
books instead of clothing.

Rowan Rover looked reproachfully at
his selection of summer trousers as if
holding the garments personally responsible for their unfashionable condition.
His late employment in tropical Sri Lanka
had left him with a superfluity of light-
weight trousers, which, given the few
weeks' wear per annum allowed by the

English climate, threatened to outlast the millennium. They had been purchased at that unfortunate period in the history of couture when flared trousers were in fashion, and the ridiculousness of this bygone splendor no doubt contributed to their dogged indestructibility. He *could* have consigned them to the rubbish bin, and invested in more elegantly tailored apparel, but since financially and philosophically he could not bring himself to dispose of usable clothing, he had attempted to improve their appearance by narrowing the trouser legs himself, an act he undertook with more zeal than skill. Thus, he occasionally appeared to have one leg thicker than the other.

The trousers were in need of other types of alteration as well, because, as the years wore on, his girth increased, causing the trousers' zippers to slip inexorably out of a securely closed position. After one disastrous attempt at trouser-widening, resulting in the complete destruction of the garment, he had given up the prospect of further do-it-yourself tailoring, and he now relied on safety pins inserted in the fly below the desired level of the zipper to protect him from embarrassing moments. He liked to think that no one noticed these little economies.

Rowan Rover selected two pairs of trousers, tan and black, and folded them carefully at the bottom of the suitcase, tossing on top of them as many shirts and undergarments as would fit without disturbing his cache of books: a British Heritage guidebook of Britain, a road atlas, a volume of English folklore, and a pocket encyclopedia of true crime.

The Murder Mystery Tour of Southern England would begin tomorrow, September 5, when he was scheduled to meet his charges—and the coach and driver—at Gatwick. The weather promised to be perfect. The English summer had been unseasonably warm (if this be global warming, make the most of it, he thought, paraphrasing an early American patriot), and current forecasts promised sunshine and balmy breezes for the next few weeks. Hence the need for his tropical wardrobe. In case the weather forecast was as inaccurate as usual, he would take sweaters.

He glanced at the list of people signed up for the tour: a dozen Americans, mostly from the West Coast, and one Scotswoman named MacPherson, from Edinburgh. It was the third name on the list that gave him pause: Susan.

His encounter with Mr. Kosminski (whom he still thought of as The Businessman) on the Ripper tour last March had faded in his memory to the insubstantiality of a bad dream. He had mentioned it to no one.

He remembered sitting in the Aldgate pub, making polite after-tour chitchat with the American, thinking he was about to be invited to lecture at some university, when, in the middle of his sip of Scotch, the man had plumped out his request: that Rowan Rover should murder his niece on the September mystery tour.

Rowan's initial reply had been a coughing fit, as a swallow of Glenlivet took a wrong turn down his throat in the tension of the moment.

Aaron Kosminski smiled, while endeavoring to look concerned. "Can I get you a glass of water?" he asked pleasantly.

Rowan Rover shook his head, unable to trust his throat to produce words. He took several deep breaths, interspersed with more coughs, before he managed to wheeze out a reply. "Sorry. I must have misunderstood you. Were you talking about one of those murder weekends with actors, by any chance? I don't do those."

"I don't blame you," said Kosminski. "They always struck me as rather undignified." He glanced around to make sure that Rowan's coughing fit had not attracted any undue attention. Satisfied on this point, he continued, "I was, in fact, proposing that you should—how shall I put it?—practice what you preach. Confirm your morbid and childish fascination with murder most foul. Why don't you give it a try? See what it's like. It could give you all kinds of insight in your chosen profession."

Rowan Rover stared at the man in amazement. He was the calmest and most reasonable of persuaders. Just so must the New York killer David Berkowitz have explained to the police about his neighbor's dog, Sam, who told him to go out and shoot people. Kosminski had the serenity of Edmund Kemper, apologizing for accidentally touching the breast of the kidnapped woman he would murder an hour later. Rowan had met loonies before, but never one so cheerfully secure in his delusions.

As if reading his thoughts, Aaron Kosminski, still smiling, shook his head. "I assure you that I am quite sane," he said. "After all, psychotics go out and commit their own murders, don't they? They don't hire people to do it for them. What I am suggesting to you is a simple business proposition, made to someone of good reputation—finances aside—who has no motive for causing the death of a total stranger from another country. That seems straightforward enough."

Rowan Rover hazarded another sip of his Scotch. "You want me to kill your niece."

Kosminski fingered his butter-soft leather gloves with a thoughtful expression. "Perhaps I could rephrase it. My niece Susan will embark on your murder tour of England this fall, and I would like her, while on this tour, to have a fatal accident, which shall be viewed by the police and all concerned as a regrettable but wholly unavoidable mishap. In return for your orchestrating this event, I am prepared to pay you the sum of fifty thousand dollars, whatever that happens to be in pounds at the time of the transaction."

Rowan Rover blinked. "Why do you want to kill your niece?"

Kosminski sighed. "It is apparent, Mr. Rover, that you have never met my niece.

But apart from aesthetics, the answer is the usual one: money. Dear Susan, her personal failings aside, has inherited the family money from her doting, but misguided grandfather. My father, a shrewd businessman, but with a dangerous flaw of sentimentality."

"No family resemblance there, then," said Rowan cheerfully.

Kosminski ignored the interruption. "Rather than sensibly investing this money into the family business, my niece Susan has decided to—as she puts it—retire."

"How old is she?"

Kosminski's frown deepened. "Thirty-six."

"I see. So she has a good bit of time in which to frivol away the family fortunes."

"We rather hope not, Mr. Rover," said Kosminski with a piercing stare. "That is where *you* come in."

Rowan squirmed under the businessman's earnest stare. "Pardon my curiosity," he said timidly, "but why bring me into this? Surely as an American you have access to any amount of professional assassins."

Kosminski sighed. "Not in Minneapolis," he said, in the tone of one who is loath to admit his hometown's inadequacies. "Besides, hit men usually use guns, making it all too obvious that a murder has been committed. That would mean an investigation. What we want is an unfortunate accident. And the farther from home the better."

"Preferably in rural England, I take it."

"Precisely. When Susan announced that she wanted to waste yet more of her inheritance on this frivolous mystery tour, I came over to make inquiries. A background check on the proposed guide indicated that you might be eminently suitable for our purposes, and that the offer of a large sum of cash might be most welcome."

"A large sum of cash is always welcome," said Rowan evasively.

"This much money should last you a good while. That is, if you don't invest in any more wives," said Kosminski with a nasty smile.

"No, it's a bad habit," said Rowan. "I've forsaken it. I smoke now instead. Packs and packs a day. Would you care for one? Cigarette, I mean. Though I've wives to spare as well."

"Fifty . . . thousand . . . dollars," said Kosminski slowly.

Somehow, between the double Scotches and Aaron Kosminski's quiet insistence,

Rowan Rover had found himself tentatively agreeing to accept employment. It had seemed rather logical at the time. After all, the tour was months away, and just as likely to be canceled as not. Besides, Kosminski had done a thorough job of researching his prospective assassin. When the preliminaries were over, he had produced a budget of Rowan Rover's projected yearly income, offset with his ominous new expenditures. The resulting deficit was so crushing that murder seemed a small price to pay to make it all go away. By the time Kosminski had finished his murder talk, and was advising his hired assassin on sound investments and the virtues of a strict budget, the whole interview had assumed the surreal quality of one of Richard Jones' well-planned practical jokes. Rowan had found himself agreeing as if the conversation were part of a script. In time, the incident became just another pub conversation.

Until today.

Today he found in his mailbox a business envelope bearing American postage stamps, with a post office box for a return address. Inside the envelope was a cashier's check for ten thousand pounds, and a note that said, "Remainder upon completion of the task. Bon voyage. A.K."

So it hadn't been a practical joke, after all. That gave him pause. For several minutes he stood there with the letter in his hand, staring stupidly into space while he considered all the implications of the message. How could he possibly have allowed himself to get mixed up in such lunacy? Finally he put the letter aside, and withdrew the rest of the mail from the box. There was the usual assortment of bills, a window-enveloped letter from the bursar's office of Sebastian's public school (marked URGENT), and a circular from a company that specialized in boat repair. Rowan Rover glanced at his watch. There was still time to deposit the cashier's check before the bank closed. At least that would eliminate all his nagging financial problems, leaving him with one enormous moral one: the contemplation of murder.

Now, ten thousand pounds richer and on the verge of paying his debts, he was solvent, but no less apprehensive. He began to contemplate his next course of action. "After all," he told himself, as he nervously rearranged the books in his suitcase, "I am an authority on murder. I've written books on British murder cases. Don't I stand up and tell people that if Crippen hadn't used hyoscine—of all the improbable poisons!—he'd have gone free? Don't I laugh when I talk about that stupid solicitor Herbert Rowse Armstrong, who kept inviting his enemies to tea long after they'd begun to notice that having tea with Herbert gave them stomach cramps symptomatic of arsenic poisoning? And he paid for his stupidity on the gallows, right enough." The thought of the gallows was chilling, but, after all, Britain had abolished capital punishment in the early Sixties, and, much as the public wanted it back when they caught the Moors Murderers, it had stayed abolished. No worries about the hangman, then.

Rowan Rover was an expert on every tantalizing murder Britain had ever seen. He knew who was caught and why, and in most of the so-called unsolved cases, he knew who had done it and how they managed to get away with it. This knowledge was, after all, the reason he had been engaged to host the September murder tour. "If I wanted to," he told himself cautiously, "I'm sure I could get away with murder. I've been studying it all my life."

Then in his best imitation of American

ex-president Richard Nixon, he shook imaginary jowls, and said, "But it would be wro-ong!"

He picked up the paperback encyclopedia of crime and stared at its cover, a collage of murderers' faces, all very ordinary and respectable-looking. "Still," he said thoughtfully, "it would be interesting to see if I could stage a convincing accident. I could certainly name a few killers who managed it. I wouldn't mind seeing if I could get away scot-free."

Suddenly he pictured his own face adorning the cover of a future edition of the encyclopedia of crime: the carefully dyed black hair, the distinguished bulbous nose, and his dark eyes narrowed into the menacing slits indicative of a merciless killer. It didn't bear thinking about. He buried the offending volume beneath a couple of handkerchiefs in the suitcase, then turned his attention to the *Guide to England*. It was all very well to speculate on the fanciful, but his immediate responsibility was to lead a well-researched and entertaining tour for the travel company. They, after all, might wish to hire him again. Whereas the Kosminski offer was, while generous, hardly the thing he would wish to turn into a career.

(He pictured himself in a cell next to the surviving Kray twin, swapping grisly business tips. No, definitely not a career.)

He took out his tour itinerary and hotel brochures, supplied by his employers. There were to be eleven travelers, and, judging from the names, ten of them were women. After he met them, he could make decisions about how strenuous the tour could be. If most of them were upwards of seventy, then he must curb his desire for three-mile walks before lunch. Also, before he planned a detailed list of places to visit, he must gauge their knowledge of and interest in true crime. (Would they want to see the pond where Agatha Christie began her famous disappearance? Or would they want seamier stuff—the field near Alton where Sweet Fanny Adams was dismembered in 1867, thus giving the Royal Navy a new slang term for canned meat? Truthfully, Rowan Rover hoped for the former: the case of poor, young Fanny Adams sickened even his Ripper-hardened soul.)

The tour would begin with a two-night stay in Winchester, in the hotel next to the cathedral. From there he could plan day-trips to nearby places of interest. He consulted the atlas to see what locales lay within an hour's drive of Winchester. He wouldn't think about Susan just now, he decided. There would be time enough to worry about that once he got the tour well under way. Besides, Rowan Rover was from Cornwall; Hampshire was not familiar country to him. Accidents would be much easier to arrange on home turf, he thought. Wait until we get to the West Country. The phrase *poor Susan went west* sprang unbidden to mind, and he actually laughed out loud—before the implication of the entire plan sent him pawing through the guidebook for safer subjects to contemplate. He found the assassination of Thomas à Becket at Canterbury; the Peasenhall case: throat-cutting in Suffolk; ritual sacrifices at Stonehenge. No matter where he looked, it all came back to murder.

CHAPTER 4

*"Let him go abroad to a distant country;
let him go to some place where he is not
known; Don't let him go to the Devil,
where he is known!"*

—Jonathan Swift

GATWICK

"EXCUSE ME," SAID Elizabeth MacPherson to the nearest Gatwick airport official. "I just got off a plane. Do I have to go through customs?"

The guard, or whatever he was, paused in mid-dash to consider her question. "Where did you fly in from?" he asked.

"Edinburgh."

The man gave her a pitying smile. "Then it won't be necessary, ma'am. Scotland is a part of this country, you see."

It was on the tip of Elizabeth's unrepentant Jacobite tongue to snap back, "Well, it oughtn't to be!" But she realized that airport officials take a dim view of unsanctioned patriots, and that such a reply could lead to an unpleasant half-hour search of herself and her belongings, on the off chance that she was that rarest of political animals: a Scottish terrorist. In any case, the man looked much too harried to be interested in a discussion of Bonnie Prince Charlie and the Rebellion of 1745, so she smiled sweetly, hoisted her bags, and hurried away to find the airport lobby.

It would be several hours yet before all of the tour members' planes arrived, since they had set out from half a dozen different cities. Elizabeth, the only one not flying in from the United States, had arrived just after nine in the morning, which gave her at least four hours to wait for the coach and guide, scheduled to meet the party at two o'clock. The rendezvous point for the murder mystery tour was to be the luggage carousel on the first floor of the airport. Until then, lacking name tags with which to identify each other as fellow travelers, the early-arriving tour members would prowl the airport shops and restaurants, killing time until someone came to collect them.

Elizabeth first looked round all the eating places, marveling at the exorbitant food prices. Although she had been in Scotland for a little over two months, her mind still ran on the U.S. currency system, which, at the current exchange rate, meant doubling the stated price of everything, in order to get an emotional understanding of how much anything cost. Inevitably, the short answer was: too much. She read the McDonald's sign with an expression of disbelief usually reserved for UFO sightings.

"They're charging *four dollars* for a hamburger!" she muttered. "I wouldn't pay that if they were making them out of last year's Derby winner."

Similar responses to menu prices in Edinburgh had caused Cameron to remark that after only eight weeks in residence, she was out-Scottishing the Scots. Elizabeth replied that it was culture shock, and began muttering threats about CARE packages whenever she went out shopping.

"Anyway," she said, turning her back on the metaphorical golden arches, "the last thing I want to eat in Britain is American food. I'll go back to the cafeteria and have tea and scones."

The return trek to the upstairs restaurant took longer than it should have, because the hallway led past Elizabeth's main weakness: a row of gift shops. Her cousin Geoffrey liked to remark that had Elizabeth been aboard the *Titanic,* she would have checked the gift shop for a Going Out of Business Sale before proceeding to the lifeboat. She glanced at an enticing window display of Beefeater teddy bears and scenic linen towels. It wouldn't hurt to browse for a little while, she thought. It's not as if I'm short of time.

Once inside she went straight to the postcard rack, assuring herself that she was only looking, because it would be stupid to buy postcards in the airport on the first day of a three-week tour. Well, maybe just a couple, to give herself a head start on correspondence. There didn't seem to be much point in attempting to correspond with Cameron, who would be at sea for five more weeks, annoying the seals of the north Atlantic. "Perhaps you could toss a note in a Guinness bottle into the sea at Land's End," he'd suggested, when she brought up the subject of writing. To which she replied that there'd be enough Guinness bottles aboard the research vessel without her contributing to the supply.

With Cameron incommunicado, the list of correspondents dwindled to her parents, her brother Bill, her insufferable cousin Geoffrey, and her new in-laws. She was searching the postcard rack for cards suitably impertinent for Bill and Geoffrey, when a tall young woman beside her picked up a postcard portrait of Princess Diana and said, "Back in the States we have a mystery writer who looks just like her!"

Elizabeth was unable to think of a reply to this gambit, and she wasn't entirely sure that this total stranger was addressing her. (There is nothing worse than replying to a stranger's pleasantry, only to discover that the intended recipient of the remark is the person standing directly behind you.)

She smiled vaguely to indicate polite disinterest, then went back to studying the postcards.

"You're American, aren't you?" the woman persisted.

Elizabeth, suspecting insult, longed to reply in the negative, but such an accusation is difficult to deny with a Virginia accent. She took a long look at her interrogator. The woman was the personification of Cheerleader: shoulder-length blonde hair, trim figure, and a perky beauty-pageant smile. Just the sort of person that Elizabeth wished the Japanese would hunt, instead of whales. She summoned up a chilling smile. "I'm from Virginia. How did you guess?"

The woman shrugged. "You just look American, I guess. Anyway, you're wearing a fairystone necklace, and you can only get them in Virginia. They're a natural crystal formation, right? Only found in the mountains. I know because I traveled the Blue Ridge Parkway with my parents when I was twelve."

"Good detective work," said Elizabeth grudgingly, fingering her staurolite necklace. She made a mental note to give fairy-stones to every British woman she knew next Christmas. (Take that, Sherlock!)

"I guess some of it rubbed off," came the complacent reply. "I read a lot of murder mysteries."

Elizabeth stared at her and at last the penny dropped. (Or, at the current exchange rate, two cents did.) "Are you, by any chance, with the murder mystery tour that's meeting here this afternoon?"

"That's right!" said the woman, beaming. "My name is Susan Cohen. Are you on it, too?"

Elizabeth nodded slowly. "Elizabeth MacPherson," she said, withholding her title in a rare gesture of modesty. "Where are you from?"

"Minneapolis," said Susan eagerly. "Have you ever been there? It's in the Midwest, but it isn't at all provincial like the coastal people think it is. It's the most gorgeous city in the world."

Elizabeth managed to refrain from asking why Susan had bothered to leave this Shangri-la for a mere excursion to England. "I'm from Virginia originally," she said, "but I just got married in July, so now I live in Edinburgh. For a while, at least. We're still negotiating careers."

Susan looked around. "But your husband didn't come on the tour?"

"No," said Elizabeth. "He had better fish to fry." She explained about the oceangoing expedition, and the six-week separation that she decided to fill with a package tour. She looked appraisingly at the youthful Susan. "So I'm not manhunting or anything on this trip. In fact I was sure that everyone else on this tour was going to be much older than I."

"I expect they will be," said Susan Cohen complacently. "After all, we can't all be heiresses."

We all are so far, thought Elizabeth, mindful of the receipt of her great-aunt Augusta's money which came to her upon her marriage. She didn't think it was a topic you ought to broach with strangers in an airport, though. "I was just going to get some tea," she said.

"Great!" said Susan, cheerfully abandoning the postcards. "The airline breakfast was lousy. The French toast tasted like they made it with Play-Doh. I'm going to write a letter of complaint to the airline."

They started off together down the hall, dodging baggage-laden passengers. "It sounds like a very interesting tour, doesn't it?" said Elizabeth.

"The perfect combination," Susan agreed. "I just love England, and I love mysteries. My uncle Aaron says that my house will probably collapse under the weight of all the books I have. See, I used to read *all* the time. I mean all the time. I was an only child, you know, and I didn't have a lot of friends." She laughed. "I guess I was kind of an ugly duckling."

Whereas now you are a nonstop parrot, thought Elizabeth. But, she had to admit, a pretty one. Aloud she said, "You seem to have made a satisfactory transition to swandom."

"I know. Isn't it amazing? After Grandpa Benjie died and left me a fortune, one of the girls down at the library where I worked—her name was Claire, and she was the children's librarian—anyway, Claire said, 'If I were you, I'd take some of that money and become gorgeous.' And I thought to myself, 'Well, why not?' Because in Minnesota, even though it's cold for a lot of the year, we have gyms and health clubs, so there's really no excuse not to exercise." She looked appraisingly at Elizabeth. "I suppose you haven't found any gyms yet in Edinburgh? *Anyhow,* I'd never bothered before, because I went to an all-girls' college, and I was so shy and all, that there really didn't seem to be any point in it, But about a year ago, after Grandpa Benjie left me his money, I could afford to quit my library job . . ."

By this time they had found the cafeteria, selected their tea and scones, and paid for them, found a table and settled in for elevenses, during the course of which Susan had recited her biography without pausing for breath. *Three weeks,* Elizabeth kept thinking. *Three weeks.*

"Look at this passport picture," said

Susan triumphantly. "It stops them cold in customs."

Dutifully, Elizabeth accepted the blue passport booklet, and turned to look at Susan's photograph. "This is *you?*" she blurted out. Sure enough, the identification page said Susan Cohen, 420 North Fifth Street, Minneapolis, but the face that looked back from the passport was a round-faced woman with short mouse-brown hair and thick horn-rimmed glasses balanced on a Roman nose. Her protruding front teeth made her look like an intellectual beaver. Elizabeth could see why the photo gave the immigration people pause. The Susan Cohen who sat across the table from her wolfing down a scone bore little resemblance to the dumpling girl in the passport. "That's quite a change," she murmured, handing it back.

"I know. Isn't money wonderful? I went to a dear old plastic surgeon in Long Beach. My doctor recommended him. He's a friend of the family. I've always called him Uncle Bob, and he told me to go to this friend of his up the coast. Anyhow, I went to see him for a consultation. He took this computer thingamabob and scanned in a picture of me, and then he adjusted the machine to show me various changes that we could make. Noses, jawline, everything! Do you like this nose? It's Katharine Hepburn's. After that, I had my teeth fixed, and I went to one of those fat farms, and got a wardrobe consultant, and now I'm perfect."

"How amusing for you," said Elizabeth, who had heard that the Queen said that to people who were being completely obnoxious.

The sarcasm was lost on her table partner. "I suppose so," said Susan. "If you can afford it, you ought to give it a try. I think they all did a nice job on me, but I'm not sure what to do next. It's not like I want to be an actress or anything. And I don't need a job. I mean, sometimes I say to myself: what's the point? But you know what? People are nicer to you if you're pretty. Isn't that weird? It seems so unfair, doesn't it?"

Elizabeth managed to get a nod in edgewise.

"Actually, I haven't exactly turned into a party girl. 1 guess I was too old to learn to like it. What's the point of talking to a bunch of boring strangers while you overeat? So I do my exercises and read my books and stay at home with my cats—there's Dickens and Waldo and Wilkie and Trollope. Trollope is female, get it? I had her fixed, though. And as I said, I read a lot. I think people are much nicer in books than they are in person, don't you?"

At least, thought Elizabeth, *they are easier to shut up.* Aloud she said, "Actually, in the books I usually read, the people are nowhere near as nice as those I meet in real life. I like true crime."

Susan appeared less than thrilled by this revelation. "True crime? That's pretty ghoulish. Sort of perverted, I mean. How did you get interested in that?"

"I am a forensic anthropologist," Elizabeth reminded her in icy tones, "But actually, it all began a few years ago on an archaeological dig in Scotland. One of the other diggers was a crime buff and he sparked my interest." She neglected to mention what fate befell this crime buff. Besides, the truth was that Elizabeth's fervors were short-lived, lasting for approximately six months each. Having gone through her Brontë phase, her sea lion fixation, and her most recent (and to her loved ones particularly trying) royal flush, she was now occupying her intellect with murder most foul, until the next idée fixe happened along.

"In fact, I brought along a true crime book today. I kept it with me in case I had time to read." She reached into her purse and brought out a copy of *Death Takes A Holiday: A Murder Guide* to Britain by Rowan Rover. "It covers old murder cases in just the areas we will visit on this tour."

"Do you think the guide will take us to those?" asked Susan. "I hope not. I wanted to see things of real cultural importance, like Agatha Christie's home, and the cathedral of Brother Cadfael, and—"

"But those aren't real crimes!" Elizabeth protested.

"But they were set in real places," said Susan with unshakable logic. "And they're much more famous. Besides, those PBS *Mystery!* adaptations are always filmed on location. Wouldn't it be great to visit a movie set?"

"No," said Elizabeth. "I want to see the roof where Charles Bravo threw up the poison his wife gave him. And I thought that as long as I was here early, I'd use this book to find some other places of interest to the group just in case the guide isn't familiar with this text.

"Lucky for you that I turned up, isn't it?' said Susan. "Imagine being stuck here all day with that nasty reference book. I find it impossible to read in airports with all the noise and confusion."

Elizabeth managed a feeble smile. "Lucky me," she said.

◆　◆　◆

ELSEWHERE IN THE airport Alice MacKenzie, her finger inserted in a cup of ice water, was debarking from a flight that had seemed to last six months. Under these circumstances, she bore a newfound indifference to the charms of Britain.

Alice was a gray-haired woman in her mid-fifties with a penchant for pantsuits and sensible shoes, and she was not the least bit embarrassed to enter Great Britain wearing a Dixie cup on her forefinger. It would be silly to value appearances more than comfort, in her oft-stated opinion.

Alice had boarded the plane many time zones earlier in southern California, full of excitement about the upcoming murder mystery tour of England. A retired teacher from San Diego, she was a mystery buff who combined a keen love of travel with an interest in the island origins of her Mac-

Kenzie ancestors. When she read about the tour in a local newspaper, it seemed the perfect combination of both her passions.

"Go," said her second husband Richard, who was not retired. "I have enough work at the office for two people. Besides, as long as the sports channel doesn't go on the fritz and the pizzeria doesn't stop delivering, I can manage."

So Alice had boarded the plane with last minute instructions about the houseplants and the cat, and promises to call each weekend to check on him and give him tour updates. Once the plane began to taxi down the runway, Alice relegated the cat, the houseplants, and Richard to a mental broom closet. She settled back happily with her guidebook to anticipate the coming adventure. She was going to keep a journal of the trip, so that she could relive it privately in the months to come. Perhaps she would write it up for her book club. She pictured herself guest speaker at one of the winter meetings, regaling her friends with details of her sojourn in England.

Several cramped, monotonous hours later, Alice was beginning to feel like the modern equivalent of a wagon train pioneer. At least the forty-niners got more to eat than salted peanuts and Diet Coke. And they didn't have to sit next to a snoring businessman for three thousand miles.

As the plane droned on toward Chicago over dark empty prairies, she found herself wondering if it would have been faster to get to England from the other direction. She supposed not. The Pacific was rather large, not to mention China and Russia. Still, it did seem to take forever to inch across North America and finally into the sky above the vast blackness of the Atlantic.

To make matters worse, just about the time she could have gone to sleep from sheer exhaustion, she managed to burn herself on that stupid light fixture above her seat, causing her to spend most of the Atlantic stretch of the journey in absolute agony. She was trying to turn off the light so that she could sleep, she explained tearfully to the flight attendant. On other airlines (better airlines, her tone suggested) the switch was beside the bulb. In this plane, it was on the armrest, but how was she to know that? In groping for it, she had put her forefinger directly on the white-hot bulb, sending a wave of unbelievable pain through her body. It seemed hours before

59

a flight attendant strolled by to answer her call button. She asked for ice for her finger, which was by now beginning to blister. The stewardess brought it with all the casualness of someone indulging an irrational whim. Alice, mindful of her dependence on this creature's goodwill for more ice, managed to thank her politely.

Ice, she discovered, made it possible for her to stand the pain without weeping, but she was still unable to sleep. She stared at the meager cup encasing her enflamed forefinger and watched the ice melt and turn tepid, sending stabs of pain through her injured flesh.

The necessity of staving off the pain forced her to make quite a nuisance of herself with the cabin crew for the remainder of the flight, ringing them whenever her balm melted, and in one instance, when no one answered her summons, venturing for ice herself, much to the dismay of the stewardesses, who were lounging around gossiping in the galley.

Alice remained civil to these slackers, but she was firm in her request for assistance in her medical dilemma. That's what they were paid for, wasn't it? Why shouldn't they help a stricken passenger?

She supposed that they were delighted to see her go when the plane finally touched down at Gatwick. For once she didn't fret about the plane crashing on the runway. Now, however, she was having considerable misgivings about her ability to enjoy the tour. She exited the plane with her finger thrust into a cup of rapidly melting ice, wondering what would become of her next. An airport attendant told her that Gatwick had a first aid station—not that anything could be done for minor burns, he added. His directions on how to get there were so endless and complicated that Alice resolved to look for a restaurant instead. Surely someone would sell her some ice.

But first she had to get through customs. Before the plane landed, the flight attendant had recited some carefully memorized instructions on how to proceed. It boiled down to: get your luggage, stand in the appropriate line.

Alice wondered how she was going to carry two suitcases with her finger in a paper cup. She managed to find the metal shopping carts, and was debating the best way to steer one with a hand and a foot, when a slender auburn-haired woman of about her own age approached her. "You look like you could use some help," she said in familiar California English.

Alice heaved a sigh of relief. "I sure could," she said. "I burned my finger on the airplane reading lamp! Did you just get here, too? Were you on Flight 304?"

The woman picked up Alice's suitcases and set them on the cart. "Yes," she said. "I'm Frances Coles, from La Mesa. I'm taking a mystery tour of southern England."

After they had expressed delight and astonishment that they were both on the same tour, Alice reflected that it was not such a remarkable coincidence after all, since they were both from southern California. The travel agency had quite naturally booked them on the same flight, albeit twenty rows apart. But she was nonetheless delighted to find an ally so soon.

"I'll hold your passport for you," said Frances, as they waited in the nonresidents' line for customs.

"Thanks," said Alice. "I hope we get through fast." She indicated her paper cup. "My ice is melting."

"That would be a great way to smuggle diamonds into the country," Frances remarked. "Burn your finger and hide the diamonds in the ice."

"You're welcome to it," Alice said. "After this experience, I wouldn't burn my finger on purpose for all the diamonds in South Africa."

The customs official was cheerful, but brisk, and apparently unthreatened by a couple of middle-aged women with well-worn suitcases, one of whom had a finger immersed in a cup of ice. He was an expert on American eccentricities. He wished the ladies a pleasant stay in England and waved them through.

Frances Coles glanced at her watch. "We still have four hours before the tour assembles. How is your finger feeling now?"

Alice took a deep breath and eased her finger out of the puddle of ice. She shut her eyes, waiting for the stab of pain. Instead there was only a mild twinge of discomfort. "It's better," she admitted.

"Good. I think you should switch from ice to something else now. Aloe, if we can find any. Do you suppose there's a drug-store in the airport?"

"Bound to be," said Alice. "I suppose we'd better change some money first."

Together they trundled off down the halls of Gatwick. The adventure had begun.

63

◆ ◆ ◆

AT TWO-FIFTEEN that afternoon a small group of travelers began to assemble in the ground floor lobby of the airport: a married couple, an English-looking mother and daughter in tweeds and sensible shoes, a pretty young nurse, a Canadian doctor's wife, a silver-haired lady from Berkeley, Frances Coles, and her new friend Alice MacKenzie, whose burned finger was now shiny with aloe ointment.

Elizabeth MacPherson was the last to arrive, followed by the beautiful Susan Cohen, who had reached chapter thirty-one in the oral history of her life. "And then I got my *second* cat, Wilkie. He's the tortoiseshell one with the yellow eyes. I have a picture of him somewhere—"

"Oh look!" cried Elizabeth, more with relief than surprise. "This must be the rest of the tour!" She wondered hopefully if any of them were hard of hearing. "Mystery tour?" she asked, striding toward the group.

Several of the travelers nodded.

Elizabeth and Susan added their suitcases to the pile of luggage in the circle.

"Is the guide here yet?" Elizabeth inquired.

64

"Not yet," said the tall silver-haired woman consulting her watch. "Oh dear," she said. "It's still on Berkeley time."

The rest of the tour members offered her local times ranging from two-twenty to two-forty. Elizabeth noticed that there was only one man in the group, a tanned and genial-looking gentleman with peppery hair. He wore a T-shirt that proclaimed ERIK BROADAXE RULES PRETTY GOOD. From this evidence, Elizabeth deduced that he was an American; that he had been to the Jorvik, the Norse exhibit at York (whence the T-shirt); and that he had a good sense of humor, always a pleasant discovery in a fellow traveler. His wife, who was half a head shorter than he, was blonde and smiling, and looked equally good-tempered.

"Is everybody here from California?" asked Mrs. Broadaxe (as Elizabeth had begun to characterize her.)

"San Diego," said the pretty, dark-eyed nurse.

"So am I!" said Alice MacKenzie. "And Frances is from La Mesa, which amounts to the same thing."

"We're from Colorado," said the lady in tweeds. Her daughter nodded and smiled.

"Vancouver."

"Berkeley," said the silver-haired woman, eldest of the party.

"I'm from Minneapolis," said Susan, "And our airport, the Minneapolis-St. Paul International, is much more—"

"Edinburgh," said Elizabeth MacPherson—and instantly regretted it. She then had to admit that she was, in fact, an American; she started to explain how she came to be living in Scotland and why her new husband hadn't come along.

She was still relating all this when a man in a beige leisure suit approached the group, carrying a canvas shoulder bag and a sheaf of typed papers. "Tour?" he said briskly. "South of England mystery tour? I am your guide."

There was a moment of silence while the assembly took in the sight of their guide. He was a desperately stately five feet, eight inches, with longish blue-black hair that conjured up images of shoe polish in the minds of the beholders. Such a hue did, of course, exist in nature. Innumerable species of crows possessed it without resorting to artifice, and, among homo sapiens, certain bands of Comanches may in their youth rejoice in a similarly stygian shade; but in an aging Englishman whose face

66

sported the crow's-feet to accompany the crow's color, the shade suggested hairstyling of a suicidal nature: dyed by his own hand and with a reckless disregard for plausibility. His eyes behind dark-framed glasses were similarly dark, and his expression radiated a confidence and self-esteem that belied his unevenly cut, safety-pinned trousers.

"My name is Rowan Rover," said the personage.

With an exclamation of surprise Elizabeth held aloft her copy of *Death Takes a Holiday.*

"Yes, I'll sign it for you later," said Rowan Rover soothingly. "Now, I'll just read out the names on my list to make sure that we are all here. Elizabeth MacPherson?"

"Here," mumbled Elizabeth, chagrined at having been mistaken for a groupie. She wondered if she could arrange for him to sit with Susan on the bus trip to Winchester.

"It may take me a while to learn your names. Ah, only one gentleman, I see. *That* should be easy." He beamed at Erik Broadaxe. "Charles Warren, I presume?"

"That's right, and this is my wife Nancy."

"Martha Tabram?" The well-dressed woman from Vancouver raised her hand.

"Frances Coles? Alice MacKenzie? Ah, there you are together. Very convenient. Both from California, aren't you? How lovely. And two Colorado ladies, where are they? Miriam Angel and Emma Smith?"

"We're mother and daughter," said Miriam Angel.

"Splendid. No one's mistaken you for the Judds, have they, dear?" Rowan said under his breath. He had become conversant in country music during the period he referred to as his exile in the academic gulag, by which he meant the state of Wisconsin. "Any more Californians? Kate Conway?"

The pretty young nurse in the red sweater raised her hand.

"And one more—Maud Marsh." He nodded toward the silver-haired lady from Berkeley. "That's it, I think."

"Excuse me. You forgot me."

Rowan Rover looked up from his list. "Did I? I thought I had read out all the names. You are . . ."

"Susan Cohen. From Minneapolis."

Rowan Rover's smile faded as he stared at the belligerent-looking blonde. He made a show of consulting his list again. "Susan

Cohen. It's here, of course. It's just that I thought I'd already said it. No, I wouldn't forget you."

After a moment's silence, during which the color grudgingly returned to Rowan Rover's face, the members of the group picked up their belongings and surged at him with questions.

He held up a hand to forestall the onslaught. "I am told that the tour coach will be waiting for us in the loading zone just outside. Our driver should be there now unless he has been delayed in the interminable traffic that one inevitably encounters on the motorway. I don't know who thought up the road system out here, but he evidently came from a family not known for precognition, because he certainly didn't foresee—"

Alice MacKenzie interrupted his tirade. "Do you want us to go outside now?"

"Yes," said Rowan. "Let us be optimistic."

"And will there be a sign on the side of the bus that says MURDER TOUR?"

Rowan Rover sighed. "No, madam. Definitely not. We don't want to be mistaken for the IRA." He ended further discussion by turning and marching for the glass doors

69

of the exit, while the tour members scrambled behind him, balancing suitcases and handbags as they ran.

Once assembled on the sidewalk outside, Rowan Rover turned and faced his charges. "Ladies," he intoned, *"and* Charles." He nodded toward the lone gentleman in the party. "If you will all stay here, I will attempt to locate the coach."

With a reassuring wave, Rowan Rover hurried away. Once out of sight of the party, he took out a cigarette and lit it with trembling hands. Susan Cohen. There she was: undeniably real and unavoidably doomed. He had three weeks in which to kill her. Somehow, despite the arrival of a fiscally sound ten thousand pound check, the murder scheme had never seemed more than an idle exercise in theory. Until now. Rowan Rover had spent the past few years making a living out of idle murder theories, and this one had seemed little different from the others. "Suppose Florence Maybrick knew that her husband was an arsenic eater," he would say in one of his crime lectures. "It would be very easy then for her to purchase some arsenic, or even to steal some of his own private stock . . ." It was great fun to speculate. But he, Rowan Rover, had never had to buy any arsenic. Or to watch the death throes of the subsequent victim. Now, suddenly, he had to move from the theoretical to the practical—and to accomplish the task before ten potential witnesses, all of them avowed crime buffs. Was he mad?

He looked up to find that a large tour coach had pulled up alongside him. "Mr. Rover?" the driver inquired in a working-class twang. "Mystery tour?"

Rowan took a long drag on his cigarette. "Right," he wheezed. "They're just around the corner."

"Climb aboard, then, and we'll go and get them."

Rowan Rover hesitated. "Mind if I smoke?"

"Not me, mate. But if you're ferrying about a load of American ladies, there's sure to be objections. Regular health nuts, some of them." He was young and blond and he looked as if he should be running across a rugby field rather than driving a bus. He smiled again as Rowan Rover mounted the steps to the coach. "My name's Bernard," he said. "I'm from Kensington."

"And you know where you're going, I take it?"

"Complete instructions," said Bernard. "Not as if it ever changes, though. All the tourists want to go to the same dreary places."

Rowan Rover smirked. "I think this lot may surprise you."

CHAPTER 5

"Alas, regardless of their doom,
The little victims play!
No sense have they of ills to come,
Nor care beyond today."
—Thomas Gray

WINCHESTER

WHEN ALL THE luggage had been stowed into the undercarriage of the coach, and the travelers had boarded the bus two by two, like Noah's passengers on an earlier tour, Rowan Rover turned to address the group. First he introduced Bernard, their friendly and experienced coach driver, who would be the final authority on where the bus could and could not go. "England is not all motorways yet," he reminded them. "Medieval towns were not constructed to accommodate lorries. Some of the rural counties are quite unspoiled. When we get down into the West Country, you will see some narrow lanes that wouldn't take horses two abreast,

73

much less allow this tin beast an unscathed passage."

They looked up at Rowan with polite interest, possibly subdued by the fact that as far as their bodies were concerned it was ten A.M. after a grueling transatlantic all-nighter. Although the coach would have held three times their number comfortably, they still insisted upon sitting two by two, and they were all concentrated in the front six rows. He must, he realized, make a start at learning their names. His eyes strayed toward the right front seat, where a sleepy-looking Susan Cohen sat alone. He knew *her* name well enough; ten to go.

The bus left the airport terminal, and for the first time the members of the tour got a glimpse of English scenery. It was not an auspicious beginning. Acres of scrub woodland and pasture stretched out on either side of the congested motorway, looking less than glamorous under a buttermilk sky that threatened rain at any moment.

After a moment's experimentation with the coach microphone, Rowan Rover resumed his briefing. "Our first destination is Winchester, appropriately enough. After all, Winchester was the first capital of England, both before and after the Norman

Conquest. It was the capital of Saxon Wessex, and later William the Conqueror's capital of Norman England. He built a palace there after the invasion."

"It's a bakery now," said Emma Smith.

The guide stopped in mid-vowel. "I beg your pardon?"

"The site of William the Conqueror's palace is now occupied by a bakery. It's beside the market cross. The bakery has a little sign in the window."

"Specializing in French rolls, no doubt," said Rowan acidly. He consulted his lecture notes. "And many of the early kings are buried in Winchester Cathedral. We will be staying at the Wessex, a Trusthouse Forte Hotel right on the cathedral green."

"I don't remember any hotel there," muttered Emma Smith to her mother.

Elizabeth, who was sitting in the seat in front of them, overheard this remark and turned around. "Have you been to Winchester before?"

"Yes, when I was in college, I went on an archaeological dig to Winchester. We were digging for the old Saxon cathedral that had been destroyed by William the Conqueror in 1066. Its ruins are beneath the present churchyard. But there wasn't a hotel next to the cathedral. I'm sure of it."

"You went on the dig when you were in college?" said Maud Marsh, momentarily distracted from the indifferent scenery of the motorway. "How did American students happen to be allowed on the dig?"

"I think the British may have needed the money to do it in a hurry," said Emma. "As I recall, a private company was planning to build something on land that had once been part of the cathedral holdings. When they started excavating, they found ruins, so they gave the archaeologists a certain amount of time to excavate the site before it was destroyed. Two American universities—Duke and North Carolina—put up the money in exchange for being allowed to send their own archaeology students over for field study. At least I think that's how it went."

Miriam Angel laughed at the memory of her daughter's adventure. "Emma wrote us twice a week, telling us about what they were finding and what work she had been assigned. Once, I remember we got a letter from her that said, 'Dear Mom and Dad, This week we are finding mass graves in the old churchyard. We have dug up lepers

76

from the Crusades, and plague victims from the Black Death. How long do germs live?' Her father wrote her back: 'We don't know, but we burned your letters.' "

"One of our daughters wanted to major in archaeology," said Nancy Warren, with a glance at her husband. "Did you become an archaeologist, Emma?"

"No. That was the Sixties, when you did things that had no bearing on real life. I majored in math after that, and I taught for a while before I got married. This will be my first trip back to Winchester since the dig."

"I expect a lot has changed since you were there, Emma," said her mother. "Twenty years."

Emma Smith frowned. "I hope it isn't too commercialized," she sighed.

Across the aisle Frances Coles giggled. "If William the Conqueror is running a bakery, I'd expect the worst, if I were you."

By this time Rowan Rover had finished his introductory speech and the coach was pulling onto the motorway, heading south for Winchester. Rowan slid into the seat beside Elizabeth MacPherson and consulted his notes, with a view to scheduling a fatal accident.

"Any murders in Winchester?" asked Elizabeth.

With heroic effort Rowan Rover managed not to spring from his seat and run screaming down the aisle. Instead he reached for a cigarette and took particular care to note which end to light. Once it was lit, he exercised even greater care not to stick that end into his mouth. Drawing a few calming puffs of nicotine into his lungs, he turned to his companion and murmured, "I'm sorry. Didn't catch that over the noise of the engine. What was it you were saying?"

"I wondered if there were any famous murders associated with Winchester," Elizabeth said. "The only one I can think of is Sweet Fanny Adams."

Rowan stifled a cough. "That was in Alton," he wheezed. "Dreadful story. Dismembered girl in a meadow a hundred and twenty-odd years ago. Couldn't be much to see there now."

"I expect not," said Elizabeth wistfully. "I suppose they buried her?"

"The British Navy has its doubts," said Rowan. "Why do you ask?"

"I'm a forensic anthropologist. I was hoping to get a chance to use my training at least once on this tour."

Rowan Rover inhaled another column of smoke down the wrong passage. When his coughing fit subsided and he had waved away all inquiries about his health, he said, "I expect you will have a chance to do a bit of that at Madame Tussaud's when the tour concludes in London. You know about the Chamber of Horrors, of course?"

Elizabeth nodded. "And I'm looking forward to taking your Ripper tour as well. Incidentally, I've read your book, *Death Takes a Holiday*. What an array of crimes. Do you remember the Alexander Evans case?"

"I believe so," said Rowan Rover, trying to channel his thoughts back to murder in the abstract. "Glasgow, wasn't it? Young boy who poisoned his family and was sent to Broadmoor?"

"Right," said Elizabeth. "I knew him."

"Did you really?" asked Rowan Rover happily. "This was after he got out, I take it? Oh! Were you on that dig in the Highlands with him where he started up again? Were you really?"

For the next thirty miles they prattled on, dropping killers' names left and right, while Alice MacKenzie dropped off to sleep and Susan Cohen, refreshened after her own nap, told Bernard the bus driver in agonizing detail all about beautiful downtown Minneapolis.

◆　◆　◆

NEARLY TWO HOURS later the coach left the motorway and negotiated a series of increasingly smaller thoroughfares, until it finally pulled in to the city of Winchester. Emma Smith studied the narrow streets, flanked by rose brick buildings, sporting shop names and pub signs. "I don't recognize any of this," she said.

"We may have come in the back way, so to speak," said Frances Coles soothingly. "After all, the driver has to choose a route wide enough to accommodate the bus."

"Look, Emma!" said her mother, who was gazing out the window. "Isn't that the market cross? I recognized it from one of the coasters you brought me."

Emma studied the street scene with a frown of recognition. "That was the high street," she said. "But it isn't a street anymore. Apparently, they have made it into a mall." Her frown suggested that she disapproved of the giddy town planners who were mucking about with the design of an ancient city. She braced herself for a renovated cathedral with neon lights and a petting zoo.

Fortunately, however, civic irresponsibility stopped short of architectural sacrilege. A moment later the bus rounded a corner. "Winchester Cathedral," Bernard announced.

"Right over there." It was quite unchanged. The gray Gothic edifice with its spires and buttresses sat in the middle of a well-kept green, looking much as it had for centuries, unaltered since Cromwell's men shot out the huge pictorial stained-glass window for cannon practice and the puzzle-inept churchmen had glued it back in as a mosaic. Twentieth-century visitors to the cathedral often praised its twelfth-century builders for their modern design instincts, when, in fact, the credit should have been given to the Roundhead Artillery.

"And here's your hotel," said Bernard, stopping the coach in the driveway of a very modern brick and glass building a hundred yards from a wing of the cathedral.

"I see," said Emma Smith thoughtfully. "This is what they were planning to build back in the Sixties when they found the artifacts. This is where the cathedral outbuildings would have been."

Rowan Rover was on his feet with more immediate concerns. "Ladies and Charles," he announced, "this is what the tour calls a free evening, which you are soon to learn means that it is *not* free in any monetary sense. On free evenings your meal is not paid for. You are welcome to find a reasonably priced pub or to dine here at the Wessex. We have nothing planned for you this evening except a glass of wine in the lounge at seven—optimistically referred to in the schedule as a sherry party. I hope at that time that we can talk a bit about what your interests are and perhaps get more acquainted. After that, you may have dinner on your own."

He braced himself for a storm of protest from budget-bound Americans, who were, he knew, already reeling from the unexpected rise of the pound, making their dollars worth half as much as last year. To his surprise, no one objected to an evening at leisure. "It's only money," said Susan Cohen with her grating laugh. "I wonder if Winchester has any pizza parlors."

When the coach door opened, Rowan stationed himself on the pavement in case anyone needed help getting out. They looked fit enough, but you could never be certain. "Bernard and the hotel porter will assist you with your cases. After that, we shan't be seeing Bernard until tomorrow afternoon."

After he shepherded them into the Wessex and saw to it that everyone had a room, Rowan Rover ascended to his own assigned quarters on the third floor to spend the remainder of the afternoon plotting his murder. He discovered that either by chance or as an expression of divine sarcasm, his tiny bedroom was graced with an enormous picture window, affording him an inescapable view of Winchester Cathedral. It loomed reproachfully before him in the fading sunlight, as he sat down with his itinerary to schedule in an unfortunate accident.

His most optimistic maiden aunt wouldn't have called Rowan Rover a religious person, but years of public school chapel-going had left a lingering impression upon his soul that was more superstition than piety; besides, his keenly developed sense of irony could not fail to miss the omen of the cathedral view overlooking his plottings of murder.

"Well, look here," he said to the ceiling, and to anything that might or might not lie infinitely above it, "I've already spent the money, all right? It's for a good cause. Surely you don't disapprove of a public school education? I could donate a bit to the Church, if you like."

He glanced out at the church, a squat gray pile of granite that seemed crouched like a hound of hell, ready to leap at his window. He tried to bolster his resolve by picturing the Deity as an ethereal version of Alec Guinness, nodding understandingly at his plight as one gentleman to another, but instead he kept seeing his first wife, with that *do-come-off-it, Rowan* expression that seemed permanently ingrained into her features.

"Look, it's just this one murder," said Rowan reasonably. "And then I shan't break that particular commandment ever again. I could do something commendable to atone for it. Give up smoking—no, perhaps not that. It isn't a commandment anyhow." He wandered over to the bureau and began idly stuffing the complimentary chocolate packets and tea bags into his suitcase, next to the extra bars of soap and vials of shampoo already liberated from the bathroom. "Well, I'll think of something."

♦　♦　♦

ALICE MACKENZIE AND Frances Coles, who had paid tour fees based on a double occupancy rate, decided to be roommates. They had followed the porter upstairs to a spacious third floor room overlooking the car park. Once they settled in, they boiled water for tea in the electric kettle provided in each room by the management.

Frances' eyes shone with excitement as she savored her first trip to England. She was a primary school teacher, with that delightful quality of unjaded enthusiasm that one sometimes finds in people who enjoy small children and spend considerable time among them. With her winsome smile and jogger's figure, she made an appealing contrast to Alice's bluff heartiness.

"What do you think so far?" asked Frances.

Alice was reading the little packets in the china bowl beside the teapot. "Too early to tell," she said, selecting two tea bags and placing them in the pot, which she filled to the brim with the boiling water. "I thought our guide was a little strange at first, but he seems very knowledgeable."

"I want to buy his book," said Frances.

85

"If we see any bookshops, I'll go in and look for it. I also collect cat figurines." She fingered the emerald-eyed cat pinned to the shawl collar of her black sweater.

"We have time for a walk before dinner," said Alice cheerily. With a fresh application of aloe cream, her finger had ceased to trouble her, and she felt refreshed after her nap in the coach.

Frances looked doubtful. "Walking by ourselves? Suppose we got lost?"

"Emma Smith and her mother are in the room next to us. We could see if they want to go. Emma spent a summer here once." Alice poured a cup of tea for each of them. "I'd hate to spend my first day in England doing nothing. Such a waste."

"True," said Frances. "You never know when it might rain. Let's ask them."

Twenty minutes later Alice MacKenzie, Frances Coles, and Emma Smith were strolling across the lawn of Winchester Cathedral. Emma's mother had decided to take an afternoon nap.

"There used to be more tombstones," said Emma, frowning to summon up her memories of the Winchester of 1968. "There used to be gravesites on this green every few feet."

"Where did they go?" asked Frances, looking around as if she expected to see grave robbers lurking behind the yew tree.

"I expect the bodies are still there," said Emma. "As for the tombstones, look down at the sidewalk."

Alice leaned down to inspect the paving stones and for the first time she noticed faint Gothic lettering, spelling out names and dates, with an occasional carved lamb or flower in relief. "The sidewalk is made of recycled tombstones!" she exclaimed.

"Of course," said Emma. "This has been a cemetery for a thousand years. They would have run out of room centuries ago, if they hadn't removed the old stones every so often."

"I don't see any signs of an archaeological dig," said Frances, looking out at the smooth expanse of grass.

"They had to fill it back in after the dig was completed. The main excavation was right over here between the West Door, which is the main entrance, and the North Transept." She indicated a plot of grass just beyond the paved path.

"What did you find there?"

"The ruins of the original Saxon cathedral," Emma replied. "You see, when William the Conqueror invaded England, the Church sent monks in armor to fight against him. After the Battle of Hastings, he took revenge on the bishoprics who opposed him by destroying their churches and building Norman-style ones in their place. We call this the *new* cathedral." Emma pointed to the great Gothic church. "It dates from 1066."

"And William just tore down the old one?"

"Yes. He used many of the stones from the Saxon cathedral to build his Gothic one, but in Winchester he didn't build his new church on top of the old one. He did that everywhere else, but here his architects chose to construct the new building on a site several feet to the right of the ruined church. It's the only Saxon cathedral that will ever be found."

"Why?" asked Alice, who hadn't quite followed the explanation.

Emma sighed. "Because in order to find any of the other Saxon cathedrals, you'd have to tear down the present cathedrals. Canterbury, for example."

"What a cruel thing for William to have done!" exclaimed Frances.

"He was French," Alice reminded her.

"It made very good sense politically," said Emma. "If you destroy the old church, the people you conquered have to worship in your church. I expect it cut down on dissension considerably."

"Should we go inside the cathedral?" asked Alice, as they passed the West Door.

"That is scheduled for the group tomorrow morning," said Emma. "I wonder if Thomas Thetcher is still here, though. Come on!" She left the path and began to walk away from the church toward a small group of tombstones near the outer wall of the green.

"Who is Thomas Thetcher?" asked Frances. "Anyone famous?"

"Only posthumously," said Emma. "According to his tombstone, he was a grenadier who died from drinking small beer."

"What's small beer?"

"Not very alcoholic. More like soda pop. Anyway, they put the whole story in verse on his tombstone, which is what made him so infamous. When I was on the dig here in Winchester, we used to love to show him off to tourists. They couldn't have got rid of that gravestone!"

They split up and began wandering

around the upper green, reading the inscriptions on the remaining stones.

"Here it is!" cried Alice, pointing to a well-tended gravestone of old-fashioned design. "Thomas Thetcher."

Together they read the inscription, lamenting the overheated young soldier's death from drinking overly cold small beer. The epitaph ended with a warning to passersby: "And when you're hot, drink strong or not at all."

Alice MacKenzie noted it all down carefully for future inclusion in her journal. "When I die, I hope nobody puts anything silly on my tombstone," she said in a tone that left no doubt of her opinions on the subject of prankster stonemasons.

"Oh, don't talk about dying!" laughed Frances. "I've never seen a healthier group of tourists, have you?"

◆ ◆ ◆

ELIZABETH MACPHERSON FOUND that she had a small, but comfortable second-floor room with a beautiful view of the cathedral out her picture window. She sat for several minutes admiring the splendor of the medieval architecture, the serenity of the cathedral grounds, and the intricacy of light and shadow on the stonework. All this ethereal pleasure was considerably enhanced by the consumption of the chocolate bar that the Wessex Hotel had thoughtfully provided for each guest.

After several moments' contemplation of a blank sheet of hotel stationery while considering her adventures thus far (that is, since her eight A.M. departure from Edinburgh), she regretfully decided that, while she certainly had the time just now to communicate with her various correspondents, she had, alas, nothing to say. To write *Having wonderful time, wish you were here* would do nothing to enhance her reputation for cleverness.

She considered taking a nice bracing walk to enjoy the beauties of the English countryside, but a glance at her watch confirmed her suspicion that the shops were closed.

She decided to have another look at Rowan Rover's book. Since the author was an authority on British murder cases, his presence would provide an excellent opportunity for her to discuss some of the famous unsolved crimes with an expert. Because of the inexactness of forensic science in the old days, quite a number of nineteenth-century murder cases were unsolved; at least a good many people were acquitted, rightfully or not. Elizabeth enjoyed second-guessing the expert witnesses in the vintage trials. How *did* Adelaide Bartlett get corrosive chloroform down her husband's throat without leaving a trace? Did the man on the green bicycle murder pretty Bella Wright on a country road near Leicester? Did Ethel LeNeve know that her lover Dr. Crippen had murdered his wife when she ran away with him to Canada?

Elizabeth was delighted at the prospect of discussing these crimes with Rowan Rover. She felt that she knew him already. After all, they had about a hundred mutual *friends,* most of whom had ended up on the gallows for the crime of murder. True, Rover had seemed nervous when she tried to discuss true crime with him earlier, but she put that down to a natural shyness on his part, and she was sure that his reserve would dissolve after everyone became better acquainted, especially if he was pressed to discuss his pet subject. Elizabeth decided she could help their diffident guide overcome his nervousness by discussing murder with him at every possible opportunity.

AT SEVEN O´CLOCK Rowan Rover changed his clothes and decided that he could probably do without an evening shave. He opted for a last cigarette instead. It was time to meet the troops. He supposed it would be a good idea to get better acquainted with the lovely Susan: useful to know whether she was afraid of heights, what she drank, and so on. Rowan Rover's greatest fear was that his susceptibility to attractive women would be his undoing. He pictured himself like the huntsman in Snow White, falling on one knee before fair Susan Cohen, telling her that her wicked uncle wished her dead and urging her to flee into the forest so that he would not have to kill her. He had a feeling, though, that besides the probability that she would not believe a word of it, such altruism might be hazardous to his own health, as well as to his financial well-being. While there might indeed be a shortage of assassins in Minneapolis, Rowan had no doubt that, if double-crossed, the resourceful Mr. Kosminski could locate one elsewhere, and that no expense would be spared in enabling the thug to track down Rowan himself and kill him in the alleys of Whitechapel or the lanes of Cornwall. Anywhere, really.

He looked at his watch. Time to go down for the glass of sherry and to learn more about the other tourists in the party. Elizabeth MacPherson, the Scot with the southern drawl, was a forensic anthropologist. He must discover more about that. Could she just identify bodies from skeletal remains, or could she also figure out cause of death, if she happened to be on the spot when one occurred? Just his luck to get a bloody medical vulture on his tour. And the Conway girl was a nurse. Who else was along for the ride? A mortician? A coroner? A bloody police inspector? Rowan reflected that he was about to express more polite interest in a group of tourists than he had ever exhibited before. He hoped they appreciated his efforts.

As he flipped off the light switch, he took one last look at the dark cathedral, silent beneath a pale oval moon. He thought he detected a definite smirk etched on the lunar surface.

◆ ◆ ◆

IN THE WESSEX lounge two semicircular sofas had been reserved for the mystery

94

tour participants. A low table held a bottle of sherry and the requisite number of glasses.

Rowan Rover waited until everyone was present before addressing his charges. "Now," he said, "suppose we go round the group and get everyone's name—and perhaps a word from each of you about how you happened to come on the tour, and what you'd like to see." He smiled at Charles Warren, who was no longer advertising the governing skills of Erik Broadaxe. He was now looking considerably more distinguished in a navy jacket and tie. "Suppose we start with you, Charles. No one's likely to forget who you are."

Charles Warren reddened a bit, and it was apparent that Nancy was the one who did most of the talking in social situations. "I'm Charles Warren. We're from San Diego, and I own a computer electronics firm. I guess we came on this trip because we've always wanted to see England, and mostly because Nancy likes mysteries." He nodded toward his wife, obviously ready to relinquish the floor.

"I'm Nancy Warren and I just adore British mysteries," said the small blonde beside him. "I grew up with Nancy Drew and then

I moved on to Agatha Christie." She reminded Rowan Rover of the sweet-girl-next-door movie actress, June Allyson. *Lucky I don't have to kill her,* he was thinking.

"Am I next?" said the elderly woman beside her. She was tall and slender, and her energy and alertness belied her age. "My name is Maud Marsh and I'm seventy-seven. I'm from Berkeley, and I read Agatha Christie and Dorothy Sayers. I like the sort of mysteries that don't have gangsters in them."

"Will you be able to keep up with us on a walking tour?" asked Susan.

Maud Marsh gave her a mirthless smile. "I usually walk five miles a day at home. I doubt we'll be doing more than that."

"Some of us may have trouble keeping up with you," said Rowan gallantly. "Who's next?"

"Martha Tabram," said the well-dressed brunette with the Canadian accent. "My husband is a surgeon in Vancouver, and since he couldn't get away this fall for a real vacation, I decided to try this tour. I wanted to see the south of England again, and this seemed like an ideal way to do it."

"Susan Cohen, from Minneapolis," said

the intended victim, swishing her blonde hair like a model in a shampoo ad. "I'm young, so I don't have to exercise yet, but I thought a tour might be a fun way to see England, and maybe enlarge my book collection. I admire British mysteries, too—those by Colin Dexter and P. D. James—but we also have a lot of good mystery writers around Minneapolis. Has anybody read R. D. Zimmerman? He has this one book called—"

Rowan Rover realized that henceforth they might all have to pretend to have read a good many books that they had actually never heard of. "Fascinating," he said hurriedly. "And you are Elizabeth . . . ?"

"Yes. Elizabeth MacPherson. I'm a forensic anthropologist, with a doctorate but no job yet. My husband is a marine biologist. He went off to do seal research, so I decided to take this tour. I've read a few murder mysteries, but I really love true crime."

"Having a husband who comes home with the Gulf Stream could drive anybody to true crime," murmured Rowan, "but we're glad to have you, anyhow. And you are . . . ?"

"Kate Conway," said the youngest member of the group, flashing her dark eyes at him. She was wearing a simple blue sheath dress and a string of pearls. "I'm an emergency room nurse. I like to travel. I enjoyed the public television presentations of Sherlock Holmes."

When the discussion of Jeremy Brett's interpretations of the Sleuth of Baker Street versus those of Mr. Basil Rathbone had subsided, Rowan Rover invited Alice Mac-Kenzie to identify herself to the group. She announced herself in sympathy with the Christie readers and the Jeremy Brett watchers. Thereupon the attention turned to her roommate, Frances Coles.

Frances managed to smile and look terrified at the same time. She tugged at a lock of auburn hair and smoothed imaginary wrinkles out of her corduroy skirt. Rowan, who was hopeless at guessing ages, thought she might be in her early forties, but since she was a Californian it was hard to tell, since they cheated by exercising and going on diets. "I just wanted to come to England because I read so much about it," she said softly. "I used to teach second grade. I'm a great fan of Ellis Peters."

"You are in luck," said Rowan Rover magnanimously. "We shall be visiting

Brother Cadfael's home city of Shrewsbury at the end of next week and you will be able to see the settings for the Ellis Peters novels." Rowan Rover had never read Ellis Peters himself, but he was well-briefed on the tour itinerary. Besides, years of association with university English departments had left him able to bluff his way through almost any literary discussion. Sometimes he even fooled himself into thinking that he had read *Moby Dick* and *War and Peace*.

"Am I next?" said the serious-looking young woman in rimless glasses. "My name is Emma Smith and this is my mother, Miriam Angel."

Her mother was the most English-looking of the bunch, pale with softly waved brown hair and green eyes in a gentle heart-shaped face. In her good-but-not-new tweed jacket and well-cut skirt, she fitted Rowan's idea of a duchess—or she would if she gained forty pounds or so. In Rowan's experience, duchesses seldom came in small packages.

"We're from Colorado," Emma was saying. "My husband thought we'd both enjoy coming on this trip. He's at home minding the two kids."

Miriam beamed with pride. "Emma's husband is an attorney. And such a dear!"

Rowan Rover was unable to imagine any reason why a sane man who was capable of supporting himself would offer to babysit for two children while sending his wife and mother-in-law on an extended European vacation. Knowing lawyers, though, the motives were bound to be devious. He gave the assembly a bright smile. "How lovely," he said. "So there we all are. No real crime experts here, then." (Thank God, he finished silently.)

"I hear you're a crime expert," said Alice MacKenzie.

For a moment he froze. Then he realized that the comment pertained to his theoretical connections with crime history—not his future plans to practice what he preached. "Oh, me? You want to know about me?"

The group nodded solemnly. They still had an ounce or two of sherry to finish, after all.

"Well, I am from Cornwall originally," said Rowan Rover. "I attended a minor public school in the West Country, and then went on to Oxford. We shall be going to Oxford near the end of our tour, by the way. As some of you know, I give the Jack the Ripper tour in Whitechapel for one of the city tour companies—when I am not otherwise engaged as a media consultant on crime. And I write books about English crimes. I hope you will find me knowledgeable about your areas of interest. Certainly I shall be helpful in history and geography; fictional mystery stories are not, alas, within my realm of expertise."

"Don't worry," said Susan Cohen cheerfully. "I've read most of them, and I'll be happy to fill everyone in on the books pertaining to the areas we visit."

"How nice," said Rowan, from the depths of a plaster smile. "And now, before we adjourn for dinner, let me tell you tomorrow's schedule. The hotel will serve you breakfast, anytime between seven and nine—"

"I eat breakfast at six-thirty," said Maud Marsh.

"So do I if I still happen to be up," said Rowan. "Well, let me inquire for you. Perhaps they can provide something earlier than seven. At nine o'clock you will all assemble in the Wessex lobby and we'll walk over across the green for your tour of the cathedral, to be followed by a quick tour of Winchester College and a look round the city. Lunch is on your own, but be back in the lobby at one. Bernard will bring the coach to the car park, and we will go off on our afternoon tour, to see the New Forest site where King William Rufus was murdered in the year 1100. We shall also visit the grave of Sir Arthur Conan Doyle, the creator of Sherlock Holmes."

Elizabeth MacPherson frowned. "Conan Doyle was Scottish. He was born in Edinburgh."

Rowan Rover acknowledged the fact with a bland smile. "His heart may have been in the Highlands, madam, but the rest of him is under a stone cross in Minstead. I shall prove it to you tomorrow. Any more questions? No? Off you go, then."

CHAPTER 6

*"For God's sake, let us sit upon the ground
And tell sad stories of the death of
kings . . ."*
                              Richard II, iii, 2

THE NEW FOREST

ROWAN ROVER ABSENTED himself from the
morning tour of Winchester, leaving his
charges in the capable hands of one of the
cathedral's volunteer guides, a tall silver-
haired gentleman who identified himself as
a retired physician. He began by telling them
that they were standing in the longest church
in Europe, except for St. Peter's in Rome.
"When Winchester was the capital of England, kings were crowned here in this cathedral, not in Westminster Abbey," he said,
in tones suggesting that he considered the
move to London a recent bureaucratic whim.

"Isn't it beautiful?" whispered Frances
Coles, gazing up at the graceful succession
of carved Gothic arches high above their
heads.

Alice MacKenzie wasn't ready to forgive the Conqueror for his destruction of the original church. "It's a bit showy. What did the Saxon cathedral look like, Emma?" she whispered.

"Not so upscale," Emma whispered back. "Based on what we found on the dig, I'd say it was a lot smaller, and the architecture was simpler. Besides, even before William trashed it, it had been damaged by the Danes during the tenth-century Viking raids."

"Go, Vikings!" whispered Susan, who had heard only the last few words of the conversation and had assumed they were talking about her hometown football team.

Emma pretended not to have heard. "When we were excavating the ruins of the old cathedral, we found a few Viking graves. You could always tell when you'd found one who had converted to Christianity late in life. The deceased would have a cross on his chest, but just in case Odin was the right god after all, the bones would be lying in a layer of charcoal—symbolizing the flaming ship burials of the Norse religion."

"Did you find any treasure?" asked Frances. "My pupils love stories about buried treasure."

Emma shook her head. "Nothing much. A few Roman coins. It's the knowledge of Saxon Britain that we valued."

"It hardly seems worth the bother of excavating for a few lousy coins," said Susan. "I'd want to work on a dig where there was a chance of finding treasure. Like Egypt. I'll bet you could smuggle a lot of stuff out of the country without the authorities ever knowing. If your dig didn't find anything worth selling, how could they afford to pay you diggers?"

"We only got four shillings a day," Emma admitted. "That was lunch money."

Susan hooted. "Boy, talk about your migrant workers!"

Her fellow tourists glanced at each other, but no one said anything in reply.

They walked on in silence, reading the grave markers that made up the flooring of the cathedral and listening to the explanations provided by their distinguished guide. Charles Warren, armed with a complex-looking 35 mm. camera, was taking light readings and discreetly photographing the points of interest.

They admired the nave, built in 1079 by Bishop Walkelyn, a kinsman of William the Conqueror. ("Two hundred fifty feet long and seventy-seven feet high at the ridge rib," the guide informed them.)

After that, Elizabeth's attention began to flag. She followed the group dutifully through the south aisle, thinking about the gift shop and the hour of free time before the one o'clock departure of the coach. She only half listened to the details of Bishop Wykeham's transformation of the nave from three tiers to two; her admiration of the elaborately carved choir stalls of Norwegian oak was only perfunctory. She came back to full alert when the guide stopped before a collection of decorated wooden chests balanced on top of the stone side screens of the choir. "Boxes of bones," the guide repeated.

"Bones?" echoed Elizabeth with renewed ardor.

"That is correct. In 1524 Bishop Fox placed the bones in these chests. Kings, queens, and bishops are all collected together in the boxes atop that wall. We have most of the early monarchs of England. Westminster Abbey has many of the later ones."

"Do you ever open the boxes?" asked Elizabeth, hoping for a professional perusal of a royal skull. Examining the suture closures of William the Conqueror would be even better than waving at the present Queen from a distance of ten feet, her only royal encounter thus far.

"No," said the guide. "We never open the boxes."

A disappointed silence followed before the guide resumed his lecture. "Besides providing us with these boxes of royal bones, Bishop Fox has other claims to fame. He founded the college of Corpus Christi at Oxford and he served as Secretary and Lord Privy Seal to Henry VII."

Everyone nodded politely.

"I can take you down to see the crypt if you like," he offered.

This cheered them up immensely.

Alice MacKenzie, after wandering about the choir enclosure examining the carvings, had strayed farther afield. She called out, "Look what I found!"

The others turned to see her pointing to a simple stone slab, located beneath the tower in the very center of the cathedral. "It's King William Rufus!" she announced.

"This afternoon we're going to visit his death scene," Elizabeth told the guide.

The old gentleman cleared his throat. "Ah . . . hmmm. It was in Winchester Cathedral that Mary Tudor married Philip II of Spain in 1554. This marriage later gave Philip some claim to the throne of England and resulted in his sending of the Spanish Armada to reinforce that claim."

"William Rufus was murdered, you know," said Elizabeth happily. "It's unsolved."

After this exchange, the old gentleman became so distracted that he had to be reminded to show the group the grave of Jane Austen as they were leaving the church.

◆　◆　◆

AFTER A PICTURESQUE but tedious walkthrough of Winchester College, whose gates lay a few hundred yards from the cathedral, the group was temporarily disbanded for lunch, money-changing, or whatever other necessities suggested themselves to the ladies and Charles. They met again shortly before one o'clock in the lobby of the Wessex, where a smiling Rowan Rover awaited them, notes in hand.

"Good afternoon. Everyone behaved this morning, I trust? No going round saying 'We have two of those at home,' or making the vicar an offer for the altar silver?"

Wisely leaving the murder discussion unmentioned, they swore that they had behaved in an exemplary fashion. Then they allowed themselves to be shepherded aboard the bus for the afternoon's outing to the New Forest. They still occupied the front half of the vehicle, sitting two by two, like good schoolchildren. Rowan Rover took up his accustomed front row seat next to the coach door. Elizabeth, who obviously considered herself the tour's other murder specialist, slid in beside him. Susan Cohen sat alone in the other front seat and directed most of her remarks to Bernard, who pretended to be inordinately occupied with driving.

The day was bright and sunny, too warm even for a sweater: perfect weather for exploring the country lanes of rural Hampshire. Bernard eased the coach out of the parking lot. The coach rumbled slowly through the narrow streets of Winchester and headed for the A303 motorway south. A few miles outside the city, they would pick up the A31, which would take them southwest, bypassing Southampton, and in an hour's time they would be exploring the winding lanes of the New Forest.

"We will, of course, return to the hotel tonight for dinner and our second night's stay. Meanwhile, to start off this afternoon's jaunt, I must tell you a thing or two about the New Forest," said Rowan Rover, leaning into his microphone like a rock star. "It isn't new—and it isn't a forest."

"I'm not surprised," said Maud Marsh. "The British are always misnaming things. At lunch today they gave me a 7-Up and tried to tell me it was lemonade."

Kate Conway leaned forward in her seat, her pretty face the picture of bewilderment. "But, Rowan, if it isn't a new forest, then what is *the* New Forest?"

"For one thing, it's a thousand years old. In this country, I suppose that millennium-old things can be considered relatively new. It was the hunting preserve of William the Conqueror."

"Him again!" snapped Alice MacKenzie. "I suppose he destroyed a few villages to make this wilderness?"

"There are rumors to that effect," Rowan agreed. "And the preserve isn't a forest in the usual sense of the word. It is simply a wilderness area, comprised of heath, bog, and woodland that was not to be farmed or built upon. It was a game preserve for the noblemen—and only for the noblemen. Poachers were hanged. In fact, a commoner could have his eyes put out just for disturbing the huntsmen at their sport."

"Then how pleasant that the king should have been murdered there," said Elizabeth, with a republican glint in her eye.

Rowan Rover beamed. "Yes, I thought you colonials would feel that way. It was not, alas, William the Conqueror who met with this poetic justice. It was his son and successor William the Red, or William Rufus, as they called him, in lieu, perhaps of *Junior.*"

"Was he killed by a rebellious peasant?" asked Alice hopefully.

"No, it's much more sinister than that. Are you at all familiar with the case?" They all shook their heads.

"We saw his grave in the cathedral this morning," said Frances Coles.

"Interesting the way he ended up there," said Rowan with a knowing smile. "Here's what happened. On the evening of August second, in the year 1100, the red-haired King William II was finishing up a day's hunting with his seven fellow sportsmen. Incidentally, the way the Normans hunted game is absurd."

"Bow and arrow?" guessed Charles Warren.

"Yes, but they were complete idiots about it. For a stag hunt the band of archers would hide behind trees surrounding a clearing. When the beaters drove the deer forward into the clearing, all seven hunters would shoot wildly in the general direction of the other six."

"That sounds more like Russian roulette than deer hunting," said Charles Warren, shaking his head.

"It was madly dangerous. The wonder isn't that the king was shot, but that *anybody* ever came out of such a hunting party alive."

The group digested this information. Finally Martha Tabram said thoughtfully, "I suppose that such a system might be useful if you were interested in arranging a number of plausible accidents."

"Yes, I thought of that," said Rowan. "If the king was angry with any of his henchmen, he could arrange a hunting party and tell the other six not to aim at the deer. Anyhow, on that August evening, the stag got away, and it was the king who took an arrow in the heart."

Kate Conway, the nurse, looked shocked. "Was he shot deliberately?"

"I'm rather fond of the official story,"

Rowan said with a grin. "According to the other five hunters, the king's companion Walter Tyrrel shot an arrow at the stag; it *ricocheted off the animal's back*—and struck the king in the heart."

Charles Warren burst out laughing. "What a line! Did anybody actually believe it?"

"I myself consider it on a par with Woody Allen's joke about the man who committed suicide by shooting himself from a passing car. Walter Tyrrel was not charged with regicide. That does not, of course, mean that he wasn't guilty. It may simply mean that influential people were glad it happened. The fascinating element about the accident is that as soon as Tyrrel had killed the king, the entire hunting party fled the New Forest without a backward glance."

"What did they do with the king?" asked Kate, frowning at this medieval example of hit-and-run. "He would have gone into shock almost immediately."

Rowan chuckled. "So did they, I expect. They left him right where he had fallen. Several hours later a peasant passing through the forest found the body abandoned in the clearing. He loaded it onto his cart and carried it the twenty miles to Winchester."

"They left the king's body unattended? That seems rather disrespectful of his companions," said Elizabeth, whose royalist tendencies were never far from the surface.

"It suggests that their loyalties lay elsewhere," Rowan agreed.

"Wasn't the king a nice person?" asked Miriam Angel, who evidently pictured the late king as a Dark Ages version of Prince Charles. She drew her tweed jacket close around her, as if the chill of terrorism still lingered.

"Chroniclers of the time suggest that he was quite depraved," the guide told her. "They mention vices that delicacy forbids them to enumerate."

"French," said Alice darkly.

Rowan Rover shook his head. "I don't think sexual misconduct would have upset them much, no matter what his choice of partner: choirboys, sheep, whatever. Kings were entitled to their hobbies. Besides, in those days it was religion, not sex, that scandalized decent people."

"Religion?" said Kate.

"They think he may have belonged to some sort of occult group. I'm not an authority on such matters, though. I think we can assume that he was not held in esteem by anyone. But when one is discussing the monarchy, personal popularity is only incidental, don't you think?"

"Somebody wanted his job," Emma Smith said, by way of translation.

Rowan Rover nodded sagely. "Almost certainly. And they may have had excellent reasons for wanting him off the throne. Students of detection will be interested to learn that the king was killed on Thursday evening; his body reached Winchester by cart on Friday morning. By Friday noon he was buried, and that afternoon, his younger brother Henry had seized the Treasury, and was making his way to London to be crowned himself. There was no funeral for William, by the way, and no masses were said for his soul. He was simply dumped in his grave without ceremony."

"How very odd," said Martha Tabram with her usual air of calm detachment. "Kings are divinely appointed, according to tradition. Surely the priests at Winchester would have been in awe of the royal person, dead or not, and would have felt obliged to give him some sort of Christian burial."

"There are rumors," said Rowan Rover

in ominous tones. "Legend has it that the wooden arrow was never removed from William's chest. Does that remind you of anything?"

"A wooden stake through the vampire's heart!" cried Elizabeth.

"Something of the sort." Trust the Yanks to know Bram Stoker better than the Venerable Bede, he thought. Rowan sneaked a look at his notes. "The coffin was opened in 1868—I'm not sure why—and a wooden shaft was found among the bones."

"The arrow!" cried Frances Coles.

"But we still don't know who wanted him killed," said Kate, frowning.

"One doesn't like to be suspicious," said Elizabeth, who was always willing to give royalty the benefit of the doubt, "but did William's successor seem like the sort of person who would have had his own brother killed in order to seize power for himself?"

Rowan Rover shrugged. "Henry the First? Well, he had his other brother's eyes put out for trying to escape from house arrest."

Alice MacKenzie nodded triumphantly. "Bad blood in that family! I'll bet he wasn't much of an improvement as monarch."

"Thank God my relatives aren't like that," said Susan Cohen.

The guide paused for a moment with his mouth open. Finally he recovered enough to say, "As the Victorian lady said when she saw a production of *Antony and Cleopatra:* 'How very different from the home life of our own dear Queen.' "

Elizabeth was still considering the list of suspects. "Did Walter Tyrrel get anything from the new king? Was he made Lord Chancellor, or archbishop, or anything?"

"Not that I know of," said Rowan. "After eight hundred and ninety years, it's a bit late to be checking bank balances, and testing alibis."

Alice MacKenzie made a note in her travel diary: *Find out what became of Walter Tyrrel.*

Rowan pointed to the coach windows. "We are coming into more intriguing country," he remarked. "We have been traveling southwest and we are now between Salisbury and Bournemouth, heading for the tiny village of Minstead, in the heart of the New Forest. Has anyone read anything of Conan Doyle besides the Sherlock Holmes stories?"

They shook their heads.

"Did he write something else?" asked Frances.

Rowan Rover did not trust himself to elaborate. "He did. Sir Nigel, a character in *The White Company*, lives at Minstead. Conan Doyle himself lived east of here in Crowborough."

"What beautiful hedges!" said Nancy Warren. "Lovely gardens—and no billboards or gas stations. You can't tell it's the twentieth century here at all."

"The price of a pint in the pub will give you a hint," muttered Bernard from the driver's seat.

"Notice these picturesque cottages with their thatched roofs," said Rowan into the microphone. "Don't be fooled by all this rustic simplicity. These places cost the earth."

Susan Cohen looked unimpressed. "If you knew what my grandfather's house cost, you'd probably faint." She stifled a yawn.

"A pony!" cried Frances. "Look! He's wandering around loose beside the road."

"It's a New Forest pony," said Rowan. "They're wild. They still roam about wherever they like, so it's just as well that these narrow roads force one to go slow."

There was a pause while everyone in the coach waited to hear if there were wild ponies in Minnesota, but Susan had nodded off to sleep and was unavailable for comment. Rowan Rover leaned back in his seat and contemplated the hazardous possibilities of pastoral Hampshire. Fortunately or unfortunately, incompetent Norman archers no longer roamed the wilderness. It also seemed unlikely on this first day of the tour that Rowan would be able to bonk his victim on the head with a log in a peaceful forest glade without the presence of a gaggle of horrified onlookers. He knew that he could not expect to share Walter Tyrrel's good fortune in his witnesses: this lot would not run away in terror and say no more about the incident. Trust them to fight each other for pride of place on the evening news in their eagerness to shop him to the CID. He daren't risk anything. Rowan hunched down in his seat, oblivious to the glorious warmth of the late summer day.

♦ ♦ ♦

AFTER A FEW more minutes of travel through country lanes scarcely wider than the coach, Bernard eased into an expanse of grass at a crossroads facing a half-

119

timbered pub. "Minstead," he announced. "I'm not sure that road will take this vehicle, though." He indicated an even smaller hedge-lined road that led uphill from the pub.

Rowan Rover consulted his notes. "It can't be far. Minstead is a small village. Why don't we get out and walk to the church? It's just a little way up this road."

The tourists stood up and began to collect purses and cameras. "Should we wake up Susan?" asked Kate Conway, flashing her Bambi eyelashes at the guide.

No, let's leave her here with the bus running and a handkerchief stuffed in the tailpipe. Aloud Rowan Rover managed to say, "Yes, indeed. She wouldn't want to miss seeing the grave of Sir Arthur Conan Doyle. She may have heard of him."

Bernard had opened the coach door and was waiting outside to assist the travelers as they stepped down.

"Are you coming with us?" Maud Marsh asked him as she descended.

Bernard laughed. "Not me. I'll be having a cigarette break. Take your time, though."

Susan, stifling a yawn, grabbed her cardigan sweater and ambled off the bus. She looked around at the thatched cottage across the road, the ponies wandering about the green, the ancient pub, and finally at the steep and narrow road that curved away through trees and hedges.

"We have to walk?" she wailed. "Can't we get any closer?"

"No," said Maud, tying the laces of her running shoes. "The bus wouldn't make it up that narrow lane."

Susan sighed. "I hope it's worth seeing. I can't believe we have to walk a mile to look at some pokey old church. These are Italian leather shoes I'm wearing! And it's *uphill!*"

The pathos of this statement was diminished somewhat by the sight of Maud Marsh, some forty years her senior, striding briskly along as if she were on level ground.

"What flowers are those?" asked Nancy Warren, appearing at Rowan's elbow as they began the climb.

The guide peered over the privet hedge into a cottage garden, praying for a glimpse of a Michaelmas daisy. "I don't know," he said, frowning at a clump of dark pink blossoms in the direction of Nancy's pointing. "I'm afraid I'm no gardener. Now, if you could poison someone with it, I might possibly know."

"Impatiens," said Maud Marsh without breaking stride as she elbowed past.

"Nancy loves to garden," said Charles Warren. "Of course, in San Diego it's probably easier to get the stuff to grow. Warmer climate."

"What do you use for water?" asked Susan Cohen. "Stale Perrier? In Minnesota, we never have water rationing."

The Californians exchanged glances that suggested they'd like to hold her head under a basin full of it.

The road ended at a wrought-iron fence surrounding the small stone church. They stood for a moment before the arched entrance to the churchyard, taking in the beauty of the weathered stone, bathed in fading sunlight, and the serenity of the grounds, dotted only with simple crosses and gravestones. They felt out of place with their cameras and running shoes.

While Rowan Rover waited for the non-Californians to make it up the hill, he took another look at his notes. "I think we'll find Conan Doyle past the church, under one of the trees in the western part of the churchyard. Perhaps we ought to split up and have a go at reading tombstones."

Charles Warren took a few carefully me-tered shots of the church, and then followed the others into the churchyard. "This is an out-of-the-way place for Doyle to be buried, isn't it?" he asked the guide.

"Surely this is the only church at Minstead," said Rowan. "Oh, I see! You expected such a famous writer to be buried somewhere more grand? Westminster Abbey, perhaps?"

"Something like that," Warren admitted. "After all, they had Jane Austen in the cathedral at Winchester—and she wrote romance novels."

Rowan pictured certain Victorian scholars of his acquaintance ranting in apoplectic rage at this cavalier dismissal of their favorite novelist. The vision pleased him immensely. "Life is hardly fair, is it?" he remarked to Charles.

Up ahead they saw Emma Smith and her mother standing in front of a simple stone cross and waving semaphore-style to indicate that they found the grave. Soon everyone had gathered around it for a moment of silent homage, followed by an orgy of photography.

"You'd think he could have afforded a better monument than that," said Susan, lowering her camera.

"I'm surprised that it didn't say anything

about his books on the tombstone," said Kate Conway. "I thought someone might have chiseled CREATOR OF SHERLOCK HOLMS or something like that."

"Perhaps as a writer he felt that it was too late to advertise," said Rowan with all the solemnity he could muster. "Is everyone finished here? Pictures all taken? Then, I think we should move on. Before we start back, though, I thought we might have a look inside the church itself. My references indicate that there is a private pew that is most unusual."

He led the way to the church entrance and ushered his party inside the small sanctuary. It was a simple country church with worn wooden pews, a tiny balcony, and a Victorian stained-glass window that blazed in the golden light of afternoon. The three-paneled window featured a kneeling angel on each side in a landscape of trees and a bright blue sky. They faced the image of an armored knight leading a white horse. The inscription below was a memorial to a lieutenant in the Coldstream Guards, dead at twenty-four.

"Good heavens!" said Martha Tabram, staring up at the stained-glass window. "Do you know who that is?"

124

"Sir Galahad, I expect," said Rowan Rover, reading the inscription. "It's a memorial to a young soldier, you see."

"It's Ellen Terry," she replied. "I never expected to see *her* in a church."

"Who's Ellen Terry?" asked Elizabeth, hoping, at least, for a lady poisoner.

"She was the first actress to receive a knighthood, I believe, but she had a rather scandalous life. Two illegitimate children! At seventeen she married the painter George Frederick Watts, which is when she posed for that picture of Sir Galahad that the stained-glass window people so shamelessly copied. Perhaps they didn't know who posed for it."

"Perhaps they didn't care," Rowan observed. "After all, she has the face of an angel, doesn't she? Whereas Eleanor Roosevelt was a virtuous woman, full of good works, but hardly anybody's idea of a celestial being."

"But Ellen Terry isn't connected to any murder cases?" Elizabeth persisted.

"No, she seems to have had no trouble keeping that particular commandment," said Rowan. "It was the Seventh she found difficult to manage."

"Is that what we came to see?" asked

Susan, appearing at Rowan's elbow. "A stained-glass window? In Minneapolis, we have much bigger and more ornate—"

"No, actually, I didn't know about Miss Terry's cameo appearance in the Minstead church," said Rowan, hastening to shut her up. "My guidebooks advise me that the most renowned facets of this sanctuary are the ancient marble font and the squire's pew. The latter dates from Victorian times. I believe it is this way." He led them back down the aisle toward the altar and indicated a small windowed alcove in the front of the church to the left of the altar. The spacious compartment contained cushioned pews and footstools, all enclosed by a low wooden barricade. In the white wall in front of the pews was a coal fireplace, so that the squire's party could listen to the sermon in warm comfort.

For a moment of bemused silence, the group stared at the deluxe accommodations, contemplating the privileges of Victorian gentry. Finally Rowan Rover said, "I trust that the flames of their private fireplace provided them a foretaste of their own hereafter." In his student days, Rowan had dabbled in fashionable Socialism, and he had not entirely lost the habit of making egalitarian noises.

When everyone had finished exploring the little country church, Rowan Rover led the downhill march to the parking area, where Bernard sprawled in the driver's seat, cushioned in the blare of rock music from the radio. Maud Marsh, who hadn't had quite enough exercise yet, trotted past the group with a cheerful wave. As soon as she tapped on the door, he straightened up and adjusted the dial until somnolent classical strains again issued forth from the dashboard. "Hullo, again," he said, pushing the door lever. "Did you have a good walk?"

"Lovely, thank you!" Maud assured him. "The others will be along soon."

Bernard consulted his map. "And the next stop is the Rufus Stone, isn't it? That shouldn't be far from here."

Several minutes later Rowan Rover escorted the rest of the group back to the coach. He counted them off one by one as they climbed on board. "Eleven. All here, then." He nodded to Bernard. "Can you get us to the Rufus Stone?"

"No bother," said Bernard. "Tea first or after?"

"After, I think," said Rowan, glancing at his watch. "Murder first."

The road to the heart of the New Forest reminded Elizabeth of a stretch of woodland in the Virginia Shenandoah, where trees shrouded the road. Modern pavement aside, it could be any century at all. Sunlight filtered through the spreading leaves, dappling the road with patches of light, and an unfettered brown pony ambled along the verge, untroubled by the passing coach. A few miles beyond the village of Minstead, Bernard pulled off into a gravel parking lot situated next to the road in a grove of trees. No buildings were in sight.

"This is where we park to go and see the stone," he explained as he cut the engine. "It's just across the road there."

They filed out of the bus and waited for Rowan Rover to lead the expedition twenty yards across an empty road to the clearing where William II had died like a deer.

Susan Cohen was reminded of Loring Park, the city park across from the Walker Sculpture Garden in downtown Minneapolis. She was making her comparison in exhaustive narrative detail.

"Susan, be careful!" murmured Elizabeth as they stepped out onto the pavement.

"What do you mean? Nothing is coming."

"Yes, but you looked the wrong way before you crossed," Elizabeth pointed out. "In Britain they drive on the left side of the road."

"Well, I've only been here one day," said Susan. "It's hard to remember petty details like that."

It might help if you got your mind out of Minnesota, thought Elizabeth. "Just be careful, will you? London traffic will be a lot less forgiving than this New Forest bridle path."

As royal monuments go, the Rufus Stone was relatively modest, even casual. It stood near the center of the clearing, well within sight of the coach: a waist-high slab of stone recording the king's fate matter-of-factly in small chiseled letters along the side of the marker.

While the group took turns posing beside the Rufus Stone, Rowan Rover evidently felt that some sort of summation was called for. "On this spot, at approximately seven o'clock on the evening of August second, in the year 1100, King William Rufus was felled by an arrow and died."

"Do people die instantly from arrow wounds?" asked Elizabeth, who was back on the case.

"They do if it gets them directly in the heart," said Kate Conway with medical authority. "And aside from that, they might go pretty fast anyway if the wound was severe enough. I work in the emergency room, and you'd be surprised how fast people can die if they go into shock."

"Pretty lucky shot for a deer ricochet, though," Charles Warren observed with a touch of sarcasm in his voice.

"August second," Emma Smith repeated. "I wonder if that means anything."

Rowan Rover nodded approvingly. "It's the day after Lammas, a pagan festival generally requiring human sacrifice. Did I mention that the king's son had died of an arrow in the New Forest just three months earlier on the eve of the spring festival— Beltane!"

Alice MacKenzie was shocked. "The king was killed by a cult?"

"The theory has been proposed," Rowan Rover admitted, following his Ripper custom of never saying whodunit. "There has always been a tradition of the divine victim, the king who must be sacrificed to ensure the harvest. The mumming rituals are based on those old beliefs, and so is the legend that inspired *King Lear.*"

"It would explain why the Christian priests gave him no funeral, and said no masses for him," Emma mused.

Her mother nodded in agreement. "They surely would have said a mass for him otherwise."

"I suppose the treeline here has changed in the past nine hundred years," said Elizabeth. "Because if it hasn't, that's suspicious. The legend says the hunters took cover behind trees, but there are no trees within twenty feet of this stone that marks the death scene."

"My sources say that the treeline hasn't changed," Rowan told her. "Apparently, the clearing itself is marshy and incapable of supporting trees, so the scene should look approximately as it did then."

"It wasn't a hunting accident," Elizabeth declared. "He was deliberately assassinated."

"Ritual sacrifices can't be considered murder," said Emma Smith.

"That's true," said Martha Tabram. "It isn't as if he were done in by some shabby thug for *money.*"

Rowan Rover reddened slightly, and drowned out further comments with a smoker's cough. "All very interesting," he managed to say at last. "But it is getting a bit late and I for one could use a drink. Do you suppose we might continue this postmortem in a pub? I believe there's one within walking distance, just down the road."

He ushered his charges back across the road, signaled to Bernard to follow in the coach, and marched them a few hundred yards around the bend to a large half-timbered pub set in its own graveled parking lot. One look at the quaintly-lettered inn sign caused everyone to burst out laughing.

"Good heavens!" said Alice MacKenzie. "The Walter Tyrrel Pub!" She pointed to the inn sign, with its carefully painted illustration depicting the deer and the deflected arrow striking William.

Martha Tabram shook her head. "Oh, dear. How gauche. They've named the local pub after the king's murderer!"

"Sometimes crime does pay," said Rowan Rover with a smile.

CHAPTER 7

*"The reports of my death
have been greatly exaggerated."*
—Mark Twain

STONEHENGE TO TORQUAY

BREAKFAST ON DAY two of the tour was an eight o'clock buffet in the Wessex Hotel, after which they would be departing for the wilds of Devonshire. Rowan Rover, who had no objections to early hours or free meals, joined the breakfasters and found himself at a table with the smuggest of the party's early birds: Alice MacKenzie, Maud Marsh, and Susan Cohen. Rowan, in an aging sky-blue pullover and black pants, looked rather like an early bird himself, or perhaps like an insomniac parakeet.

Rowan began the meal with a bowl of shredded cereal, topped with milk and figs. After bidding his tablemates a brisk good morning and noting that they also had plates of food before them, he began

133

to attack this first course in cheerful anticipation of his just-ordered coffee.

"Aren't you supposed to drink tea?"
asked Susan, whose own cup sported a
dangling string and a square of card-
board.

"I prefer coffee," said Rowan, halting a
spoonful of cereal inches from his lips.

"But you're English. I thought Americans drank coffee and English people drank
tea."

"I am a defector."

"And what's that stuff you're eating?"
Susan persisted. "Ee-ooo. It looks like the
sort of wood shavings they put in boxes
of china to keep them from breaking.
Sawdust. I ordered an English breakfast."

Rowan showed his teeth in a parody of
a smile. "You must try the blood pudding,"
he purred.

"I know all about British customs," she
informed him. "I have all of *Upstairs Downstairs* on video. And I've read all of Dorothy
Sayers."

This remark inspired Alice MacKenzie to
a new line of questioning. "I love Dorothy
Sayers! Especially *Gaudy Night*. You went
to Oxford, didn't you, Rowan?"

"Somewhat after Miss Sayers' own time

in residence there, yes," said Rowan Rover cautiously.

"I'm really looking forward to touring Oxford," said Alice. "In the footsteps of Peter Wimsey! Are *you* a Balliol man as well?"

"Ah . . . no," said Rowan, balancing another spoonful of cereal within loading distance.

"Christ Church?"

"No, that's a rather exalted place, and I was just a clever youth without peer." Rowan smiled at his own pun.

Alice cast about for other possibilities. "Magadalen? Trinity? Merton?"

"Ah!" said Maud Marsh. "T. S. Eliot *and* J. R. R. Tolkien both went to Merton." They looked at Rowan expectantly.

He looked longingly at his soggy cereal. "No, actually . . . I went to Keeble."

This admission was received with a silence that made it patently obvious that they had never heard of Keeble. They may have been entertaining some doubt as to whether there was such a college. Rowan felt himself redden at this impugning of his credentials.

"It's one of the modern colleges," he said petulantly. "Founded in the early part of this century. Not as arty and hidebound as some of the old ones, where they want blue blood instead of brains."

"I expect it was a lot cheaper, too," Susan remarked, eyeing his ratty pullover.

At that moment a white-coated teenager arrived, bearing a stainless steel pot which he set before Rowan Rover with a flourish of personal triumph at having remembered both the beverage and the existence of the diner. "Ah, my coffee," said Rowan, grateful for the diversion. He poured a few drops into his cup and inspected the result. "This doesn't look like . . ." He raised the cup to his lips and, seconds later, sputtered out his verdict. "Bloody Earl Grey!"

"Do you want to call the waiter back?" asked Alice.

"No, it took him an age to bring this. God knows how long he'd be if we asked for something else. Since the Americans evidently expect it of me, and the waiters conspire to abet them, I shall drink tea." He reached for the cream jug.

"Milk in first?" asked Susan, raising her eyebrows. "I thought you weren't supposed to do that. Isn't it—what's the phrase?—non-U?"

"If it's me, it's U," muttered Rowan, stirring the fawn-colored beverage. Suddenly the prospect of doing away with Susan Cohen had become a little less dreadful to contemplate.

◆ ◆ ◆

FIRST BERNARD COUNTED the suitcases, counted them again, and stowed them into the coach's luggage compartment. Then Rowan Rover took a head count of the passengers, and, satisfied that all were accounted for, he ushered them onto the bus, where they took up their accustomed positions, sitting two by two in a clump at the front.

"Good morning, ladies and Charles!" said Rowan, standing in the aisle and addressing them without benefit of microphone. "Does everyone have sweaters out? It's a bit chillier today and we are going to do a bit of walking, as our first stop is Stonehenge. Did everyone have breakfast? I hope so, because lunch today is as usual—*on your own,* which means that we'll stop in a pub somewhere along the route."

"Aren't there any pizza places in England?" asked Susan plaintively.

"Not as many as in Minneapolis," said Rowan between clinched teeth.

137

"I went to Stonehenge when I was over on the archaeological dig in 'sixty-eight," said Emma Smith. "I don't suppose it has changed much since then."

From the driver's seat came Bernard's short laugh. "Don't bet on it, miss!"

An hour later Emma had to admit the truth of Bernard's remark. The coach made its way out of the narrow streets of Winchester; from the A34 to the A303, a large modern motorway that took them across the chalk downs of Wiltshire and straight to Stonehenge. *Straight to Stonehenge.*

As they approached the great neolithic monument, Maud Marsh said sadly, "I never pictured a highway going ten feet past the heelstone."

"That was there in 1968," said Emma, studying the scene. "But the fence wasn't."

"Vandals," said Bernard over his shoulder. "Stonehenge draws loonies like a flame draws moths."

He pulled the coach into the paved car park across the road from the great stone circle. It was already crowded with other tour buses and dozens of private cars. They stood in the lot beside the coach, braving the chill wind, while Rowan consulted his notes. "I have a pass here to get us in as a group," he announced. "Everyone follow me, please."

"They sell tickets?" asked Miriam Angel, sounding shocked and grieved. "To Stonehenge? We don't charge people to go into the Lincoln Memorial."

Bernard shrugged. "Maybe the Druids need the money." He got back on board and adjusted his radio to a rock station to while away the tour time.

"It wasn't built by the Druids," Emma was explaining to her comrades as they trotted after Rowan across the parking lot. They discovered that the south end of the lot was equipped with concrete steps leading to a subterranean level, containing lavatories, a gift shop, and the ticket booth. In order to reach Stonehenge, tourists had to pass through an iron gate and walk through a tunnel built under the highway, which brought them out near the monument on the other side.

Rowan shepherded the group through the admission gates with his British Heritage tour pass, but he lost control as soon as they were through the gate. Elizabeth MacPherson led a charge to the gift shop, followed by Kate Conway and Nancy Warren.

"I promised a couple of the student nurses that I'd send postcards," Kate explained to the scowling guide.

"One of my daughters wanted a Stonehenge poster," murmured Nancy.

"It's cold out there," said Elizabeth, when Rowan attempted to round them up. "We're just getting warm before we walk out to the monument."

"You have ten minutes," said Rowan in his most authoritative voice. He then stalked off toward the lavatory.

Twelve minutes later the renegades emerged from gift shop and ladies' room, laden with packages and ready to inspect the great stone circle. They followed Rowan through the tunnel and up the other set of stairs.

Fifty yards in front of them the great stones towered against a watery blue sky, but the majesty of the monument was diminished considerably by the chain-link fence surrounding it—and the paved path that encircled it, currently full of other tourists. An icy wind pushed them along toward the stone uprights.

"The stones in the outer ring are made of a material called *sarsen*," Rowan Rover shouted above the wind. "Which is a type of sandstone formed on chalk deposits in prehistoric seas. The horseshoe of uprights within the sarsen circle are called bluestones, because in dry weather there is a bluish-gray tinge to their surfaces. They are made of a crystalline rock called dolerite. Actually, though, the first circle is one that can hardly be seen. It lies beyond the path on which we are walking. If you look closely at the field, you may see traces of chalk from some of the fifty-six Aubrey holes that surround Stonehenge in a circle 288 feet in diameter."

"What were these holes for?" asked Kate Conway, scanning the field of scrub grass for traces of the outer ring.

"There were bodies in them, weren't there?" asked Emma Smith, summoning up memories from her days on the dig.

Before Rowan Rover could find a note to cover that question, Elizabeth MacPherson, the other amateur archaeologist, said, "Yes, but they were put in after the holes were dug and refilled. Maybe not by the original builders."

"One theory," said Rowan, who had found his place in the guidebook, "is that they reflect the same beliefs that caused the Greeks to dig similar pits, called *bothros,* in ancient times. If so, then they indicate a belief in a netherworld—like Hades—and the pits are symbolic passageways to the gods below. And the worshipers may have filled the holes with sacrifices to these gods from time to time."

"The Druids practiced human sacrifice, didn't they?" asked Susan.

"They didn't build Stonehenge!" said Emma and Elizabeth together.

Susan looked puzzled. "Who did?"

Rowan Rover, who was fortunately a fast reader, flipped through page after page of his guidebook. "Good luck getting a straight answer on that one," he said at last. "Apparently, Stonehenge was modified by a succession of prehistoric builders, so that you can't attribute the thing to just one group. British archaeologists go on about the Windmill Hill culture, and the Beaker culture, and the Secondary Neolithic, until you scarcely remember what it was you wanted to know in the first place."

"They sound like Grammy nominees, don't they?" giggled Kate Conway.

"I wouldn't know," snapped Rowan. "Does anyone else have any questions? Several of the Californians are beginning to turn blue with cold."

"It's not cold by Canadian standards," said Martha Tabram, smiling. "I wanted to ask how prehistoric people could build such a huge structure."

"You mean the standing stones? We think they went up much later than the first circle—around 1700 B.C. I think we can assume that it was laborious work, requiring years of skill and patience."

"When I was on the dig in Winchester, our archaeologist lectured on Stonehenge. He said that they excavated the field next to it, and found a cemetery full of crushed skeletons."

"The sign of a bad construction worker," said Rowan, eyeing the carefully balanced stones and the chain-link fence with a curious expression of regret.

Charles Warren, sensibly attired in a red ski parka, and not shivering, said, "I saw a TV special once that claimed that Stonehenge was a prehistoric observatory, designed to tell when it was midsummer and midwinter. Something about the way the sun rose in relation to the rocks. Is there any truth to that?"

"That's what we were told when I was here in 'sixty-eight," said Emma Smith.

Rowan Rover smiled. "Like most academic theories, that one went out of fashion after a decade or so. The current one, I believe, is that the neolithic people danced here. Archaeologists have found buried surfaces that they say were compacted by the pounding of dancing feet many centuries ago. I find that theory compelling, because a number of similar local legends survive about various rings of standing stones. Tradition always says that the stones themselves are dancers forever frozen in their tracks as punishment for some sin they committed, like breaking the Sabbath."

"It is definitely a holy place," said Maud Marsh, gazing admiringly at the ring of stones. "I get the same feeling here that I got in Winchester Cathedral."

"I don't doubt it," said Rowan. "I'm sure it was a temple to its builders, whatever uses they made of it, and despite the tacky little fence and the tourists, quite a bit of that majesty survives."

"There is a stone circle in Scotland," said Elizabeth. "It's called Callanish, and it's on the island of Lewis. Luckily, there is no fence around that one. Of course, it isn't as famous as Stonehenge, or as accessible."

"Just as well," said Rowan. "The world is too much with us late and soon."

Frances Coles waved her tiny automatic camera. "Just stand together, everybody, would you? I want to get a group shot with Stonehenge in the background. Everybody smile!"

◆ ◆ ◆

"TORQUAY, ISN´T IT?" asked Bernard, when the freezing tourists had been loaded back into the coach. "Any particular route you'd fancy?"

Rowan Rover knelt down beside the driver's seat and studied the road atlas. "Here we are above Salisbury," he murmured, tracing the A303 with his finger. "And we have to get down to the Devon coast in reasonably good time. Shops tend to close at five, don't they? Not tourist season anymore, really."

"We should stay on the A303 to Honiton, I should think," said Bernard. "Lunch there? By then it ought to be about one o'clock. Then the A30, bypass Exeter, pick up the A18, and take it to the A380. That will take us straight in. We should be there by half past three, if you don't take too long eating your lunch."

Rowan cast a steely eye at the shopping members of the party, who were happily engaged in comparing Stonehenge postcards, tea towels, and tiny replicas of the circle itself. "I'll be ruthless," he promised, reaching for the microphone. "Ladies and Charles, as you know from your schedule, you will be staying tonight in Exeter, but for this afternoon's outing, it will be necessary for us to bypass Exeter and drive on to Torquay, where we will view the Agatha Christie exhibit in Torre Abbey. After that, it will be a drive of an hour or so to get you back to Exeter to your hotel. Any questions?"

Charles Warren raised his hand. "Lunch?"

"Bernard and I think that Honiton will provide a few suitable restaurants—"

"Honiton lace," said Martha Tabram. "Is it the same place?"

Rowan Rover frowned. "If you wish to get to Torre Abbey before it closes, you will confine yourselves to a brief lunch stop. Are we all agreed?"

There was a mutinous set to Elizabeth's jaw, but it was early days yet on the tour. There would be time to shop later. The others agreed cheerfully.

"Well then, say goodbye to the Beaker People. We're off to the English Riviera."

♦ ♦ ♦

TRUE TO THEIR word, the group passed up a street full of inviting curio and antique shops and descended en masse into the Three Tuns Pub on the Honiton High Street, immediately outnumbering the bemused locals. They packed themselves in fours around wooden tables the size of poker chips, sharing one paper menu per table and speculating on the entrees like sharks at a swim meet. Rowan Rover explained, between sips of a pint of ale, that prawns were shrimp, cider was not synonymous with apple juice, and there were no waitresses in pubs. If they wanted to eat, they'd better join the queue at the bar.

"Can't you get anything nonalcoholic?" asked Susan. "I hate beer. And why are these tables so tiny? And no waitresses?"

Rowan Rover sighed. "A far cry from the Minneapolis Burger King, I have no doubt."

She frowned at the menu. "What is this stuff anyway. What are you having, Rowan?"

"A double Scotch and three cigarettes. For my nerves."

Bernard, who did not appear in the

147

crowded pub, had presumably found somewhere else to eat, because precisely forty-
five minutes later, when Rowan had herded
the flock back to the appointed meeting
place on a corner of the high street, Bernard
was already there, with the door open and
classical music to aid the digestive process.

For the next couple of hours, as they
passed through Dorset, Rowan Rover confined his remarks to explaining points of interest on the landscape ("That rounded hill
is believed to be the site of King Arthur's
great battle at Badon Hill, as are the
Badbury Hill in Oxfordshire, and the one
near Swindon in Wiltshire") and answering
questions about objects sighted by the tourists as they rode along ("That, madam, is
a goat"). Several members of the party took
advantage of the indifferent motorway scenery and the inducement of a full stomach.
They slept the untroubled sleep of the jet-
lagged.

At one point, noticing the mention of
Torquay on a highway sign, Frances Coles
asked, "Are we by any chance going to pass
the spot where Agatha Christie staged her
disappearance in the Twenties?"

Rowan Rover, whose knowledge of English literature did not extend to the private

controversies of mystery writers, met this query with a blank stare. "I know she went missing for a week or so," he said at last. "Somebody produced a movie based on the case. I don't know where she took off from, though. She was born in Torquay, but I don't think she lived there as an adult."

"She disappeared near Guilford," said Alice MacKenzie, who maintained that Agatha Christie's work reached a plane of literary perfection to which Thomas Hardy could only aspire. "I've read two biographies of her."

"Oh, *Guilford*," said Rowan Rover, in tones suggesting that it might as well be Hoboken. "That's practically on the outskirts of London. We're nowhere near it."

"What do you make of her disappearance?" asked Elizabeth MacPherson, grasping at this straw of a crime.

"Amnesia under a strain isn't all that uncommon," Rowan suggested.

"It's more common if there has been a head injury," said Kate Conway. "Personally, I've never seen a case."

"Amnesia!" said Alice MacKenzie. "Ha!"

"I really know very little about the incident, but she was a very shy woman, wasn't she? Hardly the sort of person to stage a publicity stunt."

"I don't think it was a publicity stunt," said Alice, leaning forward and speaking in a stage whisper, so as not to disturb the sleeping Frances. "But I do think she did it on purpose."

"Wasn't her husband having an affair?" asked Kate Conway.

"Yes! And he had gone off to spend the weekend with his girlfriend," said Alice triumphantly. "So Agatha crashes her car into a pond, leaves her expensive fur coat on the seat, and vanishes. The police assume foul play, of course, and guess who they suspect?"

"The husband," sighed Rowan Rover. "They always do."

"Right! He gets a grilling from the authorities, and his private life *and* the girlfriend's name become front page news. Hundreds of people are out combing the woods for Agatha's body. It's the nine days' wonder of all of England."

"Where was she?" asked Charles Warren, postponing his nap.

"In a fancy hotel in Harrogate, attending tea dances and reading newspaper accounts of her own disappearance," Alice informed

him. "If she hadn't planned her disappearance, how did she happen to be carrying
enough money for a two-week stay at an
expensive hotel? And what name do you
suppose she registered under?"

"The girlfriend's," said Rowan with a
sinking heart. His second wife was just the
sort of person who would have done that.

"Exactly! Agatha wasn't ill. She was brilliant. She humiliated her rotten husband in
front of the entire world. Serves him right!"

"And did he give up the other woman and
go back to Agatha?"

"No!" cried Rowan, Charles, and Bernard in unison.

Alice regarded them with the look of an
entomologist who has just identified their
species. "You're right," she said evenly. "A
year later Archie Christie divorced her and
married the other woman."

"But he probably wasn't worth having
anyway," Kate Conway pointed out. "I
know a plastic surgeon who's just like that.
He's married two nurses so far and made
them both miserable. Archie Christie
sounds rather heartless to me."

"True," said Alice. "And at least Agatha
made him suffer."

"We're coming into Torquay now," Bernard told Rowan. "So you're all going to tour this sneaky lady's museum, eh?"

"Isn't it thrilling," said the guide, without any trace of enthusiasm. He was envisioning a Rowan Rover exhibit in a museum, should one be dedicated to his second wife, who, fortunately, was not famous. The Rover Husband display would feature his most unflattering portrait (the hangover one, perhaps) with concentric circles drawn around it, and a list of his faults in easily readable red letters: WEARS SAFETY PINS IN FLY.

With a sigh of resignation, he turned to his notes on Torre Abbey.

◆ ◆ ◆

BECAUSE OF THEIR proximity to the Gulf Stream, Cornwall and the coast of Devon enjoy a much warmer climate than most of the rest of Britain, and the south coast's balmy beaches and palm trees had earned it the title of English Riviera. It was evident that Torquay was the holiday spot for a goodly number of Britons, because the road into the city was lined with large houses displaying bed and breakfast signs on their well-tended lawns.

Since the majority of people on the mystery tour were southern Californians, they were less impressed with Torquay than they might have been. Kate Conway was comparing the city to San Diego's own island of Coronado and Elizabeth MacPherson, the representative of the other American coast, sniffed and said, "Virginia Beach." Clearly the group preferred thatched cottages and half-timbered pubs to the twentieth-century bustle of a British seaside community, with its traffic and its commercialism.

"This looks very familiar," said Nancy Warren, peering out at a motel with balconies and wrought-iron railings. "Doesn't it remind you of San Diego, Charles?"

Her husband grunted. "Yeah, we could have seen this at home and saved six grand."

While Bernard navigated through the late afternoon traffic, Rowan Rover consulted a city map and called out street names to look for in order to reach the abbey. Fifteen minutes and several orbits later, Bernard pulled the bus up to the curb on Falkland Road and said, "I don't think there's going to be any place to park nearby. Why don't I let you out here, and come back for you in a bit. All right?"

"Fair enough," said Rowan, standing up and stretching. "It's only a block up to the abbey. Ladies and Charles, we're getting off here."

As he marched them up the street toward the abbey, Rowan recited the particulars of the afternoon's attraction. "Torre Abbey has belonged to the city of Torquay since 1930. Before that it was the home of the Cary family, and before that it was a monastery for . . ." He took a deep breath. "Premonstratensian Canons. Built in 1196."

"What is . . . what you said?" asked Kate Conway.

"I haven't the faintest idea," Rowan assured her. "Some species of monk, I presume. Ask your guide at the abbey. They provide their own tours." *And I shall wait out in the garden and smoke copious quantities of cigarettes in blissful solitude,* he finished silently.

A few moments later they turned the corner and came within sight of Torte Abbey. Very little of the original twelfth-century architecture remained, except some ruins away from the converted abbey. Most of the structure was a solid red-brick building with white-trimmed windows, reminiscent of an American elementary school. It certainly did not resemble the group's idea of an eight-hundred-year-old edifice.

"And what is its connection with Agatha Christie?" asked Maud Marsh.

"Only that this is the city of her birth," said Rowan. "And since this is the city's museum, they have set aside a room in her honor. The abbey also has a restored Victorian kitchen that serves teas. Off we go."

He bounded up the steps and into the spacious main hallway. Beside the door was an information desk, manned by a guard/ticket-taker.

"Good afternoon," said Rowan briskly. "I believe you have a reservation for a mystery tour of a dozen persons booked to see the abbey today."

The man behind the counter glanced at a chart and assured the group that they were expected. "We haven't any guides this afternoon, though," he said. "We were terribly busy earlier in the month, and now they've all taken advantage of the lull to get a bit of time off themselves."

"No guides!" Rowan looked stricken.

"Don't worry. You can take them round yerself, sir. I have a sheet here that specifies what all the exhibits are. Everything is numbered so you can't get it wrong. All right? Off you go, then!"

Rowan Rover, still parchment-pale and muttering under his breath, stalked off in the direction indicated by the guard, while the mystery tourists pattered happily in his wake. *Bloody ad-libbing. What if they ask me something not on this handout?*

They entered a small room filled with ship models in glass cases. "Ladies and Charles, here we have a collection of ship models in glass cases, no doubt of sentimental importance to the folk of a coastal town," said the impromptu guide in the hearty tone one uses to persuade children to eat asparagus. "Aren't they neatly painted?"

The group dutifully admired the tiny ships for several seconds. Thereupon they proceeded to further exhibits. "Here we have one of the Cary family drawing rooms. It is called the Blue Room, perhaps because of its blue walls. That constitutes a guess on my part. This paper does not actually say that." Rowan looked around. "The room contains a crystal chandelier, a fireplace, the sort of marble statue that unscrupulous Italian con men-cum-antique dealers used to sell to . . ." He checked himself in mid-editorial. "Never mind. Some sculptures. And some landscape paintings of the Christmas card school of art. Take a moment to admire it." He ran his finger down the page of exhibit listings.

"My aunt Amanda would enjoy this room," said Elizabeth. "She has several very much like it."

"It doesn't look like an abbey to me," sniffed Frances Coles. "I have read *all* of the Brother Cadfael novels, and I know about twelfth-century monasteries."

"I expect the family did extensive renovations," said Martha Tabram. "People usually do when they buy an older home. We did. The Carys had over two hundred years of ownership in which to redecorate."

"I wonder if it would be expensive to redecorate a place like this," mused Susan. "We have some wonderful old mansions along the Mississippi."

"I thought you lived in Minnesota," said Rowan.

"I do. On the Mississippi."

Right, thought Rowan, *and I am king of the Belgians.* American geography had eluded him completely. "And I am sure that Minneapolis has museums just as fine as this one," he said carefully.

"It does remind me of the Sibley House in Mendota," said Susan, serenely unconscious of self-incrimination. "It was the home of Minnesota's first state governor. Of course, it isn't as old as this."

"Perhaps if the Vikings had been more politically inclined, it could have been," Rowan murmured. "Of course, then it would have been the Leif Erickson House."

"I wonder if it would cost much to heat this place," said Charles Warren, eager to change the subject.

His wife shivered. "To get it as warm as I'd want, you'd have to set fire to it."

"Ah!" said Rowan Rover. "The guide sheet informs me that there is an exhibit of marble statuary through this passage in another small room. Supposedly by a local sculptor . . . nineteenth century . . . Ah, here we are . . ." He looked appraisingly at the conglomeration of carved figures jamming the tiny room. "Oh, dear, yes. He *was* a local sculptor, wasn't he? I believe his name was . . ." Rowan had lost his place on the fact sheet, so he improvised. ". . . Fred Smith."

"*The* Fred Smith?" asked Elizabeth solemnly.

"No," said Rowan Rover. "*A* Fred Smith."

A few more rooms finished the ground-floor exhibits, and Rowan led them up a wide marble staircase festooned with paintings which, after the first shudder, he steadfastly ignored. "The Agatha Christie room is tucked away somewhere up here," he muttered. "I suppose we'll have to plow through more of this to find it, though."

He poked his nose into one dimly lit room. "Ah!" he cried, turning to face his party. "There seems to be a real painting here. Come on, come in. That large picture over there is *The Children's Holiday* by Holman Hunt. It is the showpiece of the collection." He stepped back to what he hoped was out of earshot and murmured, "Dear God, I never thought I'd see Holman Hunt seem so exalted. I think they use him at the Tate to prop doors open."

Frances Coles, who quite liked Victorian art, was gazing admiringly at the happy scene of a matronly woman presiding over a silver-laden tea table at an outing with her five children and their various pets. It was as exact as a photograph, and seemed to capture the children's personalities in their varying expressions.

"You can tell *she* had domestic help," said Alice MacKenzie, who was also studying the painting.

"I wonder if they had to cook all those things for the picnic every time Mr. Hunt came to paint some more on the picture," mused Kate Conway.

Having already given Mr. Holman Hunt considerably more than his due, in Rowan's jaded opinion, the guide shooed them out into another passageway. "Now this is more like it!" he exclaimed, catching a glimpse of the framed drawings that lined the corridor. "These are William Blake's own illustrations for *Songs of Innocence*. Wonderful! I thought these were in the Tate!" While the group congregated around the first few etchings, Rowan took another look at his crib sheets. "Reproductions!" he exclaimed. "The originals *are* in the Tate!" Seeing the questioning expression on the faces of his followers, Rowan forced a note of enthusiasm back into his voice. "But these are very good copies. Quite recognizable. And should you ever visit the Tate, you will know what to look for. Let's move along, shall we."

The next room proved to be the Carys' dining room, formally decorated eighteenth-century style, with pale green walls and an ornate ceiling, all adorned with white bas-relief scenes of Roman figures and other ancient images.

"You have heard of the famous architect Robert Adam and the term *Adam room?*" Rowan solemnly inquired.

Eagerly, they all nodded that they had indeed.

"Well, this isn't one." He turned on his heel and walked out.

He was more enthusiastic about an unconverted part of the ancient building, with its thick stone walls and simple medieval lines. These rooms were used as workrooms for the servants. As they wound their way up the twisting stone staircase, Nancy Warren noticed a small slit in an alcove by the stairs. "What is this hole for, Rowan?" she asked. "It reminds me of a laundry chute, but it's too small."

"You're on the right track," he said. "It's . . . why don't you lean over and take a deep breath just above it."

After a moment's hesitation, Nancy and Alice did as he suggested.

"It smells like my catbox," Alice declared.

Rowan nodded approvingly. "Identical

purpose, but for people instead of cats. The smell never quite comes out of the stone."

Elizabeth MacPherson muttered, "Remind me not to buy a castle."

"But where is the Agatha Christie room?" asked Maud Marsh, tugging at the sleeve of the guide's sweater.

He ran his finger along the map. "I think if we go through this door, we should be there. So, if no one wishes to try out the laundry chute, let us proceed."

They emerged again into the renovated part of the ancient abbey, in a carpeted upstairs hallway. "Here we are," Rowan announced, peering into an open door. "This door on the right. Go right in."

There was barely space for a dozen people in the tiny room with its casement window—and its air of having been a bedroom before the museum people started stashing exhibits in every cranny. The walls were now taken up with bookcases, all filled with various editions of Agatha Christie's eighty-odd novels, and amidst this literary display were a few framed, unautographed photos, a *Mousetrap* program, and a battered manual typewriter. Gravely the group studied these tributes to the city's most famous author.

Finally Susan Cohen broke the leaden silence. "I have a better collection than this," she said quietly. "I have a copy of every book she ever wrote, too, and I have seen all these photos elsewhere. Except that one over there, of her brother's dog."

"I have a movie poster from *Death on the Nile*," said Frances Coles.

Maud Marsh peered at the photographs and frowned. "I don't get any feeling of the woman herself from this room."

"That would have pleased her," said Rowan. "I do know that much about her."

"Did you say this place served teas?" asked Charles Warren, who had endured the afternoon's enlightenment with remarkable forbearance.

"Yes, and I think it's time we sampled them," said Rowan. "Nearly five. Everyone ready? I think there's a staircase we haven't tried at the end of this hall." His voice trailed off into a mutter. "God knows what they'll have stuck up on it. Stuffed badgers in choir robes, I expect."

Alice MacKenzie caught up with him on the way downstairs. "Look, Rowan," she said. "This month is the centennial of Agatha Christie's birth. There's bound to be some sort of commemoration here in

Torquay. God knows it isn't *here*. Maybe there's another museum, or if we could just go into a few shops. I promised Phyllis back at Grounds for Murder—that's our mystery bookstore in San Diego—that I'd bring her back something on the centennial for the shop, a tea towel or something. Couldn't we just go into town and look?"

Rowan shook his head. "Sorry," he told her. "We're on a tight schedule, and I have to get you back to Exeter in time for a seven o'clock reception." *Really,* he thought to himself, *if this lot had been on the Crusades, they would have bought the Holy Land.*

Elizabeth MacPherson, who was just behind them on the stairs, had overheard this exchange. "Yes, Alice," she said eagerly. "We have to get to the hotel in Exeter as soon as possible. Someone's going to be murdered!"

"Oh, dear! Rowan, are you all right? These stairs *are* treacherous, aren't they?"

CHAPTER 8

"Well, that's over. I hope my tea won't be late."

Eric Holt,
upon leaving the dock after receiving the death sentence (1920)

EXETER

THE MURDER PARTY pronounced Torre Abbey's cream tea with fresh scones and clotted cream infinitely superior to its exhibits. They dawdled for nearly an hour in the cheery cafe next to the abbey kitchen, wolfing down their allotment of homemade pastry and discussing the weekend's entertainment at the hotel in Exeter. The hotel had scheduled a murder mystery event, wherein an acting troupe stages a participatory drama, killing off several cast members during the course of the weekend. The guests play bit parts in the charade while they attempt to solve the murders, trying to make sense of the very Christie-like clues put before them. All is revealed on Sunday morning after breakfast, and prizes are awarded to the correct guessers.

"And you're sure you won't be able to stay for it?" Elizabeth MacPherson said to the guide. "Considering all that you and I know about real murders, we'd be sure to solve it."

Rowan Rover disguised his relief with a sorrowful countenance. "Alas, no. The tour company does not wish to pay for my services over the weekend, when all of you will be otherwise occupied. So Bernard and I will go to our respective homes, and we shall rejoin you on Sunday afternoon. I'm afraid you will have to solve the case without me."

Privately he pitied the troupe of actors who were staging the murder mystery weekend at the hotel, blissfully ignorant of the fact that they were about to be descended upon by ten well-read amateur sleuths and one relentless forensic anthropologist. He had heard of the zeal that possessed amateurs in such puzzle games —and he had resolved to avoid them. A friend of his who attended a similar event reported that one lady guest actually got so carried away that she began searching the handbags of her fellow guests. To one

166

who made a profession of the study of murder, the entire charade sounded very dismal indeed. Besides, it would be an uncomfortable reminder of his own little drama, which would have to be staged within the coming week. He intended to devote his free weekend to meticulously planning the most perfect of all murders: one that would not be recognized as a murder at all.

The journey out of Torquay was uneventful, except that Martha Tabram spotted a hotel bearing the name Fawlty Towers, and several tour members pleaded to be allowed to stop and photograph it. Bernard told them that neither their schedule nor the traffic would permit such a scheme, so they contented themselves with a lengthy discussion over whether the television sitcom of the same name had been inspired by the Torquay hotel, or whether it was the other way round.

An hour later they arrived in Exeter. Rowan Rover bade them a hasty goodbye at the train station, promising to reappear at one on Sunday. "You won't be seeing me for the next day and a half," he reminded them for the third time. "Is there anything you want to know before I leave? Anything you want me to investigate while I'm at home with my reference books?"

Elizabeth MacPherson raised her hand. "Could you find out if we'll be going near Constance Kent's house? I'm intrigued by her, and I'd like to see it."

"Who's Constance Kent?" asked Susan. "What did she write?"

"I'll check on it," Rowan promised. "And as to who she was—we will discuss that on some future evening. Just now, I've a train to catch."

Bernard drove them to their lodgings and parked the bus at the far end of the hotel parking lot. He then proceeded to his own home in Kensington.

Elizabeth, who had been reveling in anticipation of all the wonderful old castles they would stay in, was chagrined to find that she had sweaters older than the Exeter Trusthouse Forte. She had to admit, though, that a luxurious room with a private bath and a view of the old city wall and the spires of the cathedral beyond it went a long way toward compensating for a lack of Olde World Charm.

In her room was an invitation to a cocktail party and dinner, beginning at seven that evening. According to the typewritten note, the purpose of the party was to enable her to meet some filmmakers who were scouting for extras for a Dracula movie. Since the note was dated September 7, 1928 and signed by someone named Binky, Elizabeth was fairly certain that this was the opening gambit in the murder weekend. As a concession to Roaring Twenties, she tied a silvery scarf around her forehead, put on her red cocktail dress, and made her way downstairs to the designated party room.

The cocktail party was held in a modest-sized banquet room with red carpeting and a dazzling chandelier. A dozen tables had been set for dinner. White-coated waiters glided among the guests, offering champagne and white wine. About fifty people were congregated in the room, some of them in period costumes, chatting rather uneasily with other strangers. It was impossible at this stage to tell who the actors would turn out to be. Elizabeth found Charles Warren there, decked out in a suit and tie and looking like a bank president. Nancy Warren was equally resplendent, but the change was not so startling in her case.

"Erik Broadaxe dresses pretty good," she said, smiling at them.

In a few minutes of casual circulating,

Elizabeth managed to locate all the members of her party, and some not-too-difficult eavesdropping enabled her to identify several of the players in the murder drama. They were wearing the best costumes, and they seemed to think it was 1928.

"Isn't this fun?" whispered Alice MacKenzie, whose lime-green pantsuit made no concession to the Twenties—or the Nineties, for that matter. "I brought my little notebook, in case we need to keep track of clues."

"Let's sit at different tables and compare notes afterward," said Susan Cohen. She was wearing a black silk sheath that contrasted poorly with her blonde coloring and pale skin, making her look more like the corpse than the sleuth. "We have an acting company in Minneapolis that stages murder weekends, and I—"

"Shh!" hissed Elizabeth. "They're arguing!"

They turned to stare at a monocled man in a tuxedo, who had been introduced to them as the baron, director of the vampire film. He was berating a mousy old woman in rimless glasses and a shapeless brown dress. Apparently the woman was the company secretary, and the baron had caught her going through his desk. Alice MacKenzie dutifully made notes of the accusations. In a few minutes the scene was over and a horse-faced woman in a tweed suit approached them, shaking her head. "Those two will bear watching," she said.

"She's a plant," muttered Susan Cohen, when the woman was out of earshot. "Too Miss Marple to be real. She's probably going to be the troupe's detective."

"What about that tall blond man by the door?" asked Maud Marsh, looking elegant in a short dress of white satin. "He looks rather theatrical."

"I heard him talking to the secretary," said Nancy Warren. "He says he's playing the leading man in the film."

Martha Tabram, coolly elegant in a two-piece outfit of green silk, sipped her wine and eyed the door. "Do you suppose they'll try to keep us in the hotel all weekend with this foolishness?" she asked. "I want to see Exeter again."

"I checked my schedule," Elizabeth told her. "It says that after this we're free until one o'clock tomorrow, when the baron is rehearsing a scene with his actors. Tomorrow morning our group is supposed to have

171

a tour of the city at ten with one of Exeter's volunteer guides."

"Good," smiled Martha. "I may not return for the rehearsal."

"You might miss a murder," Nancy warned her. "But it is tempting to shop, isn't it?"

"It certainly is," said Elizabeth. "Now that we haven't got Rowan Rover barking at our heels every time we stop at a postcard rack."

The escape plans were interrupted by a stir in the crowd near the punch bowl. The buzz of voices suddenly fell silent. People began to back away from the baron's mousy little secretary, who was coughing violently into her handkerchief. Thirty seconds later she dropped her wineglass and crumpled gracefully to the floor, unconscious. Kate Conway, her nurse's instincts aroused, rushed to the body, but the baron waved her back. On cue, her fellow actors flocked around her. She was carried from the room, while the baron and his leading lady expressed their shock and dismay to the rest of the party.

The Snoop Sister in the tweed suit reappeared. Her eyes sparkled with interest. "I am Miss Eylesbarrow," she told them.

"And I must say I find this very suspicious indeed! Did any of you see anyone tampering with that lady's drink?"

The mystery group members admitted that they hadn't been paying attention.

"Oh, but you must watch everyone very carefully!" the woman chided them. "You can't trust anyone, you know!"

"I hope she did it," muttered Elizabeth, as the woman walked away.

"Not a hope," said Susan Cohen. "When it's time to reveal the killer, she'll run the confrontation scene. But she's much too brash. They need somebody who's gracious and charming to be the amateur sleuth."

"Like Angela Lansbury on *Murder She Wrote?*" asked Kate.

Susan shook her head. "I was thinking more of Charlotte MacLeod."

Maud Marsh was ready to try her hand at solving the case. "What do you suppose she was killed with?" she asked the others. "Poison in the drink?"

"So they would have us believe," said Elizabeth. "We mustn't forget that it's 1928."

"This has been done in a lot of books," said Susan, with the air of one beginning a lecture. "There's *The Mirror Cracked,* and *Murder in Three Acts.* Of course, both those murders were done the same way . . ."

Nancy Warren pretended to hear her husband calling and wandered away, followed by Martha Tabram, stifling a yawn.

"Well, I guess the evening's drama is over," said Alice. "People are beginning to sit down to dinner. Let's go and sit by the baron, shall we? He looks suspicious."

"As long as we don't have to sit with Miss Eylesbarrow," muttered Elizabeth. "I wish Rowan were here. We'd show him detective work!"

Despite the watchful anticipation of the mystery weekend guests, no one pitched forward into his soup during the dinner. The members of the acting troupe stayed perfectly in character and chatted with the guests. The older leading man, Sir Herbert, seemed quite taken with pretty Kate Conway and he spent much of the meal urging her to go into film work, while she giggled prettily in response. Susan Cohen and Elizabeth MacPherson sat beside the actor playing the baron. In a German accent that was on the horizon of plausible, the movie mogul talked amiably with the young women, inquiring where they were from and what they planned to see on their tour of England.

"You should come and see Minneapolis," Susan Cohen told him. "It's the most beautiful city. Very clean and crimefree."

"I have never had any interest in visiting the United States," said the baron at his most Teutonic. "I have always wanted to go and see . . . Russia!"

Elizabeth, remembering that it was supposed to be 1928, quipped, "Oh, I expect you will! Give it ten years or so."

The baron caught this reference to the Russian front and managed to stifle a laugh just in time to stay in character. He hastily changed the subject, telling them about the film company and the new talkie they were making, about his investments, and all the problems that he was having with his actors; but Elizabeth was having too much fun pretending that it was 1928 to pay much attention to any clues he might have offered. When he mentioned that he was contemplating buying a country house, she advised him to purchase a place called High Grove.

"You will profit enormously from selling it again in fifty years time," she assured him, approximating the year that Prince

Charles acquired the property. "It will sell for a bundle!" What fun it was to parade her Anglophilia!

She was pleased to note that the baron was as clever as he was talented. One fleeting expression showed that he had caught that reference, too, but he was quick to play dumb—and to resume less prophetic topics of conversation.

When the meal was almost over, Mr. Scott, the handsome young leading man, excused himself from one of the other tables, announcing that he wanted to telephone the hospital to ask after Miss Jenkins, the secretary who had been taken ill. This sparked fresh speculation about the cause of her attack, but the baron refused to be drawn by Susan's declaration that the woman had been poisoned.

"I expect it was something she ate for lunch that didn't agree with her," he said.

Alice MacKenzie made a note of his remark in her book.

Ten minutes later Mr. Scott reappeared in the doorway looking properly, if not convincingly, stricken. "I've just had word from the hospital that poor Miss Jenkins is dead," he lamented. "The doctors say that she was poisoned with arsenic!"

A shocked silence fell over the assembly, broken two seconds later by Elizabeth Mac-Pherson, who proclaimed, "She certainly was *not.*"

This bit of unscheduled improvisation on a carefully rehearsed scenario left all the actors speechless.

"I am a doctor of forensic anthropology," said Elizabeth, more pompously than usual. "And I assure you that we can rule out arsenic as a cause of death."

"Why?" gasped the baron in spite of himself.

"Because she just fell quietly to the floor and passed out," Elizabeth informed him. "That is not what you do if you have been poisoned with arsenic. To begin with, she should have been puking her guts out—"

Kate Conway nodded vigorously. "From both ends," she said with medical authority.

"Not before *my* dinner," murmured Martha Tabram.

Elizabeth continued. "She should have been having tonic and clonic convulsions, dizzy spells, and she would have been in incredible pain from the cramping of the stomach muscles. Also, death would not occur so quickly. If you look at the Maybrick case . . ." Elizabeth was thinking how pleased Rowan Rover would have been at this evidence of her detecting ability.

The actors were thinking that a little arsenic in the wineglass of Miss MacPherson wouldn't be amiss. Too bad they only had sugar cubes for poison.

"This is such fun!" said Frances Coles happily. "I wonder what Rowan is doing this weekend without us?"

◆ ◆ ◆

IN A PICTURESQUE village in Cornwall, the last pirate of Penzance was plotting his perfect crime. At eight o'clock Friday evening Rowan Rover had got off the train at Penzance and returned to his nonaquatic residence, the family home a few miles from the city.

After an omelet supper, washed down with liberal quantities of Scotch, he had retired to his study to read his mail. There was the usual assortment of politely worded threats from his creditors, and a dutiful scrawl from his offspring Sebastian which managed to impart no information whatsoever, except a weather report for the vicinity of his school, which Sebastian always included in lieu of any information about his grades, his interests, or his most recent misdemeanors. The air mail letter bearing a Sri Lankan stamp began with the salutation *Dear Insect*. A salvo from a former wife. He tossed that one in the pile with the Inland Revenue forms and the Stop Smoking pamphlets he received regularly from meddling friends. A *royalty* statement from one of his publishers, written as usual in Sanskrit, contained a check for the beggarly sum of seven pounds, forty-three pence. You could hardly call it a royalty statement. Why couldn't those buggers manage to sell the foreign rights to the blood-thirsty Americans, or sell the movie rights for a fat fee, so that he could make a living off crime without having to practice it!

He resigned himself to the prospect at hand. Now that he had actually gotten to know the murder group, he could refine the general plans he had sketched out in London. He settled down in his leather chair and surrounded himself with piles of guidebooks and volumes on true crime.

He decided that one good plan would not suffice. Since he was an amateur, he should not rely upon success on the first venture. Accidents were tricky. People often survived the most lethal situations, while others succumbed to a fall over a footstool. The more accidents he could arrange, the better his chances for eliminating . . . the victim. Now that she was a real person to him, he hesitated to think of her as Susan when planning her demise. A study of the itinerary suggested several possibilities to the hopeful murderer. Beginning on Sunday, when he would rejoin the group in Exeter, he hoped to schedule one potential accident per day.

If that failed, there was always poison. But which one? Thallium was too slow and not completely reliable. Even the most doddering G.P. ought to be able to spot arsenic these days. Using lethal germs was out. He wasn't such a fool as to risk contaminating himself. *And* the rest of the party, naturally, he amended, somewhat belatedly.

The real question, of course, was what could he get unobtrusively. Most of the Victorian murderesses got into trouble when their names appeared on a chemist's poison register. He wouldn't make that mistake. An inventory of the medicine chest might prove helpful.

He was mulling over the toxic possibilities of soaked cigarette butts (nicotine poisoning) when the telephone rang. He answered it at once, wondering what trouble the group had managed to get into on their own.

"Is that you, Rover?" said a familiar Yorkshire voice. "Not playing nursemaid this weekend?"

Rowan groaned to disguise the fact that he was moderately glad to hear from his fellow crime writer Kenneth O'Connor. Although O'Connor could be a nuisance—always coming unexpectedly to London and wanting to stay on the boat, when Rowan was planning to use it to entertain more nubile companions—he did have the virtue of being the only other crime expert of Rowan's acquaintance who did not earn his living as a policeman. All the other crime historians had nasty suspicious minds which came of dealing with an unsavory element of society day after day in their police work. If Rowan asked them about a poison and then someone on his tour went and died of it, they might jump to the most uncomplimentary conclusions about his own character and motives. Even a perfectly executed accident after such a conversation with them might arouse suspicion. O'Connor, though, was usually too wrapped up in book deadlines and new projects to care who poisoned whom socially. Rowan decided that he could use a second opinion and Kenneth O'Connor was the ideal person to provide it.

"Good evening, Kenneth," he said pleasantly. "I've just had a nice royalty statement on my third book. How are things with you?"

"Chaotic, as usual. I wanted to know if you're going to be using your boat this week. I have to go to London to meet with those maniacs at the film studio—"

"And you infinitely prefer my hospitality to paying hotel rates?"

"I particularly enjoy your hospitality when you're not there to dispense it in person, Rowan."

"Well, as long as you've called, I have one or two questions for you."

"I take it that this means I get the boat?"

"Yes, but if you put any more cigarette burns in the seat cushions, I'll be using you for an anchor in future. Now—first question: do you know where Constance Kent lived?"

"Rode," said Kenneth O'Connor without a moment's pause. "Do I win a prize?"

"A box of chocolates from Christiana Edmunds," snapped Rowan. A laugh from the other end of the phone told him that Kenneth recognized the name of nineteenth-century Brighton's lovelorn lady poisoner. "Everybody knows Constance Kent lived near Rode, Kenneth. We want to know if the house is still standing. Can it be seen from the road? One of my tourists wants to go there."

"I'll see if I can find out for you. When will you be home again?"

"Monday night. There's one other matter."

"Yes?"

"One of the group fancies she's a mystery novelist," he lied. "Can you recommend a good poison?"

♦   ♦   ♦

THE NEXT MORNING dawned sunny and warm, a fact observed by the mystery tour members at varying times between six and nine o'clock, when they either stumbled groggily or sprinted happily into the hotel dining room for breakfast. By ten o'clock everyone was fed and armed with sweaters, comfortable walking shoes, and credit cards, ready for an enlightening tour of Exeter.

Alice MacKenzie observed that for the first time on the tour, Elizabeth MacPherson was also carrying a pen and notebook. "Are you especially interested in Exeter?" she asked.

"It is Saturday morning," said Elizabeth cryptically. "And Rowan is not within a hundred miles of here."

A tiny and earnest-looking woman wearing a red blazer met them in the hotel foyer and introduced herself as Mrs. Lacey, their city guide. She captured Elizabeth's attention at once by explaining that the hotel parking lot had been built on top of an old city plague pit. Elizabeth was still staring down wistfully at an immovable expanse of asphalt when the less ghoulish members of the party moved along toward the remains of the old city wall, just behind the hotel. As yet, she had written nothing in her notebook.

As they walked down the narrow lane that ended beside the cathedral green, Mrs. Lacey pointed out the well-preserved medieval houses, still in use, and began her recital of city history, beginning with the Roman occupation in 55 A.D.

"We will end our tour with the cathedral," she explained as she led them past the West Front, with its beautiful carved Image Screen of saints. "It is within sight of your hotel and I am sure that you can all find your way back from there. Just now we will go to another quaint old street, where the BBC filmed some scenes in one of its Dickens dramatizations."

This television reference set Susan off on a litany of her favorite British imports, and it took them another block and a half to shut her up.

As they walked through the bustling streets, Mrs. Lacey pointed out historic buildings, mentioning that the city was home to Sir Walter Raleigh, and that Queen Henrietta, wife of Charles I, had been sent here for safety during the Civil War. (Susan's response in kind left the guide silently wondering who Hubert Humphrey was.)

"There was once a statue of Henry VII, but it was destroyed in the bombing in World War II. The statue was in honor of Henry's entry into Exeter in 1497, after the city had withstood a siege by the pretender Perkin Warbeck."

"The statue was never restored?" asked Martha Tabram, who probably chaired similar civic committees in Vancouver.

"Well, there is another statue of Henry," said Mrs. Lacey. "I wouldn't call it a restoration." With some misgivings she pointed to a fiberglass image of a knight in armor on the facade of a department store.

Susan Cohen spoke up. "In Minneapolis we have an outdoor sculpture garden that has an enormous red cherry poised on the end of a giant spoon. It's called the Spoonbridge, and it's about twenty feet tall!"

Gravely the guide looked up at the fiberglass likeness of the first Tudor monarch. "Well," she conceded, "I suppose it could be worse at that."

They continued their walk through the crowded streets past the ruins of a church destroyed by Luftwaffe bombing and into a newer-looking part of the city, all built on the sites of the historic ones lost in the war. Finally they came to Princess Elizabeth Square, an open promenade lined with shops, newly constructed after World War II to replace the buildings destroyed by enemy bombing. "The present Queen—Princess Elizabeth she was then—came down and dedicated the square as the first step toward the rebuilding of Exeter."

During this part of the tour, Susan Cohen had little to contribute by way of comparison with her hometown, since Minneapolis had never been bombed by enemy forces. (Though certain members of the party were beginning to wish that it had.)

Elizabeth was scribbling furiously in her notebook, adding diagrams and arrows to her text. Alice leaned over to catch a glimpse of the writing, but she was unable to decipher it. The tour proceeded at a brisk pace, without shopping breaks, and without backtracking. Mrs. Lacey was a wealth of information on historic buildings, medieval celebrities, and dates. She said very little about the mercantile aspects of the city, past or present.

Nearly an hour later the group stood once again at the west front of Exeter Cathedral, arriving there by a circular route that did not involve the retracing of their previous paths. Elizabeth's note-taking had been steady throughout the latter part of the excursion, although Alice had been unable to determine any correlation between the guide's remarks and the fervor of Elizabeth's note-taking.

"What are you doing?" she whispered.

"Tell you later," muttered Elizabeth.

Compared to Winchester, the only other

cathedral they had seen, Exeter looked rather wide and squat. It lacked the tall spires and the sprawling length of Winchester, but the exterior decoration was much more ornate. The entire west front of the cathedral was decorated with a pantheon of life-sized figures. Jesus and his apostles had pride of place above the central doorway, above more figures of kings, confessors, and prophets. The lowest row of statues depicted angels.

"Why are the statues damaged?" asked Frances Coles, pointing to a crowned figure who was missing several facial parts.

"Not the Blitz?" asked Alice. She had about decided that the Germans and the French deserved each other.

"No," said Mrs. Lacey sadly. "The damage goes back to medieval times, I'm afraid. In those days people were very superstitious about the miraculous healing powers of saints. People used to chip off bits of the statues in hopes that the blessed stone would effect a cure for themselves or a loved one. Some of the statues have been replaced over the years. That king on the right is a new one. Now let's go inside."

Susan Cohen whispered to Elizabeth. "Since the statues are already so damaged, they probably wouldn't notice if I broke off another little piece as a souvenir."

"Try it and I'll break your arm," Elizabeth whispered back.

Elizabeth took no notes at all during the cathedral tour. She followed along in an abstracted way, while the rest of the party admired the rib vaulting of the ceiling ("finest decorated Gothic vault in existence"), and she came out of her reverie briefly to examine the carvings beneath the choir seats. The underside of the seats were fashioned with a small shelf so that weary choir members might slump against these supports and still remain in a standing position. Mrs. Lacey explained that because the choir members were going to rest their posteriors on the *misereres,* the builders considered it inappropriate to decorate them with images of saints or other divine symbols around them. Instead, they carved a variety of secular items in the choir seats, so that the wood could be decorated without impropriety.

"This is meant to be the image of an elephant," she told them, pointing to an object with tusks and hooves, carved under stall 44. "We think the artist did it from hearsay."

"Well, it isn't too bad," said Frances Coles, who had seen her second-graders do worse after an eyewitness encounter with the beast.

Charles Warren carefully photographed the elephant seat, with and without the tour members grouped around it. Emma asked a number of technical questions about cathedral restoration, and Maud Marsh made a note of the times services were held.

"I may come back for Evensong," she told the guide. "I'll come with you," said Alice.

At 11:55 Mrs. Lacey finished the whirlwind tour at the west front of the cathedral and wished them a pleasant stay in Exeter. Most of the group started back for the hotel, where lunch was being served, and Susan was complaining that her feet hurt because Italians didn't know how to make shoes. When Kate, Alice, and Frances declared themselves ready for more walking, Elizabeth looked at her watch. "We have fifty-five minutes until the baron wants us for rehearsal," she announced.

"We could go shopping," said Kate Conway wistfully. "But it would mean missing lunch."

"I'd rather shop than eat," said Elizabeth.

Frances Coles burrowed into her cavernous purse. "I saved some rolls from breakfast if anyone else would like one."

Alice MacKenzie looked longingly at the maze of streets leading away from the cathedral. "I just wish we could find our way back to some of those shops we passed on the tour."

"We can," said Elizabeth, holding up her notebook. "I mapped the entire route, and made a note of all the best shops. But we only have an hour. Run!"

◆　◆　◆

TWO WOOL SHOPS, five clothing stores, and eight curio vendors later, the weary shoppers returned to the hotel, laden with packages and too late for lunch, but triumphant in their success at having achieved an entire hour for a guide-free rampage in an English city.

"Rowan would be very disappointed in us," said Frances Coles. "We should have been visiting museums or something."

"Consider it a contribution to the local economy," Elizabeth advised her.

After depositing the packages in their respective rooms, they hurried downstairs to the lower level, where the 1928 movie company was rehearsing its screen melodrama in the room that had been a banquet hall the night before. Now it was dark and the tables were gone. In their place stood a wooden coffin on sawhorses, illuminated by a brace of candles. The spectators lined the walls watching Sir Herbert the actor (Dracula) embrace a beautiful young victim.

"Did we miss much?" asked Elizabeth, who managed to recognize Martha Tabram in the semi-darkness. Alice, Frances, and Kate crowded around to hear her whispered reply.

"They're casting stand-ins for the actors. Sir Herbert was particularly asking for you, Kate."

Kate blushed and hurried over to join the actors. Soon she was decked out in a white nightgown, ready to be the bride of Dracula.

Martha Tabram turned back to the shoppers. "Oh, before we began, the baron announced that Miss Jenkins had died of arsenic poisoning." She laughed. "He read a list of symptoms that she displayed at the hospital. They tallied exactly with the ones you mentioned last night, Elizabeth."

"Nice save on their part," muttered Elizabeth grudgingly.

"Wouldn't it be funny if she really were dead," mused Frances.

"If so, I think you'll find that she has been reincarnated," said Martha. "Look at that woman standing beside the coffin."

"The blonde?" asked Frances, squinting into the darkness. "She looks very young and beautiful to me."

"So she does," Martha agreed. "But if you put her in a frumpy gray wig and a shapeless dress, she could appear considerably older. It's the same actress. Very clever of them. There wouldn't be much point in having a member of the company out of commission after the first hour of the weekend."

"Then it isn't a clue," said Alice, disappointed.

"No," said Martha. "I just wanted to set Frances' mind at rest. The secretary may be dead, but the actress who played her is very much alive."

◆ ◆ ◆

THE CLEVERNESS OF the acting company was further exhibited later that same afternoon. On the hotel terrace a swordfight was staged between their two principal actors, with all the mystery guests watching from

193

the sidelines. As they thrust and parried, the young blond Mr. Scott was cut on the arm. Ginger, the leading lady vampire, hurried him away to have it bandaged. This time Kate did not offer her nursing skills.

"Well, he's dead," said Alice MacKenzie cheerfully.

"Oh, I don't think so," protested Frances. "It was only a little scratch."

"Hamlet," Alice replied. "A little poison on the sword and he's done for."

"Better still," said Susan Cohen, "irradiated thallium! Rick Boyer used that in *Moscow Metal.* You get it out of nuclear power plants and put it on a pellet or knife blade in order to penetrate the skin. See, in the novel—"

"Susan . . . *Susan!*" Elizabeth MacPherson was shaking her head sadly. "It's 1928, Susan. No irradiated thallium. No nuclear power plants."

"Curare?" said Susan hopefully. "There's another book . . ."

Several minutes later the answer to their speculations proved to be: none of the above. The actor reappeared with a bandaged arm, in good spirits again, and ready to resume rehearsal. It was only then that people noticed that another member of the cast was missing. Ten minutes of frantic searching by all concerned resulted in the discovery of his body in the hallway outside the banquet room. He was theatrically dead.

"Well," said Maud Marsh philosophically. "They got us on that one. Did any of you see him leave?"

"No," said Kate Conway. "I was too busy worrying about the sword wound."

Emma Smith and her mother were comparing notes. "At least this pares down the list of suspects," she remarked. "At this rate there won't be many people left by tomorrow morning."

"If we get any more clues, we'll let you know," said Elizabeth kindly.

◆　　◆　　◆

AFTER DINNER THAT night there were more goings-on. The amateur sleuths were summoned to the leading lady's room by a distraught Mr. Scott and a new murder victim was discovered, dead on the bathroom floor, with Mr. Scott's scarf wound around her neck. Clues were dispensed left and right as the actors quarreled and expressed their sorrow over the loss of the grande dame. Elizabeth had been spending a quiet evening in her room, intending to write some letters, but after the dramatic interruptions, she was out of the mood for solitary correspondence. Instead she invited Kate Conway and Frances Coles back to her room for hot chocolate.

"It's wonderful having these little electric kettles in the hotel rooms!" said Frances, as she settled in the chintz chair beside the window. She was wearing a dark green dressing gown that set off her auburn hair. "I wish American hotels would think of doing that."

"They're probably afraid the guests would burn the place down," said Elizabeth. "Which they probably would."

Kate Conway, in a white gown reminiscent of her bride of Dracula costume, sat down on the bed, nibbling on a piece of shortbread. "I still don't know who the murderer will turn out to be. I thought it was Lady Alice, but now she's dead. That was an exciting episode tonight, wasn't it?"

"I'm glad they've taken to strangling people," Elizabeth replied. "They weren't sound at all on poisons."

"Do you think they've killed everyone that they're going to?" asked Frances.

"I expect so," said Elizabeth. "It's Saturday night. They're running out of time."

Kate giggled. "Too bad they can't kill Susan Cohen."

Frances Coles gasped. "It's so odd that you should say that! I was thinking the same thing. And yet, she's really a very nice person."

Elizabeth unplugged the kettle and prepared their hot cocoa. "She's a nice person in small doses," she said. "But it's the cumulative effect that's wearing. After four days of Minneapolis travelogues and mystery fiction plot summaries, I think we're all about ready to kill her."

"I don't think she's used to interacting socially," said Frances Coles. "Sometimes I get a second-grader who alienates the rest of the class just the way Susan does. It usually means they haven't had much practice in getting along with people. I'll bet she's an only child."

"But she's very pretty," Kate Conway pointed out. "It's strange that we don't like her. She's so confrontational, which is strange. Pretty people usually find it very easy to socialize."

"I can explain that," said Elizabeth. She told them about Susan's recent plastic surgery and her transformation from ugly duckling to swan.

"So that's it," said Kate, glancing at her own pretty face in the dressing table mirror. "Susan hasn't learned how to stop acting like a wallflower. She's only pretty on the outside; she doesn't believe it yet."

"Or perhaps she talks all the time to make up for all the times that she was lonely," said Frances sadly. "It's really awful of us to be so hard on her."

Elizabeth raised her eyebrows. "Well, then . . . would you like me to invite her over for chocolate now?"

"No!" cried Kate and Frances in unison.

♦ ♦ ♦

AT BREAKFAST THE next morning Elizabeth and the other members of the mystery tour sat together, comparing notes so that they could turn in their whodunit ballots.

"Don't forget we have to consider motive," Susan reminded them. "You get points for guessing who did it and separate points for saying why."

Frances Coles groaned. "Everybody has a motive. Mr. Scott could be Sir Herbert's long-lost son, and Jackie and Ginger may

198

be sisters, and what about the diamond smuggling clue?"

"I think the baron did it," said Alice Mac-Kenzie.

"The baron? Why?"

"Because it's 1928," said Alice darkly. "And he's *German.*"

After a moment of stunned silence, Susan burst out laughing. "Don't be ridiculous! It's one of the women. The baron is so obvious that only an idiot would fall for it. Now is it Jackie or Ginger? Or maybe Gladys was only pretending to be dead . . ."

"Detecting is very difficult in 1928," Elizabeth complained. "I wish I could get hold of some decent forensic evidence."

"We'd better hurry and mark our ballots," said Kate Conway. "That Eylesbarrow woman is herding everybody toward the banquet room for the final confrontation. Who shall we put? Jackie or Ginger?"

"I'll vote for whoever you pick, Alice," said Frances Coles loyally.

"Let's split our votes," Alice suggested, glaring at Susan. "Then at least one of us will win."

AT TEN MINUTES until one the members of the murder tour assembled with their bags in the hotel lobby, still rehashing the murder mystery weekend and chatting with two of the actors, who were now out of character. Rowan Rover appeared a few minutes later, with his canvas bag slung over his shoulders, and sporting freshly laundered khaki trousers.

"Good afternoon, everybody! I see that Bernard has returned and is pulling the coach up out front. Did you enjoy the murder weekend?"

"It was quite well done," said Kate Conway with her usual look of big-eyed sincerity.

"It could have been anybody," Susan Cohen declared, scowling.

"And did you solve the crime?"

"We did!" cried Miriam Angel, holding up the bottle of wine that was their trophy. "Emma and I were the only ones who guessed who did it!"

"And who did it?" asked Rowan indulgently.

"Why the *baron,* of course!" said Miriam.

CHAPTER 9

*"There is but one step from the grotesque
to the horrible."*
—Arthur Conan Doyle

DARTMOOR

THE SUNDAY AFTERNOON drive to the next destination was a short one: seventeen miles to the edge of the Dartmoor National Park, to the Manor House Hotel, a beautiful Jacobean-style mansion nestled among the moors. Bernard maneuvered the coach up the narrow access road, past the golf course, and up to the massive stone arch that marked the entrance to the Manor House parking area. From the vantage point of a full-sized tour bus, the archway looked dangerously low and disastrously solid.

"You'll never make it," said Susan Cohen, surveying the obstacle from her usual seat behind the driver. "You'd have to be stupid to even try."

Charles Warren got up and signaled for

Bernard to open the coach door. He walked through the arch and, with a succession of nods and hand signals, he guided the coach through the archway with inches to spare. When he had parked in the paved lot on the side bordering the golf course, Bernard modestly acknowledged the cheers of the passengers and then climbed down to unload the suitcases.

The tour members stood in the parking lot and surveyed their new lodgings, the first of the accommodations that was not newly constructed. This one was imposing and ancient-looking, but a certain reticence on the part of the hotel literature led Rowan to suspect (aloud) that it was actually constructed in the late nineteenth century by a nouveau riche industrialist with aristocratic delusions. The Manor House was a sprawling beige stone building, or series of buildings, about the length of a city block, with formal archways, pitched roofs, and multiple chimneys, looking very much like the country estate it must have been once. The enormous mansion was set down in an expanse of well-tended lawn, surrounded by acres of wood and park land, some of which was now a golf course.

"This looks familiar," said Maud Marsh,

twisting a lock of silver hair. "I'm sure I've seen this place somewhere."

"I expect you have," said Rowan Rover. "It was the setting for the 1939 version of *The Hound of the Baskervilles* with Basil Rathbone."

The others gathered around. "Oh, is this Sherlock Holmes country?" asked Susan.

"*The Hound of the Baskervilles* is set in this area," Rowan replied. "Many of the place names mentioned in Conan Doyle's story are variations of actual places nearby: Hound Tor and Black Tor. Cleft Tor can only be Cleft Rock. If you know the area well, it is possible to pinpoint the locations in the story." He paused for two beats, and then said, as if the thought had just occurred to him, "Would you like to go for a walk on the moor? It's an unseasonably warm day for September. Not a cloud in the sky." He glanced at Elizabeth MacPherson. "No shops open."

Everyone assured him that they would love to go for a walk, and they agreed to meet on the south terrace of the manor in twenty minutes.

Rowan closed his personally annotated guidebook with a smile, wondering how well any of them actually remembered the

Holmes tale. He had wisely chosen not to read them the passage of his notes concerning another feature of the Baskerville story:

You see, for example, this great plain to the north here, with the queer hills breaking out of it . . . You notice those bright green spots scattered thickly over it? Rowan looked up from the page to scan the rolling grassland beyond the Manor House. He thought he *did* see such patches of green. *That is the great Grimpen Mire . . . a false step yonder means death to man or beast.*

♦ ♦ ♦

ELIZABETH MACPHERSON NEVER claimed to be psychic, not even in the dimmest candlelight in an evening of ghost-storytelling, but something about Moretonhampstead made her uneasy. She had a tiny room on the top floor of the manor, with an impressive view of the rolling green moorland, but even in the full sun of a cloudless September day; she felt chilled by the atmosphere of the place. She had walked up the flights of stairs to her room, and, while all was bright and elegant on the lower landings, the higher reaches gave way to worn green carpeting and walls in need of new paint.

"Top floor," she said aloud. "Old servants quarters. This is where the first Mrs. Rochester would have lived, I presume." The fact that her room was well-kept and tidy, with a private bath and a television, did little to dispel her feelings of gloom after the long trek up the endless flight of stairs. From her casement window she could see the south lawn and the moors beyond, but the narrow walkway outside the window made her think of cat burglars and itinerant vampires. "At least it's only for one night," she reminded herself.

Hurriedly she changed into slacks and sensible walking shoes, glad for an excuse to leave her solitary quarters. Even a walk without shopping was better than being the madwoman in the attic.

When she arrived on the south terrace, she found the rest of the group already assembled and posing for pictures on the stone balustrade overlooking the flower beds. Susan Cohen and Charles Warren took turns playing photographer with their respective cameras. Rowan Rover had put on his tan windbreaker in anticipation of windy weather on the moors. He gravely inspected the rest of the party to see that no one proposed to mountain climb in high-heeled shoes or sundresses. Satisfied that the troops were at least impersonating competent hikers, be began the march down the wide stone steps and across the grass. "There is a path through the woods at the bottom of this hill," Rowan told them. "It eventually ends up in North Bovey, but I thought that you might prefer a nice bracing walk on the moors."

He had studied *Barts Drivers Road Atlas to Britain* and discovered to his annoyance that the Great Grimpen Bog was not among the topographical landmarks featured in that august volume. Still, his annotated Sherlock Holmes had mentioned it, coyly noting that Conan Doyle had merely changed the name Great Grimpen Bog to Great Grimpen Mire in order to avoid the use of the schoolboy's word for toilet. *My plan will be in the bog without any paper if there isn't any mud,* Rowan thought, reverting to the juvenile use of the word. He had wanted to ask the hotel people about rainfall in recent months, but someone might remember the question later, so he decided not to risk it. The editors of *The Annotated Holmes* had put the Grimpen Mire west of Moretonhampstead, about three miles north of the village of Widecombe in the Moor, fabled in the folksong for its fair. *And I'm going to get them stuck,* thought Rowan sardonically. *Uncle Tom Cobleigh and all.*

As he marched the group past brilliantly sunlit flower beds and the lush greenery of the golf course, he found himself wishing for more suitable moorland weather. It should be a windy autumn night, with a sliver of pale moon occasionally visible through shrouds of rolling fog. Their steps across the steep fold of hills should have been punctuated by the baying of a gigantic hound. Instead he had to carry out his dark deed against a backdrop of green hills and blazing blue sky that suggested the opening scenes of *The Sound of Music.*

At the bottom of the sloping lawn was a wide walkway that encircled the manor. Leading off from it, a narrow trail wound its way into the woods. The group set off on the woodland trace, chattering happily about plans for tea and comparing room descriptions.

"There's a fallen tree across the path!" Alice MacKenzie announced indignantly.

They were still within sight of the golf course.

"It probably fell during the windstorms last winter and no one's bothered to clear it yet," said Rowan. "It shouldn't trouble us. I'll climb over and help each of you across."

With varying degrees of agility, each member of the party clambered over the trunk of the felled oak, assisted by the ever-patient Rowan Rover, who knew that he had to keep them busy and happy for another three miles at least before he could expect to find any dangerous patches of mire. As they trotted along the well-worn path beside a sparkling brook, Rowan pointed out wildflowers and marveled at the wonderfully summerlike weather they were enjoying. Privately, he considered a thermometer reading approaching body temperature an appalling condition for an uphill hike, but he reminded himself that Americans were accustomed to warmer weather.

"Don't you think it's a bit hot for a long walk?" panted Elizabeth MacPherson, echoing his thoughts. By this time the path had forked and they had chosen to follow the route that became a steep incline, angling toward the open moors. "I was just worried about Maud on account of her age, you know."

With great deliberation, Rowan stopped

and looked back at the rest of the party. Maud Marsh, a few yards behind them, was striding briskly along at the head of the pack, without even breathing heavily. The others were grouped together, a bit red-faced, and talking less than usual. Far in the rear, Susan Cohen glistened with sweat, her shoulders heaving as she breathed. "What is this?" she yelled out. "The Devonshire Death March?"

Rowan pretended not to have heard. "Walking the moors is one of my hobbies!" he called out encouragingly. "It's good exercise and it clears the mind wonderfully."

"Mine is certainly clear," gasped Elizabeth. "I can think of nothing except the pain in my calf muscles."

"Perhaps it would help if we put price tags on the fence posts," snapped Rowan.

They tramped into a narrow dirt lane lined by blackberry thickets. Rowan graciously invited the group to stop for a moment, catch their breath, and sample the wild berries. He walked a few yards on to the top of a slope and scanned the grassy plain for the telltale bright green spots that signified patches of bog. He thought he spotted a few likely candidates to the northwest. Now would be a good time to leave the path and strike out across open country.

"How is everyone?" Rowan asked genially, surveying the party. Enjoying your walk?"

"Nancy and I enjoy walks," said Charles Warren, looking as fit as ever. "We do about seven miles a week."

"Not uphill," his wife retorted, fanning herself.

"Of course, nurses are used to doing a lot of walking, too. I just wish I'd brought proper running shoes," said Kate Conway, looking sadly down at her espadrilles.

"Where's the village?" Susan demanded. She was beginning to sag under the weight of her camera. "I thought you said the village was a mile away. We must be damn close to Scotland by now."

The guide feigned surprise. "The village is in the other direction," he informed her. "We veered off from that path shortly after we passed the fallen tree. I thought you wanted to take a walk up here on the moors. The views are breathtaking, aren't they?"

"All I see is a bunch of pasture without any cows," Susan grumbled. "You've seen one blade of grass, you've seen 'em all."

"Tell you what," said Rowan to the

group. "Let's get up out of this lane and walk across the moors. I'll bet you can see for miles from that tor off to the right." He took a short running start and scrambled up the bank, motioning for the others to follow him.

The Warrens and Kate Conway clambered after him. And one by one the others made their way up the grassy embankment.

"We'll probably be in the guidebooks next year," Elizabeth muttered to Emma Smith. "Party of American tourists dies of heat prostration on the Devonshire Death March. There'll be a statue of Rowan Rover in Madame Tussaud's Chamber of Horrors."

Emma Smith giggled. "Well, hiking is good exercise. I've felt guilty about not keeping up with my running on this trip."

Her mother nodded in agreement. "Emma and I also play tennis together twice a week. It certainly helps you keep your wind."

Rowan Rover grabbed Susan's hand and hauled her the last few feet up the bank. "Not tired, are you?" he asked. "Youngest member of the party and all."

"I'll make it," she said through clenched teeth.

"Good. It's wonderful for burning the calories, you know. Why don't you walk up front with me?" he asked. "I notice you brought your camera. Perhaps you'd like to go on ahead and check for photo opportunities. It's fairly level up here, as you can see."

"Oh, all right," said Susan, pushing sweat-dampened strands of hair away from her forehead. "I just hope we're not going to go too far."

Rowan gave her a dazzling smile of encouragement. With any luck at all, he thought, *you* won't have to walk back.

Susan stalked ahead without any apparent enjoyment of the breathtaking scenery, while Rowan contrived to fall farther and farther behind. It had occurred to him that steering Susan toward the bog was of no use if there were a dozen people close behind, ready to pull her out again. He doubted if he could get them out of earshot, but he thought that it might help to split up the herd. Perhaps he could manage to get someone else stuck in a different patch of mire (preferably Elizabeth MacPherson); and while the others were rescuing her, he could go off and drown Susan.

He approached the stragglers, radiating

212

concern for their welfare. "Is everyone all right here? Miriam? Alice? If anyone would like to go back to the hotel, it's straight down the hill behind you."

Miriam looked doubtfully at the long stretch of grassland rolling before them. She was wearing a heavy sweater and her face glistened with perspiration. She looked doubtfully at her daughter. "Do you want to keep going, Emma?"

Taking the cue, Emma said quickly, "No, I think we've had enough exercise for one afternoon. We'll walk tomorrow morning when it's cool, if you like, Mother. Alice, do you want to come back with us?"

"I suppose so," said Alice. "I'm not much on hiking if there's nowhere in particular to go."

"Go back then," the guide said soothingly. "We shan't be long." Seven to go, he thought, as he watched the threesome wend their way back across the meadow to the blackberry lane. A few moments later he sidled up to Charles and Nancy Warren, who were chatting with Martha Tabram. Feigning a perplexed expression, he said, "According to my guidebook, there is an ancient stone circle somewhere in this area. It is quite a beautiful ring of stones, set against imposing moorland scenery, and I'm sure you'd like to photograph it. Would you like to go off to the left and see if you can catch a glimpse of it. Susan is scouting in the other direction."

Charles Warren looked at his wife. "That does sound like a good picture, doesn't it, Nancy? Shall we go and look for it?"

Martha Tabram hesitated. "I seem to remember hearing somewhere that these moors could be dangerous. Are you sure it's wise for us to separate?"

"Dangerous? Rubbish! Conan Doyle didn't know what he was talking about. *Hound of the Baskervilles* notwithstanding, I assure you that not a single moor pony has ever been lost in the bogs here." *A Land Rover and a couple of Danish hikers, yes, but not a pony,* he finished silently. "Off you go, then. If you find the stone circle, give us a shout, won't you?" And it would have to be a very loud shout, Rowan reflected, because the circle he had described to them, the Nine Maidens, was a good ten miles away at Okehampton. He waved cheerily as the Warrens and Martha Tabram wandered away.

That left Maud Marsh, Kate Conway, Frances Coles, and Elizabeth MacPherson.

214

He didn't mind Maud or Frances because he fancied they'd be fairly useless in a quicksand crisis, but a trained nurse and a forensic anthropologist constituted a considerable nuisance for a wary assassin. He didn't suppose he could get rid of them, though. Kate tended to dog his steps in a way that he might have found flattering had he not been otherwise preoccupied—and the MacPherson girl was determined to talk crime with him at every waking moment. He would have to divert them somehow. When the time came. *If* it came.

He scanned the moors for a sign of Susan, but she had disappeared between the fold of hills. Aside from the nattering of Kate and Frances, all was quiet. He could feel his scalp prickling, and a shiver of dread rippled down his spine. She would be walking closer and closer to the deadly green circle, not attending to where she was going—she never did—and suddenly, a lurch, a plunge, and it would be all over but the screaming. The viscous mire of Dartmoor would envelop her in molten earth and melt inexorably away from her thrusting feet, as she clawed for a freehold. Quicksand they called it, and, indeed, the end would come swiftly. There were worse ways to go. Rowan clenched his fists, clammy with sweat, and waited for the cry.

"Damn!" Susan's voice, unmistakable with its flat Midwestern accent, floated over the moors. "Oh, damn it! Help me, somebody!"

For an instant they all froze. Rowan could see his companions glancing at each other, wondering what to do, and he forced himself to stand still, ignoring the reflexes that urged him to run toward the cry for help. He would have killed for a cigarette.

"It's Susan," said Kate Conway, with her usual knack for stating the obvious.

"She's in trouble," said Elizabeth MacPherson. Another rocket scientist.

Rowan modulated his voice by sheer willpower. "Oh, I expect not," he managed to say. "Probably got a run in her nylons, knowing our Susan."

Ignoring all the idle speculation, Maud Marsh was striding briskly forward in the direction of the cries for help. Rowan realized that it would look too suspicious if he ignored Susan altogether. The thing to do, he decided, was to direct the rescue operation in order to irrevocably botch it. Throw Susan a branch and then manage to let go of it, for example. He hurried toward the slope, determined now to be first on the scene, while the others trotted in his wake.

As he reached the edge of the incline, preparing to stagger down it, avoiding the dangerous mire, he nearly tripped over the kneeling figure of Susan Cohen, just below the crest of the slope. She was patting the short moor grass with both hands, cursing roundly, but distinctly unmuddied.

"Look out, damn it!" she snarled, peering up at him with one eye shut.

Rowan lurched to a standstill, waving his arms for balance and examining the surrounding turf for signs of quicksand. All seemed firm and dry: outcroppings of rock and scraggly gorse bushes dotted the hillside, but there were no ominous patches of emerald green.

Elizabeth, Frances, Kate, and Maud peered at them from the summit of the hill. "What is it, Susan?" Kate called out. "Did you sprain your ankle?"

"No!" yelled Susan. "Everybody stay back! I've lost a contact lens!"

For a quarter of an hour the six of them padded about the area on all fours, looking for the transparent lens, while Susan complained about the wind that blew dust in her face and caused her to lose the lens by rubbing the irritated eye. The Warrens and Martha Tabram drifted back to the group, announcing that they had found a hill with a view for miles in every direction, and there was no stone circle within sight. Rowan muttered something about modern vandals and continued to pat the heath with his fingertips. Finally, after everyone was thoroughly dusty from grubbing in the earth, and chilled by the evening wind at sunset, Susan herself found the offending object in the folds of her corduroy skirt, whereupon she announced that she'd had all the hiking that she could stand. As the weary troop straggled back across the moors toward the Manor House, a sore and bitter Rowan Rover looked earnestly for a pool of quicksand, with a view toward using it himself—but it had been a dry summer in Devon and the moors weren't accepting any human sacrifices.

◆　◆　◆

AT NINE THAT evening the Oak Room bar was empty except for the members of the mystery tour. Even Bernard had lingered after dinner, sipping a pint of bitter and lis-

218

tening to the general chat. Charles Warren was wedged on a small love seat between his wife and Martha Tabram, and the others occupied various armchairs, which they had pulled up in a circle round a coffee table. Susan, now restored to normal vision, wanted to compare the Manor's restaurant to one in Minneapolis called Azur. Resolutely, Elizabeth MacPherson kept coming back to forensic anthropology and to murders in general, thus encouraging the few nontour patrons of the lounge to flee in a state of some anxiety. After half an hour of alternate monologues, a restful silence fell upon the group.

For once, it was Charles Warren who spoke up. "Talking about murders," he remarked by way of introduction, "we called our youngest daughter this evening, and she gave us some news from the States. Seems there's a mass murderer loose at the University of Florida."

Immediately the group fell silent, and Rowan and Elizabeth looked like firehorses who'd just heard the alarm bell. "What sort of mass murderer?" asked Rowan, exhaling clouds of smoke.

"Sounds like another Bundy to me," said Charles. "This past weekend he went on a rampage and killed four women students, I think, and one young man.

"Young man?" echoed Elizabeth. "Oh! I suppose he was in the apartment with one of the women?"

"Right."

Elizabeth nodded. "Collateral damage. He just happened to be in the way. I'd like to see the girls' pictures, wouldn't you, Rowan?"

"Only to verify that they look very much alike. They will, of course. Serial killers are very particular. Bundy liked brunettes with long, straight hair parted down the middle."

Susan Cohen patted her blonde curls and laughed. "I guess I'm safe, then!"

"You are from Bundy," said Elizabeth gravely. "So this guy killed five people over the weekend. They ought to have caught him by now."

"They have," said Charles. "Our daughter said they'd arrested an eighteen-year-old student on suspicion."

"It's not him," said Elizabeth and Rowan together. Elizabeth nodded toward the guide, inviting him to explain.

"He's too young," said Rowan, gesturing with his whiskey glass. "Serial killers may start as young as eighteen, but I cannot believe that this is that murderer's first killing spree. Doing away with five people in two days sounds very much like the fugue state one associates with the end of a serial killer's career. To use our previous example, Bundy did just such a multiple crime just before he was caught. Psychologists think they do it subconsciously wanting to be caught."

"If I were the Florida police," said Elizabeth, "I'd be looking for a trail of missing women or unsolved crimes involving victims who resembled these latest murdered girls. Whoever did this had to work up to this kill spree."

"Murdered women!" said Alice with a disapproving frown. "Always women! Aren't there any female serial killers?"

Rowan Rover shrugged. "Little old lady poisoners. But they kill boyfriends or family members. I'd hardly classify them as sex crimes."

Susan Cohen giggled. "What we need for true equality is a female serial killer!"

Elizabeth MacPherson looked thoughtful. "I suppose the closest we get to it is child killing, wouldn't you say, Rowan?"

"As far as I know," he agreed. "Although,

nothing is too bizarre these days. Somewhere in New Jersey there may be a woman karate expert picking up unsuspecting male hitchhikers and doing them in on stretches of lonely road. I find it hard to imagine, though. Yes, I should say that child killing is the closest female equivalent to the Bundys of this world. Were you, by any chance, thinking of Constance Kent?"

"I suppose I was," said Elizabeth.

"Interesting. So you think she did it?"

"All right," said Frances Coles, holding up her hand. "Time out. If you're going to talk shop, you might as well let us in on it. Who was Constance Kent?"

Rowan Rover looked pensively into his empty glass. "I wonder if I might have another double Scotch first?"

Kate Conway volunteered to stand him a drink in exchange for the story, and after she had supplied him with a fresh glass, he settled back in the leather wingchair and began the tale.

"We shall be traveling within a few miles of her house," he said. "She lived in a large house near Rode, a few miles south of Bath. This was in 1860. The murder occurred in that year—when Constance was sixteen. Her father was a factory inspector, but he insisted on living extravagantly, so that the family was always hard-up for money. I think Kent had five children by his first wife. After her death, he married the pretty young governess, Mary Pratt, and they proceeded to have several more children, including a son, Francis Savile Kent, born in 1856. In 1860 the boy was found with his throat cut in an outbuilding on the Kent property. The actual cause of death, though, was suffocation."

"How could they tell that?" asked Frances.

"From the bleeding," said Kate Conway absently. "The patient bleeds very little if cuts are made postmortem, because the heart has already ceased to pump the blood."

Rowan smiled approvingly. "Thank you, Nurse Conway."

"Why would anyone cut the throat of a dead person?" Frances persisted.

"To make it look like a stranger had done it, I expect," said Kate.

"That was the police theory, certainly," said Rowan. "But which member of the household did it? The crime was investigated at length by the local police, and the victim's half sister Constance Kent was charged with the murder, but she was released for lack of evidence. Five years later, she astonished everyone by going to the police of her own accord and confessing to the murder of Francis Kent."

"There!" said Elizabeth triumphantly. "You admit it. She confessed!"

"Oh, yes, she confessed," Rowan agreed. "Whether or not she did it is another matter."

"Oh, good! A real life murder mystery!" said Frances Coles. "Who do you think did it?"

"Before we discuss it further, I need to read up on the case again. I know the general facts, but I'm not well-informed enough to argue about it. Ask me again tomorrow night in St. Ives. I'll try to have another look at a crime book by then. Perhaps we could discuss more familiar ones in the meantime."

Martha Tabram stifled a yawn. "Not I," she said. "It's nearly ten o'clock. Good night all."

Emma Smith and her mother also bade them a hasty farewell, saying that they wanted to do some walking in the early morning. Susan announced that there was a good television program coming on at ten and she wanted to watch it. The others settled back to hear more tales of crime.

After Elizabeth and Rowan had talked shop—through two more double Scotches—about the moors murderers, the notorious Krays, and other favorite cases, the group fell silent. No one else was very keen on true crime; they simply liked a genteel whodunit to pass the time.

Finally Maud Marsh said quietly, "Have either of you ever heard of a case concerning a Chinese gentleman named Mr. Miao?"

"Derwentwater," said Elizabeth Mac-Pherson, who indexed her facts geographically.

"Yes," said Rowan, straining to recall the case. "I remember that it was the Lake District, wasn't it? Borrowdale, I think, in the late 1920s." He turned to Maud. "Yes, what about it?"

"What happened?" she asked simply. Her face bore a look of concern that people did not usually have when casually discussing sensational crimes.

"He murdered his wife," said Elizabeth, who had recently read an account of the case. (The one good thing about learning in binges is that all your information is fresh for as long as you care about it.) "She was Chinese, too. Not very pretty, judging from her photograph."

"They were on their honeymoon, weren't they?" said Rowan. "Staying at the hotel in Borrowdale. But they weren't from England."

"There was an American connection," said Elizabeth. "I think they sailed from New York."

"He was a law student at Loyola in Chicago," said Maud Marsh.

They stared at her. "That's not in the books," said Elizabeth.

"I knew him. He rented a room from my family in Chicago when I was a young girl. He was a very nice man. Later I heard that he was involved in a murder case, and I always wondered about the details. It didn't seem possible."

"What doesn't seem possible," said Rowan wonderingly, "is that I am sitting here talking to someone who knew a murderer who was executed in 1928. Amazing!"

"What was he like?" asked Elizabeth. She had known several murderers herself, but their cases seemed hardly sensational enough to make crime history. Mr. Miao, on the other hand, was a legend.

"He was very quiet," said Maud, summoning up her memories from half a century past. She looked a bit ghostlike herself in the plain white dress that matched the silver of her hair. Her hands twisted and untwisted in her lap as she spoke. "He came from a good family in Shanghai. I believe he already had a law degree from a university in China. He studied a great deal and he was always very nice to me. I never met his wife. Are you sure he killed her?"

"They went out for a walk," said Elizabeth, looking up at the ceiling as she tried to visualize her book of criminal history. "A couple of hours later, he came back, but she didn't. He told another guest at the hotel that his wife had gone to town to shop. When she hadn't returned by eight o'clock, the hotel proprietress became concerned; but apparently Mr. Miao wasn't worried that she had been gone shopping for so long."

"That's a little odd, surely, for a newly-wed," Maud conceded.

"Unless he were married to Elizabeth here," Rowan grunted.

"I don't shop *that* much! Anyhow, what

happened then? A farmer found the body by a pool of water in the woods. She had been strangled with a blind cord and her clothing was torn. Also her rings were missing."

"Rape?" said Maud. "That doesn't sound like something a husband would have done."

Rowan, thinking of previous wives, opened his mouth and closed it again. He took another sip of Scotch. "As I recall, the physical evidence incriminated him, didn't it? Didn't the blind cord match the kind used in the hotel?"

"Yes," said Elizabeth. "I remember that. And they found her missing rings hidden among his things."

Maud sighed. "How very sad. That does seem to settle it. I only wondered because of something that happened in Chicago, while he was staying with us. I remember that some Chinese men came to see him one afternoon. They were standing in the hallway, speaking very angrily at Mr. Miao in Chinese. And when I saw him later he had cuts and bruises on his face. I asked him who the men were, and he said that they were from—I think he said a rival family. Anyway, they wanted him to do something that he didn't want to do. He seemed very afraid of them."

"A tong!" muttered Rowan Rover. "Chinese gangsters in America. Of course you had them in Chicago! I wonder how he got mixed up with them?"

"I don't know," said Maud. "I never saw them again, and he didn't discuss it with my parents. But when I heard that his wife had been murdered, I wondered if those people had somehow followed him to England and killed his bride. Maybe they didn't want him to marry her."

Elizabeth looked uneasy. "The defense did call witnesses who stated that they had seen Oriental men in the area that day."

Rowan shook his head. "Japanese tourists? Korean immigrants? They never found those mysterious Orientals, did they? I think his attorney was grasping at straws."

"He was such a gentle man, though," said Maud. "What was his motive supposed to be?"

"They never really gave one," said Elizabeth. "The theories were that he killed her for her money or because he learned that she couldn't have children. I think in those days no one expected to understand the motivations of a Chinese mind."

Maud looked thoughtful. "I wonder if *they* forced him to kill her, or else . . . or else, what? I don't know."

"I can't even guess what his motive was," said Rowan. "But considering how unconcerned he was about her disappearance, we have to assume that he knew she was dead. The fact that her missing rings were found among his possessions is strong evidence that he did it. Had I been on the jury, I'd have found him guilty."

"And he was hanged?"

"Yes. At Strangeways in Manchester, I expect," said Rowan. "We'll be going past another famous prison tomorrow, incidentally. Dartmoor."

"I want to see that!" said Elizabeth. But she was a bit more subdued about crime than usual. It was difficult to know what to say to someone who mourned for a murderer. Odd how unusual even the most ordinary people could turn out to be.

She fell asleep that night thinking of Constance Kent in a bloodstained nightdress standing over the body of her brother.

CHAPTER 10

"How many were going to St. Ives?"
> —Old English Riddle

"I'LL NEVER GET used to stewed tomatoes for breakfast," said Alice MacKenzie, peering at the shriveled vegetable curled up next to a sausage patty.

"No," Frances Coles agreed. "But the bread is certainly good." She had piled a selection of baked goods next to her plate of eggs.

It was nine o'clock and those members of the tour group who had not been up for hours were finishing up a hasty breakfast in the Manor House restaurant, an elegant banquet hall decorated in pastels, with large sunny windows, and a photograph of their most famous diner, HRH the Prince of Wales, prominently displayed.

"You're going to eat all those?" asked Elizabeth MacPherson, slipping into the vacant chair at their table with a croissant and a bowl of cereal.

Frances giggled. "Eventually," she said, pointing to her cavernous handbag.

Elizabeth stifled a yawn. She was wearing a black sweatsuit that suggested a rapid transition from bed to breakfast table. "Are you already packed? We're heading out soon. Bernard was just finishing his breakfast when I came in. I hope we get to St. Ives today before five."

Alice heaved a sigh. "More shopping?"

"Actually, no. I want to visit a library."

Frances began to rummage in her handbag. "I have an extra paperback here," she said. "It's a Carolyn Hart, if you'd like to borrow it."

"Thanks, Frances, but I brought reading material. I need to find a library because I want to do some research."

"On what?" asked Frances. She was wrapping a croissant in a paper napkin and stowing it away for future consumption.

"Constance Kent," said Elizabeth. "I'm fascinated by what Rowan said last night—that just because she confessed doesn't mean she was guilty. The books I've read always assumed that she was guilty, and I had never thought to question it."

"If she didn't kill her little brother, who did?" asked Frances.

"I don't know," said Elizabeth. "But I want to find out more about the case. Maybe we can figure it out."

"Didn't Rowan say that she was only a teenager when the murder occurred? I wonder what became of her?"

"I'll ask him," said Elizabeth. "I think one of my books said that she changed her name and emigrated to Canada. The author didn't know what became of her after that."

With studied casualness, Alice and Frances turned to look at Martha Tabram, eating her porridge in blissful ignorance of their suspicions.

Elizabeth noted the direction of their stares. "No," she said. "Francis Kent was killed in 1865. That would make Constance 142 years old by now. Besides, she was a blonde."

Martha Tabram looked up from her spoon to find an entire table of her fellow travelers gazing at her in silent contemplation. She gave them a bewildered frown, and they smiled and waved before hastily looking away.

"She probably thinks we're crazy," muttered Alice.

"It's time to go anyway," Frances Coles

replied. "Aren't these tiny jam jars cute? Just the right size for one serving."

"And so portable, too," murmured Elizabeth, handing over her own unopened jar of strawberry preserves. Frances added it to the provisions already in her bag.

♦ ♦ ♦

ROWAN ROVER, IN his pseudo-uniform of khaki slacks and windcheater, took up his accustomed position at the microphone. "We have a long way to go, ladies and Charles," he said, when everyone had taken their accustomed seats. "I want us to be in Cornwall by lunchtime, and that means only short rest stops this morning. If all goes well, we shall be lunching on Bodmin Moor at Jamaica Inn."

Several of the older members of the group murmured Daphne DuMaurier's name, recognizing the coaching inn as the namesake of her classic novel about the Cornish shipwreckers.

"Although we won't be doing any walking tours this morning, this morning's route is not without its points of interest."

"That'll be the B3212, right?" said Bernard, starting the engine.

"Correct. A scenic minor road through

the heart of Dartmoor, and, incidentally, the road that leads to Dartmoor Prison."

"Can't we go inside?" said Elizabeth MacPherson.

"I'd rather not," said Rowan. Ever, he added silently, with a twinge of dread at the prospect of a long-term stay in retribution for his current project. "But you will get a good look at it from a distance."

"Is there anyone there that we know?" asked Elizabeth, referring, as Rowan well knew, to the more notorious murderers of recent years.

"I know a few gangsters currently in residence," Rowan replied, "but since your interests are confined exclusively to amateur murderers, I cannot think of anyone you'd recognize."

"Ian Brady?"

"He's up north. Scottish family."

"Peter Sutcliffe?"

"Up north. He's the Yorkshire Ripper, remember."

"Dennis Nilsen?"

"Oh, yes, the fellow in north London who cut up his victims and stuffed them down the sink—and then wrote to his landlord to complain that the drains were blocked. I'm not sure where he is. But I did hear a funny story about him. It seems that a movie company was considering making a film about his crimes, and when Nilsen heard about it, he wrote to the producer and asked that the cast be listed in the order of their *dis*appearance."

"Even if some famous murderers were in Dartmoor, the prison officials wouldn't let you talk to them, Elizabeth," Susan pointed out. She had settled into the seat behind Bernard with a paperback crime novel and the chocolate bar from her room.

Kate Conway shivered at the thought. "Why would you even want to talk to a convicted killer?"

Elizabeth considered the question. "I don't know. I know they're probably all crazy. I guess I'm just curious to see what a murderer would be like in person. Would he seem like everybody else? Would it be frightening just to be in the same room with him? What do you think, Rowan?"

He looked startled by the question. "I suppose it would depend," he stammered. "I've known one or two gangsters who had put people away. They seemed rather crass and insensitive, but then, so do many bankers and minor bureaucrats, so it's difficult to say. Some of my friends in the constabulary say that the safest prisoners to be around are those who've killed just one person, a girlfriend or a family member. They're usually model prisoners, and they seldom repeat their crime." *And I wouldn't either,* he promised silently, to whatever fates might have been listening.

◆ ◆ ◆

THE ONLY STOP that morning was at Postbridge, just over halfway between Moretonhampstead and Dartmoor Prison. "Photo opportunity," said Bernard, pulling the coach into a graveled lot alongside a country store. "People always want to take snaps of the old bridge."

The three-arched stone bridge over which the road ran seemed old enough, but fifty yards downstream from it was such a quaint-looking span that everyone sprinted from the coach, cameras in hand, to examine it. It was a footbridge over the River Dart, consisting of three thin slabs of granite laid end to end across the water, supported by two piles of balanced stone slabs in midstream and an additional pile of rocks at each bank. Had the river not been visibly shallow, no one would have ventured onto the bridge, but the sight of a retriever wading happily near the bridge encouraged the group to brave the stone span. They spent a happy quarter of an hour photographing the bridge, each other, each other on the bridge, and the red-berried rowan tree at the edge of the field (with Rowan in the foreground, as a visual pun).

As their guide herded them back to the bus, they bolted into the roadside shop for an orgy of postcard purchasing, but since the store's merchandise was limited and its floor space minuscule, they soon emerged and climbed back aboard with reasonable punctuality.

A few minutes later, before Susan had begun her nap or Frances had finished her first postcard, Rowan Rover was on the microphone again, calling their attention to an assortment of four-storied gray buildings across an expanse of fields on the left side of the road. "There it is, ladies and Charles," he said with a dramatic hush in his voice. "With the gorse in bloom and the grass still summer green, it doesn't look like such a forbidding place, I suppose. But one prisoner called it the Siberia of England. I assure you that winter on Dartmoor can be very bleak indeed."

The tour members craned their necks for

a better look at the circular granite compound, reminiscent of a nineteenth-century factory complex.

Rowan consulted his tour notes. "When I was at home this weekend, I found this quote in one of my reference books. It was written by a young American prisoner named Charles Andrews, kept here during the War of 1812. *You feel the cold of the place in your marrow. Driving rain comes through the windows, the wind rattles the slates, the walls are damp. In winter the place seems always under fog which penetrates everything. It has driven many a prisoner crazy* . . . I expect all of that is still true today."

"How old is it?" asked Charles Warren.

"It was built in the early 1800s to house prisoners from the Napoleonic wars," said Rowan. "It has been modernized over the years, of course. I believe the chief problem now is overcrowding."

"Does England have the death penalty?" asked Susan, looking up from her novel.

"No. It was abolished in the mid-Sixties."

"Too bad. It would have solved the problem." Susan went back to her book.

Bernard took a side road that enabled them to circle the prison and to come back out on the main road again. Charles and

Elizabeth snapped photos from the moving coach, but the others seemed to lose interest in the prison after their first look. Rowan, too, was glad to leave the ominous compound behind. In another hour they would cross the River Tamar and go into Cornwall, where his attempts to murder would begin in earnest. Just after lunch, in fact.

◆ ◆ ◆

BUSY WITH HIS own thoughts about the remainder of the day, Rowan Rover left the group alone to doze or enjoy the scenery from Princetown to Tavistock, and for most of the way up to Launceston, where they would pick up the A30 that led all the way through the Cornish countryside to their destination in St. Ives. Just after Dunterton, though, when the road crossed the River Tamar, Rowan Rover's sectarian feelings for his home province won out over his preoccupation with his personal plans and he felt compelled to infuse the group with enthusiasm about his native Cornwall.

"Cornwall has always been a place apart," he began. "It is surrounded on three sides by the sea and cut off from neighboring Devon by the River Tamar, which we just crossed. But the separateness is more than mere geography. Until the eighteenth century, the people of Cornwall spoke another language as well. Old Cornish is a Celtic tongue, akin to Welsh and Breton."

Susan Cohen rolled her eyes. "Oh, God! We're going someplace where they don't speak English?"

"On the contrary," said Rowan Rover, holding in his temper with a deep breath. "English is all they speak. The Cornish language died out two hundred years ago. However, other traces of the ancient culture do survive. There are dolmens and great stone circles dotting the landscape. Holy wells, remnants of a pre-Christian faith, are found all over the countryside, and in the place names and the oral tradition, you can find the remnants of the old legends. One of the legends is the tale of King Arthur."

The Sword in the Stone," said Kate Conway, whose acquisition of culture seemed entirely cinematic.

"Let us not forget *Camelot* and *Excalibur,* while we're at it," snapped Rowan. "However, for purposes of this tour, there are some less savory Cornish traditions that we should discuss. It was a culture of fishermen and seafarers, but others also depended on the sea for a living. I mean, of course, the smugglers and wreckers."

"What are wreckers?" asked Frances, scanning the road for hot-rodders.

"Ship wreckers," Rowan explained. "Back in the old days, any goods washed ashore from wrecks were considered common property, so a foundering ship would bring the entire village out to congregate on the beach, awaiting the storm-tossed booty. It was inevitable that sooner or later someone got the idea of *helping* ships to wreck. Tradition has it that they tied a lantern around a horse's neck and led it along the cliffs, so that a ship would mistake its light for the lighthouse, and wreck on the rocks."

"Nag's Head," murmured Elizabeth MacPherson. "That's the name of a beach off the North Carolina coast. Apparently, the custom went to the colonies with the Cornish immigrants."

Susan laughed. "So you're descended from crooks?"

"Times were hard in those days," said Rowan, ignoring the jibe. "Smugglers and wreckers made a better living than fishermen or those poor sods who worked in the

Cornish tin mines. Anyhow, today we shall visit Jamaica Inn, a fabled haunt of these outlaws, and, although it isn't on the schedule, I thought I might take you into some actual smugglers' caves tomorrow."

The mystery tourists looked doubtfully at each other. "Caves?" said Frances Coles.

Rowan gave her a magnanimous smile. "Yes. Won't it be exciting?" Ignoring their uneasy glances, he went on. "Besides the tales of saints and giants, we have a few great villains as well."

Alice MacKenzie raised her hand. "About these smugglers. Are there any precautions we ought to take?"

"They don't do it anymore," sighed Rowan, wondering if there were anything Americans wouldn't believe. "That was in the eighteenth century. There aren't any more robbers around here."

From the driver's seat came Bernard's hearty laugh. "I dunno, Rowan. Have you seen the prices some of these places charge tourists?"

"I stand corrected," said Rowan. "You will be robbed, but you will participate voluntarily, and to show for it you will have: postcards, cheaply turned-out horse brasses, souvenir key chains, and imitation shrimping nets, suitable for wall decoration."

A few miles farther on, the scenery changed from tree-lined hills and lush green valleys to a treeless open moorland of gorse and bracken: Bodmin Moor. Bernard pulled the coach into a gravel parking lot next to a two-story gray building with a stone courtyard in front of it. "Jamaica Inn," he announced. "Go and have lunch in the Smugglers' Bar." Turning to Elizabeth, he whispered, "The gift shop is right next door."

"Oh, goody!" said Elizabeth, snatching up her purse.

"That's right," snapped Rowan. "Go and buy some horse brasses and Old Cornish tea towels!"

Elizabeth made a face at him. "I like shopping."

"Well, don't be too long about it," said Rowan to the rest of the group. "After lunch, if anyone fancies a walk, I'll take you to Dozmary Pool, and tell you the story of Jan Tregeagle."

The tour members were delighted with the white-lettered inscription painted above the doorway to the old coaching inn: THROUGH THESE PORTALS PASSED SMUG-

GLERS, WRECKERS, VILLAINS, AND MURDER-
ERS. BUT REST EASY . . . T'WAS MANY YEARS
AGO.

"I wouldn't be too sure about that," muttered Rowan Rover, as he watched his
charges taking each other's picture beneath
the inscription.

He allowed them half an hour in the red-
carpeted Smugglers' Bar, with its ancient
wooden tables and exposed beams hung
with kettles and old pewter tankards. The
group ate ploughmen's lunches of bread,
cheese, and pickles, or Cornish pasties,
washed down with ale. Rowan himself
wolfed down a pasty and a pint of bitter
before escaping outside to smoke in the
cobblestone yard. He savored a quarter of
an hour's solitude, before routing the group
out for the afternoon hike.

Susan squinted at the bright noonday
sunlight in the inn yard. "How far is it to
this stupid pond?" she demanded. "I
bought some postcards and I need to get
them written."

"Oh, perhaps a mile," said Rowan, halving the actual figure on the theory that distance is a state of mind. "There is a
connection between this pool and our next
stop, Roche Rock. Incidentally, according

245

to legend, Dozmary Pool is the home of the Lady of the Lake, and it is from there that King Arthur received the sword Excalibur."

"Let's go," said Maud Marsh, swinging her cardigan over her shoulder. Thus shamed into obedience, the little group trudged off behind her.

As they crossed the busy A30 to the narrow lane that led to the pool, Rowan Rover began his tale of Cornwall's legendary villain. "Bodmin Moor is haunted, ladies and Charles, by the spirit of Jan Tregeagle. Whether or not he sold his soul to the devil, I cannot say, but it is beyond question that a local magistrate of that name actually existed in the early seventeenth century. They say he murdered his family and seized the estates of defenseless orphans, but he took pains to bribe the local priests and got himself buried in consecrated ground. Not that it did him much good." Rowan Rover paused, thinking of his own recent promises to the Deity. He put the parallel firmly from his mind.

"Was he murdered?" asked Elizabeth hopefully.

"No, but after the life he led, he hadn't a hope of heaven. Anyhow, they say he was called back from the dead to testify in a court case that he had participated in when he was alive. He sat there in court with the smell of the charnel house clinging to his shrunken features and he testified that he had swindled the litigants in the case. The judge decided the matter and dismissed the participants, but Tregeagle remained in court. The man who summoned the ghost said that he considered Tregeagle a problem for the court. And he left."

"I suppose they summoned an exorcist?" said Kate, who was reminded of yet another movie moment.

Rowan glanced around at the party. They all seemed to be keeping up reasonably well. No one seemed out of breath. Still, he slowed his pace, knowing that there was more than a mile to go. "They called in the clergy," he said. "And those learned gentlemen decided that their duty was to save Jan Tregeagle from Hell, and that the only way to accomplish that was to give his ghost a task that would keep him occupied for all eternity. They gave him a broken shell and commanded him to empty Dozmary Pool. In order to keep him at his task, they set a pack of demon hounds to watch over him, ready to attack if he stopped bailing."

"But the pool is still there?" asked Charles, smiling. "Has old Jan emptied much of it?"

"No. Legend has it that a great storm frightened him one night, and he took off across Bodmin Moor, with the devil hounds in hot pursuit. He made it to Roche Rock, a holy place about seven miles west of here. We shall be going there next. They say that he got his head into the window of the clifftop chapel, but his body would not fit through, and the hounds tore at him constantly."

"There's a mystery by Mary Stewart called *The Gabriel Hounds*," Susan began, with the air of someone about to deliver a plot summary.

Three people spoke as one to head her off. Alice MacKenzie, loudest of the trio, said, "So he's stuck up there on Roche Rock, being attacked by hellhounds?"

"There's more to the story," said Rowan quickly, realizing that it had been a close call. "After a few days of listening to Tregeagle's screams, the holy man of Roche Rock sent for one of Cornwall's saints to move Tregeagle elsewhere, and he was set to weaving ropes of sand on the beach at Padstow. But Padstow's patron saint grew tired of listening to the spirit's howls of torment, so he shipped him off to Berepper, where he was ordered to clear all the sand from the beach. Unfortunately, during his labors he dropped a sack of sand and managed to permanently seal off the entrance to Helston Harbour with a sandbar."

"Evicted again?" asked Emma Smith, a folklore enthusiast.

"Yes. He's at Land's End now, sweeping the sands from Porthcurno Cove into Mill Bay, but the ocean currents defeat him. They say you can hear his bellows of rage when gale winds blow the sand back on the beach."

Emma looked thoughtful. "I suppose Jan Tregeagle is really the personification of some ancient Celtic god. The geographic connections to the story make it seem much older than seventeenth century."

"Very likely," Rowan agreed. "But he makes a colorful villain, doesn't he?"

Susan piped up again. "In Minnesota, we have a legendary figure associated with lakes. He's an Indian called Hiawatha. There's a poem about him that I had to learn in the eighth grade. It's by Henry Wadsworth Longfellow. Have you heard it?" She cleared her throat, and hastened on. " '*By the shores of Gitchee Goomee, by the shining big sea waters, stood the wigwam of Nokomis, daughter of the moon, Nokomis . . .*' "

The others contrived to lag as far behind Susan as they possibly could for the remainder of the walk, but her flat voice carried very well across the moors, adding another dimension of agony to the haunted moor. Several members of the group were heard to mutter that they would much prefer to be set upon by hellhounds than listen to another stanza of "The Song of Hiawatha," and for one altruistic moment Rowan Rover felt guilty about taking Mr. Kosminski's money.

♦ ♦ ♦

AFTER A SOMEWHAT perfunctory admiration of Dozmary Pool and a few dutiful photographs taken by Charles Warren, the group trudged back to the Jamaica Inn car park, where Bernard was waiting, enveloped in a rock 'n' roll cloud.

"We shan't be going far this time," Rowan told the driver. "The turnoff for the village of Roche is about seven miles up the A30. I'll direct you from there."

"Right you are," said Bernard, switching

250

back to a classical lullaby. "Did everyone have a nice hike? What was the pool like?"

Alice MacKenzie paused on her way to her seat and scowled. "I was reminded of Lake Superior," she snapped, stalking away.

Recognizing this reference to Minnesota, the others stole furtive glances in Susan's direction and fought to keep straight faces.

Rowan Rover, pleased with the tide of popular opinion, reached for his trusty microphone and began to describe the next exhibit. "Our next destination is Roche Rock which is, as I told you, the summit to which Jan Tregeagle fled when he escaped from Dozmary Pool. It was also the home of a succession of Celtic saints, including St. Roche or St. Conan."

"Why do Celtic saints always have two names?" asked Emma Smith.

"Probably because the Latin clergy always wanted to translate everything into their own language, the bureaucratic old perishers. Anyhow, Roche Rock is a stark pillar of rock rising above the flat landscape, and at the top of it is a ruined chapel, carved into the rock itself. That dates from 1409. Perhaps the hermit in residence kept a light burning in the chapel to guide travelers across the moors.

"Not another walk!" moaned Susan Cohen, fanning herself with a postcard.

"Not at all," said Rowan cheerfully. "A *climb.*"

Several minutes later, Bernard turned off the main road and guided the coach through the narrow lanes of the village of Roche. A few hundred yards farther on he turned left, at Rowan's instruction. Almost immediately Martha Tabram cried out, "There it is!" and pointed to a barren spire of rock set among a tangle of underbrush in the wide plateau of open fields. The great pinnacle stood about sixty feet high and loomed dark and sinister between them and the afternoon sun.

Rowan leaped to his feet and motioned for Bernard to open the doors. "Here we are!" he announced, somewhat unnecessarily. "An ancient Celtic chapel that is not a tourist trap." He smiled at Miriam Angel. "As you can see, there are no guides, no gates, and no admission fee. It is a simple country relic."

A dirt trail led upward through the tangle of bushes to the foot of the rock, about a hundred yards from the road. Rowan led the way, answering questions about the shrubbery, and giving them more facts about the area. Finally, when they were all assembled on a small hill at the foot of the towering rock, the guide turned to the group and said, "Ready to go up?"

Frances Coles put her head back to survey the summit of the pinnacle. She looked up, and up, and up, until she nearly lost her balance. "Oh, my," she murmured. "Where are the steps?"

Rowan Rover shook his head. He walked to the base of the rock and climbed three rungs up a vertical iron ladder that was hammered into the rock. There were no handrails and the rungs of the ladder were circular iron bars, hardly suited to steady footing. "Magnificent view at the top!" he told them. "Tell you what: I'll go up to the top and help you up at the summit. Charles can stay at the foot of the ladder and steady you from below. That's quite safe, isn't it?"

Maud Marsh strode over to the foot of the ladder. "No guts, no glory," she said with a shrug, and she began to follow the guide up the iron rungs.

After snapping another shot of the rock, Charles Warren did as he was instructed, taking up his place at the base of the ladder.

"Who's next?" he asked, grinning at the huddle of tourists. "Nancy?"

His wife grinned back at him. "Sure," she said. "Just make sure you catch me, Charles."

"Anybody else?" asked Charles, noting that Maud had nearly reached Rowan's outstretched hand.

"I think the view is just fine from down here," said Miriam Angel. "We'll watch." She sat down on a flat boulder with Emma and Martha Tabram to watch the climbers.

"We're still deliberating!" yelled Kate Conway, who was standing with the undecided Alice MacKenzie and the horrified Frances Coles.

"You can be the next group!" Rowan called back from far above them. "There isn't much room up here, so we'd better limit ourselves to four people at a time. I can take one more now. Susan? Not afraid, are you?"

Susan hesitated for a moment and looked down at her slick-soled Italian pumps. "You'd better not, Susan," said Elizabeth, also looking at Susan's footwear. "That ladder is awfully small. And it may be slippery."

Susan cast her companion a look of

scorn. "I have excellent balance," she retorted. "In grade school I took several months of ballet." She waved her hand at the group on the summit. "Here I come, you guys!"

Elizabeth sighed. "I'd better come with you, then."

For anyone afraid of heights, the top of Roche Rock could fuel twenty years of nightmares. The roofless ruined chapel was missing walls on two sides so that only one's sense of balance separated the climber from a sixty-foot plunge to the jagged rocks below. The space within the chapel was about the size of a walk-in closet, so that the climbers had to be very careful not to bump into each other as they changed positions to look at the scenery.

"You're right about the view," said Nancy Warren. "You can see for miles. Rowan, look almost straight down on the back side. Is that a schoolyard? What are those boys playing?"

"Football. Well, soccer to you," Rowan replied. "What a perfect place to watch the game from. I wonder none of the school's football fans has thought of it."

Maud Marsh, who was looking across the fields to the northeast, motioned for Rowan to come and stand beside her. "That's an odd-looking mountain over there," she said, pointing to a bare hill with an escarpment of white clay.

"I'm afraid that what you're looking at is a bit of industrial blight," said Rowan sadly. "This part of Cornwall is the source of the clay used by the makers of fine china. You know Wedgewood . . . Spode . . . all those wonderfully delicate works of ceramic art. That mound that you're looking at is a refuse heap made by the china clay industry. They take the earth they want, and leave the rest behind in ugly mounds to sully the landscape. Ugly, isn't it?"

Maud Marsh looked stern. "They'd never get away with that in Berkeley!"

"No," said Rowan. "I expect your environmental terrorists would begin picketing before they'd deposited more than four shovels full of waste dirt." Still, he felt a pang of sympathy for the clay quarriers. They made it possible to fashion creations of great and lasting beauty, but all anyone ever seemed to notice was their refuse dump. In his darkest drinking moods, he saw his life like that: superior intelligence and achievement that went unrewarded, while the world carped about his credit rating and his marital problems. He wondered if his much-contemplated actions were about to change his luck or whether the deed would only prove to make his spiritual refuse heap so much the greater. He reminded himself that this was not the time for philosophy.

"You'd think there'd be a better way up here than that stupid iron ladder!" Susan Cohen's voice floated up to them several moments before her scowling face appeared at the top rung. She heaved herself onto the flat rock floor of the ruined chapel and looked around while she caught her breath. "No barriers!" she exclaimed, edging forward to peer over the precipice. "That's negligence if I ever saw it. If somebody fell off this thing, whoever owns this could get sued for a bundle."

"We are up here at our own risk," said Rowan. He hoped that Mr. Kosminski would not be crass enough to recoup his assassin's fee by suing the landowner of the rock. It was definitely a consideration, but unfortunately for Rowan's scruples, his time was running out and he could not afford to be overly fastidious in his choice of methods. "Walk around a bit," he said to Susan. "The views are quite spectacular."

Elizabeth MacPherson crept up the ladder, resolutely refusing to look down. She eased her way out onto the barren rock in a posture that was somewhere between a crawl and a catatonic seizure. "This is intense," she managed to whisper. "And there's nothing below us but rocks, whichever way you fall." She edged her way to the one wall of the chapel that was still standing and sat with her back to it, gripping a small outcrop of rock and taking slow deep breaths while she mustered her composure.

Susan seemed undisturbed by the imminence of death. She ambled around the tiny square of rock as if it were the interior of a gift shop. "This is a funny place for a chapel," she announced. "Like they wanted to look down on everybody. You know that Father Brown story called 'The Hammer of God'? According to him . . ."

Rowan Rover, who had been standing next to the ladder, suddenly moved in behind Susan. Furtively he took in the positions of everyone else. The group down below were talking among themselves and weren't looking up at the rock anymore. Charles Warren, still at the base of the iron ladder, was out of the line of sight. Maud

Marsh and Nancy Warren were on the eastern edge of the precipice, watching the schoolyard soccer game. Fortunately the position of the afternoon sun meant that the people in the schoolyard could not clearly see the top of the rock. Elizabeth MacPherson seemed to be taking in the scenery or recovering from the shock of the heights; at any rate, she was oblivious to her companions. *Now!* he thought.

He edged in closer to Susan, so that he was standing beside her, but a few inches back, out of her range of vision. They were six inches from the rock floor's ending in open space. He felt his stomach turn over as the wind touched him, reminding him of the emptiness beyond. Moving his arms slowly, so as not to attract attention, he maneuvered himself behind Susan, preparing to give her a fatal shove in her back and send her plummeting over the edge. He put his left foot forward and shifted his weight onto that foot as he leaned out, palms upright, ready to deliver the coup de grace.

Rowan pushed.

Susan moved.

The soccer game had caught her attention and, in the last split-second, she moved sideways along the rock to get a better view of the playing field. Rowan Rover, hands outstretched and braced for a collision, found himself pushing molecules of air that were only too willing to step aside.

Rowan Rover pitched forward into the welcoming abyss, with an obscenity caught in his throat. His mind, which was racing in overdrive, was considering all the Famous Last Words entries in reference books. If the anthologists were to be believed, people never seemed to say "Oh shit!" as their ultimate utterance, but he was willing to bet that in accidents, that phrase topped the list of final remarks. In his terror-driven brain, properties like gravity and inertia had switched to slow motion and there seemed to be endless time left to contemplate his life—and various other philosophical points of interest. And, he reflected, if he did go to hell, he might be able to find out who Jack the Ripper actually was. A tempting prospect. He wondered if he could come back as a ghost and taunt Donald Rumblelow with the information.

As he reached a horizontal position, with a clear view of the underbrush, the rocks, and eternity, something stopped his forward catapult, so that instead of diving into space, he slammed against the edge of

Roche Rock and dangled in a dizzying jack-knife position halfway over the side. The obscenity lodged in his throat managed to find its way out, meandered for a short jaunt up into his nasal passages, and finally emerged triumphantly through his open jaws, leading a parade of expelled air for maximum volume. Fortunately, perhaps, for the schoolboys' innocent ears, the word was lost amid the general screams on the precipice.

The pain of incipient bruises coursed through his body on the way to his whirling brain, and he had to sift through injury, fright, and bewilderment to ascertain why he wasn't plummeting to his death. A further check of his senses told him that someone was holding onto his leg. Shortly thereafter he noted that he was being shouted at.

"Hold on to something, Rowan! Somebody! Help!" Elizabeth MacPherson, thought Rowan idly. Amazing that her reflexes were that good and that she could manage to hold on to him. All those shopping forays must have strengthened her grip. Obligingly, he grabbed the rock. It was shortly thereafter that he lost his celestial objectivity about the situation and began to grip the rock until his knuckles whitened, bellowing to be pulled up.

A moment later he felt another weight on his legs, very like someone sitting down on them. It secured his attachment to the rock, but did nothing to remove him from his dangling position off the side.

He heard Nancy Warren say, "I've got him. Where's Charles?"

An out-of-breath masculine voice responded. "Here! I've got his feet. You grab his shoulders to steady him, Nancy!"

"It's all right, Rowan," called Elizabeth MacPherson. "It was lucky for you that I was coming over to ask you something about Constance Kent; otherwise I'd never have caught you in time."

As they hoisted him back over the rim of the rock, Rowan heard Susan Cohen saying, "You're not such a mountain goat after all, are you, Rowan?"

He closed his eyes and vowed to get safely down from Roche Rock, if only for the pleasure of seeing Susan Cohen dead and silenced.

CHAPTER 11

"We hardly know any instance of the strength and weakness of human nature so striking, and so grostesque, as the character of this haughty, vigilant, sagacious blue-stocking . . . with an ounce of poison in one pocket and a quire of bad verses in the other."
— Thomas Babington Macaulay

CORNWALL

THE ONE FORTUNATE aspect of the entire incident was that no one seemed to have noticed that Rowan had been attempting to push Susan at the time he fell. He told them that he had suffered a dizzy spell from the heights. Their concern for his health assured him that there were no suspicions to lie contrary. Aside from bruised knees and a few minor scrapes, he found that he was quite uninjured and, fearful of losing another chance at Susan, he insisted that the tour continue uninterrupted.

On his instructions Bernard continued to drive down the length of Cornwall to a picturesque castle across the inlet from Falmouth. St. Mawes, a military fortification rather than a residence, was built by Henry VIII as part of his chain of coastal defenses. Its massive guns protected Carrick Roads, still used as a berthing from oceangoing vessels. The guide took a perverse pleasure in marching his restive charges through the village high street, past any number of inviting shops, without letting them stop for even a postcard, let alone a cup of tea or a quarter of an hour of browsing. With only a trace of a limp, he led them up the hill toward the castle, past an assortment of private homes with lovely views of the inlet, and into the castle. Nancy Warren wanted to stop and examine the magnificent bushes of hydrangeas with blue flowers as big as cabbages, but Rowan was firm.

It was just past five o'clock when he herded them back to the coach, telling Bernard to forget the regular route to St. Ives. He knew a shortcut.

"We'll take the King Harry Ferry," he announced. "It's just north of here."

Bernard rolled his eyes, but, in the best British tradition, he concluded that it was not his to reason why; though if the do or die killed the bus, the company would go into fits, he was sure. Without a word of argument, he put the coach in gear and headed north on a winding, shady country road, labeled B3289 on his road atlas.

No one said very much along the way. It had been a tiring day of long walks and melodrama. The tourists were glad of a break. Rowan spent the time considering his contingency plan and wondering if the wretched Susan had nine lives—or only nine cats.

After a twenty-minute drive at a leisurely speed, they went down a long hill toward the river and joined the line of cars waiting for the ferry, which was on its way back to the dock.

"We're the only bus in the ferry line!" Frances Coles remarked.

Bernard heaved a weary sigh and shook his head. One by one the small cars ahead of them were driven onto the flat deck of the small river ferry. When the huge coach lumbered up to the embarkation point, three ferry workers crowded about to see them safely aboard. With many hand signals and shakes of the head, they succeeded in getting the coach down the ramp with only one major scraping of the fender, to which Bernard reacted as if he had felt it personally.

The river was only about a quarter of a mile wide, approximately a five-minute journey on the ferry. The tourists amused themselves by studying the large ships anchored just downstream and by looking ahead to the tiny hillside village on the other shore. When the ferry docked, Bernard managed to get the coach onto dry land without much difficulty.

"There!" said Rowan Rover heartily, to disguise his relief. "That wasn't so bad, was it?"

He had spoken prematurely. Fifty yards from the ferry dock, Bernard began to search for the road that would lead them out of the village. It was just as Rowan spoke that he discovered the route—and the fact that it involved a series of corkscrew turns up the side of the hill, at intervals approximating the length of the coach.

First Bernard stared, then he looked for another way out of the village and found none. Finally he took a deep breath and said to Rowan, "You'll owe me a pint for this one, mate."

"Done!" said Rowan, who was seeing his shortcut in a new light. "I've never been this way in a battleship before," he explained.

"I'll never do it again," Bernard assured him.

With steering maneuvers resembling acrobatics, he negotiated the twisting climb and emerged on the straightaway at the top, cheered on by the passengers.

"There's nothing else today, is there, Rowan?" asked Bernard. "First you try to throw yourself off a cliff, then you nearly wreck the coach on a bloody ferry, and finally we have to bend the coach in half to get it up a corkscrew. There won't be land mines up ahead, will there? Or bridges woven out of fraying jungle vines for us to cross?"

"No," said Rowan, reddening a bit at this recital. "We'll reach St. Ives within the hour."

For once, he happened to be right.

◆ ◆ ◆

WITHOUT FURTHER MISADVENTURE, Bernard navigated the narrow country lanes of Cornwall and drove into St. Ives, familiar to him from previous tours. Soon he was parking the coach beside the Tregenna Castle Hotel, a stately old building, perched atop the tallest hill in St. Ives, where it offered a commanding view of the bay and the city below.

"Is this old?" asked Kate Conway, gazing up at the ivy-covered castle with a tower at each corner and a row of battlements like jack-o'-lantern teeth.

"It is eighteenth century," Rowan told her. "I suppose that in southern California that is practically prehistoric. Here we don't make so much of it." He turned to the rest of the group, engaged in claiming their luggage from the below-carriage compartment. "I'm going to see you checked in and then I shall go home for a few hours. I shall be in the bar at half past seven, if anyone would like to join me for a drink. Dinner is at eight tonight. I have arranged a special treat for you." *Like a bloody fool,* he finished silently.

"Not another murder play?" sighed Martha Tabram.

"God forbid," said Rowan. "No. I have asked three of my friends to dine with us. They are police officers here in Cornwall. I'm sure you'll find it intriguing to talk to them about crime." *Especially,* he thought, *since there's going to be one.*

268

♦ ♦ ♦

KATE CONWAY AND Maud Marsh were just settling into their room when there was a knock at the door. It was Elizabeth Mac-Pherson, whose room was in the passageway across the hall. They had discovered that the castle was a rabbit warren of short corridors, long passageways, and culs-de-sac, all carpeted with the most garish floor coverings imaginable, guaranteed to clash with any decor.

Elizabeth came in and spent a long moment gazing at their avocado-green bedspreads and the curtains of turquoise and orange. "You'd think that anyone who could afford a castle would have the taste to furnish it correctly."

"They probably can't afford to," said Kate. "Imagine what it would cost to carpet this place! You wouldn't want to pull it up every time you painted the walls."

"How's your room?" asked Maud.

"About the same," said Elizabeth. "Except that mine has a door leading out to the roof so I can walk the battlements tonight like the ghost of Hamlet's father. I came to see you because I wanted to talk to everyone before we see Rowan tonight at dinner. Do you know what we're scheduled to do tomorrow?"

Kate Conway nodded without enthusiasm. "Smugglers' caves."

Maud Marsh looked solemn. "Sounds risky. And after today's performance, I think Rowan is in more danger than anyone. What do we do if he falls into a fifty-foot pit?"

"Exactly," said Elizabeth. "Besides, we've been in England for six days—and I've only shopped for an hour!"

"So you think we ought to ask him to give us a free afternoon?" asked Kate. She drew the curtain aside and peered down at the white cluster of buildings encircling the bay. "We could visit St. Ives, I suppose."

"It looks like a perfect place to shop," Elizabeth agreed. "But we have to present a united front. I'll go and present our scheme to the others. Then we'll tell Rowan in the bar before dinner."

Kate's eyes widened. "He's not going to like this one bit! You know what a stickler he is about our schedule and how much he hates shopping. He'll think we're frivolous. Who's going to tell him?"

"I will," said Elizabeth laughing. "What can he do? Kill me?"

BY HALF PAST seven the conspiracy was well-established. Elizabeth had talked to all the others and, while not everyone was keen on shopping, there was general agreement that they needed a day of peace and quiet. No one wanted to clamber through damp uncharted smugglers' caves with a man who almost fell off a sixty-foot rock. Elizabeth was the unanimous choice to break this news to Rowan Rover. She found him in the bar, clutching a double Scotch and chatting amiably with three men in business suits: the police who came to dinner. By the time she went to the bar and got herself a half of cider, the other members of the tour had come in and were being introduced to the officers and she was able to have a private word with the guide.

"Listen," she said, blinking a little bit from nervousness, "about the plans tomorrow . . ."

Rowan beamed in anticipation. "It's going to be marvelous, isn't it? I know some caves that no one ever goes to! There's no telling what we might come upon. You're lucky to have someone who really knows Cornwall to show you about, aren't you?"

271

"Er—well . . ." Elizabeth blushed to the top of her ears. "That's what I wanted to discuss. We all got to talking about the plans for tomorrow and we decided that, while it's really terribly generous of you to want to show us the local sights . . ." She took a fortifying breath. "What we really want is a free day."

Rowan Rover gaped in astonishment. "In St. Ives?" he screeched.

"Yes. We're rather toured out, you know, and we thought it might be fun to potter around the village and . . . you know . . . *shop.*"

To her acute discomfort, Rowan was staring at her in complete disbelief. "You want to shop?" he repeated. His expression suggested that he was casting about for some other, more suitable meaning for the word. "You want to pass up these historic, fascinating smugglers' caves that only I can take you to, in order to go and buy ornamental shrimping nets in that great low-brow jumble sale by the sea?"

"Yes, I'm afraid so," said Elizabeth. "After all, it will give you a bit of time off here at home."

"All of you, then?" he asked, steadying himself against a nearby table against the magnitude of this betrayal. "You all want to go shopping?"

"In the afternoon, then," said Elizabeth, feeling that some sort of compromise was indicated. "Maud and Martha did mention that they'd like to see St. Michael's Mount tomorrow morning. But no caves!"

Rowan, Samson in the hands of the Philistines, heaved a sigh of resignation. "All right, then. I suppose I can rearrange my plans." Surreptitiously he patted the pocket of his jacket. The little vial he had brought from home was still there. Now he was forced to use it.

♦ ♦ ♦

THE PARTY MADE two tables of five and one of six, with a guest policeman seated at each one. Elizabeth was sitting with Inspector George Burgess, at a table with Alice, Frances, and Martha Tabram. After duly admiring the spacious Trelawny Room (omitting any references to its carpeting), Alice leaned forward and whispered, "Did you tell him, Elizabeth?"

Before she answered, Elizabeth looked to see where Rowan Rover was sitting. She located him at the far table, sitting between Miriam Angel and Susan Cohen, who

273

seemed to be talking nonstop across the table to the policeman dining with them. Emma Smith, who sat on Susan's left, was eating her soup with the resignation of one who does not expect to get a word in edgewise. Reassured that she could not be overheard, Elizabeth recounted her conversation with the guide about the next day's schedule.

"Free at last!" sighed Frances. "But I don't envy you having to tell him."

"Somebody had to," Elizabeth replied. "Did you want to spend the day slogging through a dark cave?"

After that the talk turned to crime. The foursome listened happily to tales of police work in Penzance. Midway through the main course, Elizabeth thought of something else to ask. "Are you familiar with the case of Constance Kent?"

Burgess thought it over. "Victorian era? The teenage girl who supposedly cut her little brother's throat?"

"That's the one," said Elizabeth. "Rowan and I are arguing about whether or not she did it."

"It's been years since I read about the case," the inspector warned her, "but I seem to remember that there was insanity in the family. The girl's mother was shut up in her room for years before she died. The child who was killed was the son of the second Mrs. Kent, formerly the older children's governess. I think it was put about at the time that Constance might have taken after her mother—mentally unstable, you know. And a year or so before the murder, she tried to run away. Dressed as a boy. She wouldn't be the first neurotic teenager who resorted to murder."

"Thank you," said Elizabeth. "That seems quite conclusive. I wonder what Rowan will say to that!"

Two tables away Rowan Rover's mind was on a more immediate crime than the one at Road Hill House. He had pointed out the interesting arrangement of exposed beams in the high ceiling of the dining room, and while his tablemates were inspecting this architectural marvel, he had sprinkled some powder into Susan Cohen's untouched glass of wine. The maneuver had been completely successful: no one had noticed his sleight of hand. After a few more minutes of conversation, Rowan, anxious to get it over with, said, "I should like to propose a toast!" He lifted his glass and smiled at his tablemates from behind a film of cold sweat. "Er—here's to crime!"

Obediently they reached for their glasses.

Susan Cohen made a face. "I hate white wine," she whined. "It tastes like horse piss. Here, Emma, your glass is empty, and you haven't touched your water. You take my wine, and I'll toast with water. I don't see why they can't serve Pepsi over here—"

Before Rowan Rover could think of a way to salvage the situation, Detective Heamoor echoed, "Here's to crime!" and finished his glass.

With mounting horror, Rowan saw Emma Smith take a generous swallow of Susan Cohen's tainted wine. Immediately she made a face. "You're right, Susan," she giggled. "It does taste like . . . what you said."

After that the conversation progressed smoothly on to other topics. Rowan supposed that he must have uttered a word here and there, but he had no idea what went on at his table, beyond a vague impression that Susan had given the police officer plot summaries of a great many murder mysteries—so perhaps no one remembered much of the conversation. Rowan's own mind was reeling with the enormity of his error, and he was frantically engaged in trying to devise some excuse to persuade Emma Smith to take an emetic. (Ipecac as a traditional Cornish beverage? But where would he get any on ten minutes' notice so late at night?) His one consolation was that he hadn't been able to obtain a really good poison like arsenic. His home-made herbal concoction might, after all, prove too weak to cause serious injury. Perhaps, he thought hopefully, she will have a thundering case of indigestion, for which I shall blame the seafood. *Please let her survive,* he thought. Idly he wondered if the Deity paid any attention at all to the prayers of aspiring murderers.

♦ ♦ ♦

AFTER A SLEEPLESS night of worry and more contingency planning for Susan's demise, Rowan crept down to breakfast, half expecting his detective friends to be present in their official capacity. Instead, he found Emma Smith alive and well and eating breakfast with her mother and Maud Marsh. In his relief at this unexpected miracle, he scooped up a bowlful of Mueslix and sat down at their table.

"Good morning, ladies. How are you?

How are you, Emma?" Never had the greeting been less perfunctory.

"Oh, I'm all right, I suppose," Emma replied, but her tone suggested that she might have complained if she'd tried.

"Feeling a bit seedy?" asked Rowan. "Probably the rich food. Let me bring you a glass of milk." Milk, he knew, could also act to lessen the effects of certain poisons. It was worth a try.

Half an hour later the group was assembled in the parking lot, marveling at another perfect summer day granted to them in late September.

"It's St. Michael's Mount this morning, isn't it?" asked Nancy Warren.

"Can't we go to Land's End?" asked Elizabeth MacPherson.

"No," snapped the guide. "That place is a complete tourist trap. I do have my standards. They may be low, but I have them. St. Michael's Mount is much less commercial."

"All right," said Elizabeth. "It's just that I was reading some English folklore about the lost land of Lyonesse, now covered by the sea. It's supposed to be off the shore at Land's End, and they say that during storms you can still hear the church bells of the drowned village, tolling beneath the waves."

Rowan's glare was flint. "Perhaps you'd like to go there on a buying spree this afternoon."

This salvo ended all further discussion, and the rebellious flock boarded the bus in chastened silence. Susan managed to maintain this silence until the coach was nearly out of the grounds of Tregenna Castle. "I thought Mont St. Michel was over near France," she remarked. "Have you read Aaron Elkins' book *Old Bones?* It's set out there, and it's about this—"

Rowan lunged for the microphone and cut her off in mid-gallop. "Some of you may have confused Cornwall's Mount St. Michael with its French counterpart Mont St. Michel." *Those of you to whom the word atlas denotes a brand of tire,* he finished silently. "Actually the two differ somewhat in size and are located in entirely different places geographically. The French one is, conveniently enough, in the Channel, off the coast of France. The Cornish one was a port on the tin route to the Mediterranean in Roman times, but in 1070 a monastery was founded there by monks from Mont St. Michel."

279

"William the Conqueror's doing, I suppose?" said Alice.

"Probably. It's a captivating place. An ancient granite castle seems to rise out of the rock itself at the summit of a mound surrounded by the sea. Actually, it will be interesting to see whether it is an island when we arrive. At high tide, the Mount is a few hundred yards from shore, but when the tide is out, you can walk out to it. There is a paved path leading from the shore to the stone steps at the harbor."

"Maybe we could swim!" said Kate Conway, with rather more enthusiasm than she showed for walking.

Rowan Rover was stunned. "Swim? In the seas off Cornwall? You might as well go snorkeling in the sewage treatment plant. If it is low tide, you may walk the path to St. Michael's Mount; otherwise, you will enrich a local boatman by fifty pence for a three-minute ride to the rock."

Elizabeth, remembering the legend of Lyonesse, said, "How long ago was the island cut off from the mainland?"

"Well, the old Cornish name for the Mount means *gray rock in the middle of the forest.* There are still traces of old tree trunks in Mount's Bay. Legend has it that the rock

280

used to be five miles *inland* and in the middle of a dense forest. The forest was submerged by the sea around the time that Stonehenge was built—long before the arrival of the Romans. Or the French."

"Is it a fortress?" asked Charles Warren.

"It was once. It has been the home of the St. Aubyn family for three centuries, though. Though I believe there was fear of a Nazi sea invasion during the war. It never occurred, however." He turned to Elizabeth. "To my knowledge, there have been no lurid crimes associated with the Mount."

Elizabeth returned his smirk. "And can we trust you not to fall off it?"

The high promontory of St. Michael's Mount was visible for some distance before they actually reached it. When Bernard pulled the coach into the gravel parking lot adjoining the beach, they could see that the tide was high. Only a few feet of the paved path was visible at the shore, sinking into the blue water of the bay. As they trooped across the sand toward the embarkation point, they could see a flotilla of motorboats waiting to ferry passengers to the Mount. At midpoint in the bay an outcrop of barren rocks rose above the waterline, making a natural marker for monitoring the movement of the tide.

The castle looked like the Gothic cathedrals they had already seen, except that it was perched atop a steep hill, covered with shrubbery and scrub trees. Surrounding the stone docks at the base of the hill was a cluster of old buildings resembling a fishing village. They climbed into motorboats and reassembled on the quay for further instructions from Rowan. "We have about two hours to spend here," he told them. "I wouldn't want to cut into your shopping time. You may wander about the port here or, if you are feeling energetic, you can climb the Mount and have a look inside the castle."

"Let's go and see the castle!" said Maud. "Anyone want to come along? Miriam? Emma?"

"I don't think I'm feeling up to it," said Emma Smith.

Rowan glanced at her furtively. "There's also a tea shop here in the village. Perhaps you'd like a glass of milk, Emma?"

♦ ♦ ♦

DURING THEIR TWO-HOUR sojourn on the Mount the tide turned, halving the distance

282

from island to mainland. Now the motorboats picked up their passengers from the Mount and let them off at the outcrop of barren rocks that had formerly been in mid-bay. Now the path from those rocks to the sandy beach was clear and dry above the exposed mud floor of the bay. When they were once again on dry land, Rowan Rover said, "Bernard will now take you back to St. Ives and you will have a free afternoon and dinner on your own. Unless anyone wants to have a look at the caves. Susan?"

She shook her head. "There's a new Reginald Hill novel that isn't available in the States yet and I want to see if I can find it."

The guide looked as if he had swallowed a frog. "Very well, then. I shall see all of you tomorrow."

◆ ◆ ◆

No one would give Rowan Rover the satisfaction of admitting that he was right, but shopping in St. Ives had not been the idyllic experience they had envisioned. Like most seaside tourist attractions, the village specialized in cheap, mass-produced merchandise intended as souvenirs for day-trippers. The group ended up buying very little.

Even Susan had come away disappointed in her quest for Mr. Hill's new novel.

By ten o'clock the next morning, they were aboard the coach once more, on a day of tours inspired by the legend of King Arthur. The first stop was the ruins of Tintagel, legendary birthplace of Arthur. It was located on the north coast of Cornwall, past Bodmin and Camelford, a longish drive, but nothing compared to the walk required to reach the ruins of the castle. From the picturesque little village of Tintagel, where Bernard parked the coach, they had to follow a dirt track for several miles through a fold of green hills before they could catch a glimpse of the ruins.

Fortunately for those whose bodies were set for the California climate, the day was perfect, convincing them that Cornwall's nickname, the English Riviera, was well-deserved. The sun blazed in a brilliant blue sky without a wisp of cloud, and the weather rivaled the best day in July. They trotted along the dirt track in sunglasses and sleeveless shirts. "I don't know why everyone complains about British weather," said Kate Conway, inspecting the deepening tan on her arms.

"Come to Scotland," said Elizabeth

MacPherson. "That brown on your arms would be rust."

The setting for the castle was romantic enough, isolated as it was on a windswept cliff high above a sapphire sea, but there was little left of the structure itself.

As they stood on the path looking out at the towering peninsula of rock, Emma Smith said, "This reminds me of a saying we had when I was on the archaeological dig. "One stone is a stone . . ."

Elizabeth MacPherson, another veteran excavator, caught the reference, and chimed in, "*Two* stones a Roman wall . . ."

Together they chanted, "*Three* stones a ca-the-dral."

"It isn't as bad as that," said Rowan. "You can see a few feet of wall still standing, and the foundations of buildings are evident here and there."

"It's a very beautiful place," said Maud Marsh. "And you say King Arthur was born here?"

"I don't know that I say that," said Rowan, "but tradition maintains that belief. So far the archaeologists haven't found a shred of proof. Those ruins date from a twelfth-century castle built by Reginald of Cornwall, a son of Henry the First. But if you look into the inlet you can see an opening in the rock known as Merlin's Cave, so perhaps folklore knows best after all."

Emma Smith was consulting a newly-purchased guidebook. "It says here that recent excavations have found remnants of a fifth-century Celtic monastery here. That would be Arthur's time, wouldn't it?"

"Good heavens!" said Alice MacKenzie, pointing to the headland across the inlet from the ruins. "What is that monstrosity?" At the top of that windswept cliff stood a very solid-looking nineteenth-century stone building, incongruous with the rest of the landscape.

"That," sighed Rowan, "is the King Arthur Castle Hotel, placed above the Barras Nose by the Great Western Railway. Descendants, no doubt, of Mordred."

◆ ◆ ◆

THAT AFTERNOON ON the way to the next Arthurian shrine, Elizabeth MacPherson said, "I discussed the Constance Kent case with Inspector Burgess the other night. He thinks she's guilty, too. He says that there was insanity in her family."

"You are referring to Constance's mother, I presume? Certainly Mr. Kent said that she was insane. She did stay shut up in her room a good bit of the time—and was perhaps an invalid. Of course, considering the fact that the poor woman had borne nine children and that her husband left her in seclusion and turned over the running of the house to a high-spirited young governess of twenty-one, I think perhaps a bit of depression was in order, don't you?"

"I think the wrong person was murdered," muttered Elizabeth. "I suppose Mr. Kent was having an affair with the governess?"

Rowan grinned. "You would need a more trusting nature than I possess to doubt it. He married the spunky little governess when the first Mrs. Kent died of a mysterious bowel obstruction. Constance would have been ten or eleven at that time, I think."

"So the governess was the mother of the murdered child? Francis?"

"Yes. Incidentally, the family called the child Savile, not Francis."

"Teenage jealousy," said Elizabeth. "No doubt the child by Mr. Kent's new wife received much more attention than the older children. Perhaps Constance decided to punish everyone by killing the little usurper."

"But was it the sort of crime a teenage girl would commit? Do you know the details of the murder and on what evidence she was suspected?"

"No," Elizabeth admitted. "The crime book I read covered the case in about two paragraphs."

"We'll be staying in Bath for two nights," Rowan reminded her. "The crime happened at Road Hill House, just a few miles south of the city, you know."

"Do libraries over here keep microfilm copies of old newspapers?"

"I can't vouch for Bath's public library system, but you might try, if you really wish to pursue your little investigation."

"I do," said Elizabeth. "We'll continue this discussion tomorrow night."

◆　◆　◆

IT WAS NEARLY five o'clock before the coach arrived at their second Arthurian shrine: Glastonbury. Maud Marsh was looking eagerly out the window. "I have really been looking forward to coming here," she announced. "I've read so much about the legends of King Arthur, and Glastonbury is one of the most mystical places in the world. The isle of Avalon! Do the boats run this late in the evening, Rowan?"

Rowan Rover blinked. "Boats?"

"Oh, yes!" cried Emma Smith. "I read *The Mists of Avalon!* Wasn't it wonderful? You got into a little boat and if you just crossed the river—or whatever the water was—you ended up in Glastonbury, but if you got into the boat and said the magic words, you ended up on the magic island of Avalon!"

"It's a very holy place for the Church, too," said Rowan, postponing the answer to Maud's question and the inevitable reaction. "Joseph of Arimathea is said to have brought the Holy Grail here, and when he planted his staff in the earth, it grew into the Holy Thorn of Glastonbury."

"You might want to explain who Joseph of Arimathea was," Elizabeth whispered to the guide.

"Nonsense!" said Rowan. "Everybody knows that!"

"They're Californians," said Elizabeth gently.

"Who was Joseph What's-His-Name?" asked Kate Conway, looking blank and beautiful.

Rowan sighed. "He was the man who gave the tomb in which Jesus was buried after the Crucifixion. Legend has it that Joseph was in possession of the Holy Grail— that's the cup used by Christ during the Last Supper, for those of you who didn't see Paul Newman in *The Silver Chalice.*"

By this time Bernard had found a public parking lot on the brick-lined high street of a small country town. He was pulling the coach into a space near a cluster of other tour vehicles. "Here we are," he announced. "Abbey is just to the left there."

Radiating astonishment, Maud Marsh peered out the window. "This is Glastonbury?" she demanded.

"Right."

"It isn't an island?"

"No."

"Damned English. They lie about everything!"

As they walked up to the admission complex adjoining the entrance to the grounds, Rowan Rover explained that the geography of England does not stay the same. "You remember that St. Michael's Mount was once a mountain in a forest, and now it is an island in Mount's Bay. Glastonbury was indeed an island centuries ago. The Celts called it *Ynis Witrin,* the isle of glass. It was once a towering peak in an inland sea, but now it is surrounded only by Somerset's flat meadows and marshland, some of which has been drained in modern times, I expect. Progress, you know."

"No wonder the fairies left England," muttered Emma Smith, still thinking of *The Mists of Avalon.* She was looking paler than usual and she seemed irritable.

Rowan Rover showed the group's admission pass, and led them through the gates and into the grounds of the ruined abbey. A few yards from the iron gates, Rowan stopped beside a spreading tree, about twelve feet in height. "That," he said, "is the Holy Thorn of Glastonbury."

Nancy Warren examined a branch with the eye of a practiced gardener. "It's a hawthorn tree," she announced.

"A variation thereof," Rowan agreed. "But this tree flowers in December. A cutting of white flowering branches is sent each year to the Royal Family as a Christmas gift."

"It can't be the original tree," said Nancy Warren, whose belief in miracles did not extend to botany.

"No, Cromwell's men cut it down in their

usual rage against holy relics. This is descended from a cutting of the original. Now, if you'll come this way, I'll tell you what these ruins are and we shall find the grave of King Arthur."

For a pleasant hour they walked about the spreading green lawn amid the soaring ruins of the abbey. Charles took many pictures, conscious of the deepening twilight that would soon envelop the site. The others wandered around, strangely quiet, trying to imagine the church in all its medieval splendor.

Rowan, consulting his guidebook with great discretion, told them about the twelfth-century historian, William of Malmesbury, who wrote a chronicle of the abbey, placing its founding a thousand years before his time. According to legend, Ireland's St. Patrick ended his days as abbot of Glastonbury, and St. Bridget and Wales' patron saint, David, also visited the holy site. The Domesday Book pronounced it free from taxation, and the Viking raiders left it alone. Just after Malmesbury's time, a fire destroyed the old structures, but even that turned out to be a mixed blessing, because in the old burial ground, the monks discovered two oak coffins, containing the remains of a large man and a woman with strands of golden hair still clinging to her skull. A leaden cross found with them identified the bodies as those of King Arthur and Queen Guinevere. The bodies were reburied in a shrine within the church, and the site of that burial was located again in 1934.

"What a lot of famous people have been here!" said Kate Conway. "King Arthur! St. Patrick! Imagine a Grauman's Chinese Theatre of saints' footprints!"

"If it's so important to England, you'd think they'd have taken better care of it," said Susan disapprovingly. Seeing the others' frowns, she said, "Well, they restored the shopping mall in Exeter after the Blitz, didn't they? Why couldn't they rebuild one old church?"

Rowan Rover closed his eyes and counted to ten in several languages. Finally he glanced at his watch and, with evident relief, announced, "It is nearly six o'clock, ladies and Charles. The grounds are closing, and we are due in Bath this evening. Tomorrow we shall be seeing the ruins of the Roman baths."

Rowan was looking forward to inspecting the drowning facilities.

BY SEVEN O'CLOCK that evening, they had arrived in Bath and had been shown to their rooms in the stately Francis Hotel in the city center. The hotel, an eighteenth-century building overlooking Queen's Square, adjoined the residence occupied by Jane Austen when she visited that elegant spa of Georgian England. The natural hot springs over which the city is built was much prized by the Romans, who built the spa baths for their soldiers. *Taking the waters* became fashionable again in the eighteenth century when Beau Nash made London the playground of the aristocracy. Much of the classic Georgian architecture of the time remains, making Bath an architectural treasure, if not an English Lourdes. ("Wait until you taste the waters," Rowan kept telling them gleefully.)

At eight Rowan had exchanged his khaki windbreaker for a tweed jacket and was waiting for the rest of the party in the dining room, where they were expected for dinner en masse. His head count, though, showed that there were three people missing.

He was just trying to figure out who they were when Maud Marsh appeared in the doorway. "We can go in to dinner now," she told him. "I'm afraid Miriam and Emma won't be joining us. Emma is quite ill."

CHAPTER 12

"There stood arcades of stone, the stream hotly issued? With eddies widening up to the wall, encircling all."
—Saxon Poem, Eighth Century

BATH

NEITHER EMMA NOR her mother appeared for breakfast the next morning, but since *traveler's tummy* was a condition familiar to all of them, no one was particularly worried. They were impressed, though, by the touching concern of Rowan Rover, who appeared genuinely grieved by Emma's indisposition and who insisted that she have a doctor in to examine her.

"I almost wish that I were the one who was sick," sighed Kate Conway. "Isn't Rowan being sweet?"

"Yes," said Elizabeth. "It is most unlike him."

"I wonder if Bath's healing waters would do Emma any good," mused Maud Marsh.

"I very much doubt it," said Alice. "Jane

Austen must have drunk quite a lot of it and she died of Addison's disease at forty-two."

"Well," said Susan, "I'm still going to drink some of it."

Alice looked at her with a glint in her eye. "You do that, Susan."

After he had seen to Emma and her mother, Rowan gulped down his own breakfast, and arrived in the hotel lobby just at ten o'clock to lead the tour of the Roman baths and museum.

"This will take just over an hour," he told the group, looking particularly at Elizabeth. "After that you may have the rest of the day to sack the city. I'm sure you will make the locals forget the Romans."

"I'm going to the library," said Elizabeth, the picture of virtue.

"Before or after you shop?"

"Both."

As they were leaving the hotel, Elizabeth posted the letters she had written the night before. The one to Cameron was an unfortunate exercise in newlywed purple prose, followed by a cheerful and chatty account of her travels, mentioning the places she'd like to visit again ("Perhaps you ought to check out Dozmary Pool for seals . . .").

The letter Elizabeth wrote to her brother Bill was also a travelogue, but considerably funnier, mostly at Susan's expense. She discovered, though, that it was difficult on paper to convey just how annoying Susan really was. Quoted singly, any of Susan's remarks might seem merely dull, or at best, a trifle eccentric. It was the cumulative effect of the running commentary hour after hour that wore down one's nerves. Elizabeth felt that she could pass any test devised on the history and geography of Minnesota, or write a Cohen cat genealogy, and she could hear Susan's voice droning mystery plot summaries in her sleep. All this aggravation would be impossible to impart without a fifty-page transcript of Susan's endless monologue. She wondered at Rowan's boundless tact and patience. Susan didn't seem to annoy him at all. Perhaps he sees all of us that way, she thought with sudden humility.

Rowan Rover, leading the party in the direction of the baths, was lecturing wittily on the eighteenth-century antics of Beau Nash and the transformation of provincial Bath into the St. Tropez of Georgian England. Of all the group, only he himself was not listening. While he talked, his mind raced back and forth across a number of topics, including: contemplating an anonymous telephone call to Emma Smith's physician to disclose the probable nature of her illness; entertaining a hopeful thought that perhaps the poison hadn't worked at all, and she really did have a stomach virus; and considering the possibility of issuing a refund to an assassin-employer. He pictured the interchange at the bank when he attempted to explain that he needed a loan to pay back said assassin-employer. This unpleasant scenario dissolved into a vision of a melodrama called *The Custody Battle for Sebastian Melmoth Rover, Upon the Conviction of His Father for Murder Most Foul*, a farce in many exhausting acts, featuring all his ex-wives as the Avenging Furies.

No, it was all impossible. Not to be thought of. Every possible way out was worse than going ahead with the plan. He couldn't tip the wink to Emma's doctor, because doing so would land him on a charge of attempted murder. He couldn't give Mr. Kosminski back his money, because he had already spent it. And he couldn't persuade himself to abstain from murder for aesthetic reasons, because he had begun to view the killing of Susan Cohen as a pleasure, an intellectual duty, and an early Christmas present to the rest of the tour group.

How unfortunate that she had managed to live through their stay in Cornwall, where he was best prepared to contrive a successful murder. He was still smarting over the group's arbitrary and irrational rejection of his smugglers' caves excursion. It would have been a perfectly splendid accident, disposing of Susan neatly without a hint of murder. Besides, it would have left the group an entire week of the mystery tour which they could have enjoyed in blissful harmony, without so much as hearing the word Minneapolis uttered in their presence. As it was, Susan was alive and well. Even now he heard her saying:

"Oh, look! A bakery! In Minneapolis I buy my fresh-baked bread at . . ."

He saw the others cringe and edge away from her relentless nattering. Let them get an earful, he thought brutally. God knows I've tried to eliminate her.

The unpleasant implications of this last figure of speech forced all further reverie from his mind and concentrated his mind wonderfully on the exhibit at hand: one two-thousand-year-old swimming pool filled with water so murky and foul-tasting that one corpse more could hardly matter.

While Rowan was reflecting on his ominous intentions, the other members of the party were admiring the architecture of Bath, with its graceful Georgian buildings and its arcades of elegant boutiques. When they reached the stone building that housed the baths and museum, they found that it was in the square adjoining the cathedral. Since medieval times the English city of Bath had been built atop the ruins of the Roman city of Aquae Sulis, so that the ancient baths themselves had lain intact but undiscovered below street level for many centuries, until excavations in the eighteenth century led to the discovery of Roman ruins and the restoration of the baths.

"Is there some sort of spring here, like Old Faithful?" asked Frances Coles.

Rowan, who had no idea what Old Faithful was, replied with his stock answer. "The guidebook explains that the main spring, under the city center here, sends up a quarter of a million gallons a day, and maintains a constant temperature of 46.5 degrees centigrade. Apparently the spring water is the rain of ten thousand years ago, which penetrated deep into the earth and was warmed by geothermal heat."

"Can we bathe in the springs?" asked Maud Marsh. "Not that I'd want to."

"No bathing. But at the end of the tour in the pump room you can buy a glassful. Now come this way. First we will look at the exhibits of Roman artifacts and then we will walk through the complex containing the baths."

The dimly-lit display rooms featured exhibits of objects found over the course of several centuries of construction and excavation. Simple tombstones inscribed in Latin, intricate mosaics, and fragments of statuary were on display, each in its own little circle of light. Farther along they saw the array of objects that had been removed from the baths themselves. The placard explained that to the Romans, the springs were not only heated pools for cleanliness and recreation, but also sacred waters dedicated to the goddess Minerva Sulis. Worshipers threw coins, jewelry, and other offerings into the pools as a tribute to the deity.

"Emma would have loved seeing this," murmured Elizabeth. "It's too bad she had to miss it."

"Look at this!" cried Alice MacKenzie, pointing to the next display. "Curses!"

"Yes," said Rowen, motioning for the group. "The Sacred Spring was considered a way to bring divine retribution on one's enemies. Disgruntled Romans would write their grievance on a piece of pewter. *May he who stole my ring become covered with sores and die in agony.* That sort of thing. Then the complainant would throw the pewter message into the spring, and wait for the goddess to smite down the guilty party. Today, I suppose, we'd write a letter to the *Times.*"

"I'd be tempted to try that one," said Alice, casting a baleful glance in Susan's direction.

"Look out," said Rowan lightly. "You might get what you wish for at the shrine of the goddess."

As they proceeded into the series of rooms containing the various bathing pools, the guide took care to be close to Susan Cohen, so that he could make the most of any chance that might arise. The Great Bath was now restored and open to the outdoors, some two stories above it, but the other rooms in the complex were enclosed and lit only by the faint strains of

303

sunlight from without. Another group of tourists had proceeded into the baths just ahead of them, but they were farther along in the tour. A dark-haired young man, probably a college student, introduced himself as Nigel, their guide. Apparently, the mystery tourists would be taken round by themselves.

It must look like an accident, Rowan reminded himself. *She tripped hit her head on the stone, and she fell unconscious into the pool and drowned. Alas, none of us missed her until it was too late.*

Of course he could not maintain his running commentary during the tour, but fortunately this was not necessary. Nigel was nattering away nineteen to the dozen about the plumbing, the drains, the bathing rituals, and all sorts of other diverting things that Rowan might otherwise have listened to. He contrived to fall behind the rest of the party, who obligingly crowded around Nigel, enthralled by his command of water trivia.

Rowan bided his time through the dry east baths, the splendid open air Great Bath, and at last to the dark and inviting west bath, where he was determined to make his move. He let the others go in ahead of him, and then slipped in quietly to the back of the group, discerning a shadowy figure of the right size and shape to be Susan. *Mustn't do it now,* he thought. *She'd cry out.*

He leaned over and whispered, "Wait here a moment."

He could just make out the nod of her head in the gloom. He held his breath for what seemed like hours until Nigel finished his spiel and the rest of the party turned a corner and disappeared from view. Then with a great sigh of determination, the would-be murderer put his hands on his victim's shoulders, ready to push her into the pool and hold her head under the murky water.

She spun round at once, and he found himself looking into the shining Bambi-lashed eyes of Kate Conway. "Oh, Rowan!" she sighed, with a trace of a giggle in her voice. She threw her arms around him. "But what if somebody sees us?"

As quickly and gently as he possibly could, Rowan disengaged himself from the fervent embrace. At any other time a nubile and willing nurse would be more than he could resist, but just now his mind was on murder. "You're quite right," he murmured. "Someone might see us. Some other time perhaps."

"Of course, I'm rooming with Maud," she sighed. "But I suppose there's always your room."

"And I would like a shot, you know," said Rowan, improvising madly. "Except for my vow."

"Your vow?" echoed Kate.

"Yes. Pesky old thing." He was thinking furiously, enveloped in the scents of her duty-free perfume and the Francis Hotel complimentary shampoo. "I've sworn to remain celibate until Margaret Thatcher is no longer prime minister."

In the dimness, he could see Kate's bewildered face. "But I thought she was already married."

Rowan shuddered at the implication of *that*. "No, dear," he said gently. "It's not Mrs. Thatcher I'm waiting for. This is for political reasons. A protest. Like fasting."

"Oh," she said. "But then why did you—"

"An unfortunate lapse," he assured her. "Lost my head. Please pretend it never happened."

"Well, okay," said Kate, shrugging. "I guess we'd better find the others. I want to try some of the spring water."

Rowan motioned for her to go first. "The others are in the pump room, no doubt hearing how English mineral water compares to Minnesota's shining big sea waters."

The fact that he was quite correct in this prediction did nothing to improve his state of mind.

◆　◆　◆

THAT AFTERNOON ELIZABETH MACPHERSON and Susan Cohen spent an hour looking for Bath's famous Pulteney Bridge before discovering that they were standing on it. Their hotel brochure did not offer a photo of the bridge, but described it in the text as Florentine style, a term that left them completely baffled.

"With spinach?" suggested Susan.

After determining the whereabouts of the bridge (beneath their feet), they decided that it must mean: built up with shops on each side so that it looks like an ordinary street instead of like a bridge. Still it had some interesting stamp, coin, and antique shops perched over the river, and they spent several hours acquiring more goods than their luggage would accommodate.

"This is such fun," said Susan, gazing admiringly at her parcels. "If I were back in

Minneapolis, Uncle Aaron would be trying to lecture me on mutual funds and treasury bonds and all that boring stuff. And he's mad because I sold my stock in the business to some very nice Japanese businessmen." She giggled. "I told Uncle Aaron, 'If you want me to invest my money in the company, you'd better start publishing thrillers.' "

"I take it you two don't get along," said Elizabeth.

"I don't think Uncle Aaron likes me much. He likes making money, but he doesn't know how to enjoy it. At family gatherings he always looks bored. All he ever gave me for my birthday was a savings bond. He's my mother's brother. She died when I was born, but in the pictures we have of her, she looks lovely and silly. I think Uncle Aaron likes his women to be pretty bubblebrains who let him make all the decisions."

"Look the *other* way when you cross the street, Susan," said Elizabeth, holding out a restraining hand as they dodged traffic to investigate another antique shop. "So why wouldn't your uncle like you? You're pretty."

"Only recently," Susan reminded her.

"It's too late to impress him. He's had twenty years of ugly duckling me, and he'll never see me any other way. And I definitely don't let him make the decisions! But why should I care if he likes me? Thanks to Grandpa Benjie, I have as much money as he does! So what if I lose some of it by not putting it in stupid tax shelters or keeping it in stocks? Spending it is more fun. Anyway, I kind of enjoy annoying him by not putting it into the company."

"Does the company need your stock?"

"Probably. They're worried about a take-over or something. The business could get taken out of the family, apparently, and get a lot of longtime employees fired. I don't listen. Anyway, who cares? Oh, look at that boot scraper shaped like a hedgehog! Isn't it adorable? And it's only fifty pounds!"

This combination of search and shopping took them until two o'clock, at which time Elizabeth, with a pang of guilt, remembered her quest for Constance Kent, and went off in search of a library, while Susan, armed with her charge card, disappeared into a bookstore to amass crime novels for her collection.

Elizabeth had little difficulty in locating the public library. Half an hour of browsing in the card catalogue yielded several crime volumes with titles like *Victorian Murderesses*. Further inquiry unearthed back issues of newspapers of that era for further study. The *Trowbridge and North Wilts Advertiser,* the *Frome Times,* and the *Bath Chronicle* all took an intense and parochial interest in their local tragedy. Elizabeth photocopied the articles for further study.

She commandeered a table for her research, stacking all her parcels in a vacant chair, and setting the books and papers around her while she took notes, pawing through first one source and then another. As the minutes passed, she found the scene beginning to take shape in her mind, as if it were a play she half remembered.

There was Constance Kent, a pretty adolescent looking a bit like the young Princess Anne, turning her profile before the camera with a winsome smile. She wore a stylish brimmed bonnet that curled over the chignon at the nape of her neck, and her girlish figure was shrouded beneath the folds of a tentlike duster coat. Was that before the murder? Difficult to determine her age from that one surviving photograph, but it was a pleasant face, seeming both sensitive and intelligent.

Elizabeth thought of the surly pouts on the faces of other murderesses she had studied: Lizzie Borden with her gooseberry eyes and her pugnacious sneer; the vacant stare of husband-poisoner Adelaide Bartlett; the tight-lipped scowl of Glasgow's Madeleine Smith, who dosed her lover with arsenic. The shy smile of Constance Kent looked out of place among the faces of these older, harder women. Yet all of them had been acquitted (wrongly, Elizabeth was sure), and little Constance had been sent to prison.

What had happened at Road Hill House, a few miles south of Bath, on the night of June 29, 1860?

Elizabeth searched the sources for a list of the occupants of the house on that fatal night. Constance was there, of course. She was sixteen years old, living with her father Samuel and his new wife, the former governess Mary Pratt. There was a new young governess now, Elizabeth Gough, who took care of Mr. Kent's children by his second wife: Amelia, five; Francis three and one half; and the baby Eveline. There were also three older children, Constance's full siblings, who slept on the third floor of the house, as did Constance, the cook, and the maid.

"That shows you where they stood in the pecking order," Elizabeth muttered, noting down the locations of the rooms. The small children slept in the second-floor nursery with Miss Gough.

On the morning of June 30, 1860, Elizabeth Gough awakened at seven to find that the little boy was missing from his bed. When she knocked at his parents' door to ask if Mrs. Kent had taken the child during the night, she was told that the Kents had not seen the child since his bedtime the night before. Mrs. Kent was angry with the distraught nursemaid. Mr. Kent lay in bed with his eyes closed, silent but not asleep.

The search was on.

The older Kent daughters came down from their rooms and two of them became quite upset at the news that their half brother was missing. Constance, however, stood silently composed. The third-floor sleepers all maintained that they had slept through the night without hearing any disturbance, but the maid did recall that when she had gone downstairs at five that morning a window was open, and the door was ajar.

"I wonder if she was the suggestible type," Elizabeth mused. "Next she'll be claiming she saw tramps lurking around the grounds."

When a search of the house failed to turn up the missing child, Mr. Kent finally got up, called for his pony and trap, and set off to inform the police. Elizabeth pictured Samuel Kent, a pompous and selfish man of fifty-nine, enraged at this domestic upheaval that inconvenienced him, and perhaps terrified at the prospect of having lost his son. He was a lavish spender, eager to impress the world with his fine horses and fashionable clothes, but his squandering left the house short-staffed and sometimes created hardships for his family. Servants kept leaving because he worked them too hard and paid too little.

"Apparently the governess did double duty," drawled Elizabeth, thinking of Kent's hasty marriage to twenty-one-year-old Mary Pratt after the death of his first wife.

Perhaps now the paterfamilias wished that he'd had fewer waistcoats and more servants. Perhaps, as he hurried along the four-mile stretch of road to Trowbridge, he wondered if any of his neighbors had killed the child for revenge. Samuel Kent had prevented the neighbors from fishing in the river near his rented mansion and he had prosecuted some local boys for theft. Besides, tongues were still wagging about his second marriage. Samuel Kent was not a popular man locally.

While he was gone to summon the police, two farmworkers who had joined in the search for the missing child found Francis Savile Kent's body. It was wrapped in his own crib blanket and stuffed behind the splash board in the outdoor privy a hundred yards or so from Road Hill House. The boy's body bore a deep stab wound between the ribs and his throat had been slashed from ear to ear.

Elizabeth shivered. "Three and a half years old," she murmured, picturing the sturdy toddler. The little boy in the apartment next to theirs in Edinburgh was three. Judging from that child's development, Savile should have weighed more than thirty pounds, and he would have been talking clearly and in complete sentences.

After an hour or so, Samuel Kent returned with two Trowbridge policemen, whom he proceeded to supervise in their investigation. He ordered them to search the grounds and the outbuildings, and he accused his neighbors of killing the child over the fishing rights squabble. Then he suggested Gypsies might have done it. The police were allowed to search the servants, not the family.

"I wonder if he suspected his daughter?" Elizabeth said. "He didn't want to believe it. That's for sure." She read on quickly to see what evidence their search uncovered.

They inspected the child's bed and found that he had been suffocated there. The mattress and pillow showed deep impressions of Savile's head and thigh, as if someone had held him down, pushing very hard to smother him. Although the blanket from the bed had been used to wrap the body, the bed had been carefully remade to look undisturbed, so that the marks of the murder were not at first apparent. They also determined that Savile was already dead when his throat was cut in the outside privy.

In a search of the house, the officers found a bloodstained shift of coarse material, stuffed in the back of the scullery boiler. A shift, Elizabeth knew, was a sort of slip that might be worn as a nightgown or as an undergarment. "Oh-ho," said Elizabeth. "Wouldn't I like to run tests on those bloodstains." When was this? Eighteen sixty. It was another thirty years before Paul Uhlenhuth discovered the way to differentiate between human and animal blood. She wondered if they still had that shift.

As if anticipating her curiosity, the next sentence stated that the shift was subsequently lost before its owner could be identified. "The police obviously didn't secure the area back then," Elizabeth muttered. "Mr. Kent again?"

The officers did manage to determine that the shift was not the only missing garment in the case. Mrs. Holly, the village laundress, reported that when she received the washing from Road Hill House on the day of the crime, the laundry list indicated that three nightdresses were sent, but she only found two among the soiled clothing. The missing one belonged to Constance.

When after two weeks the local constabulary had made no headway with the case, Scotland Yard sent down Inspector Jonathan Whicher to take over. Perhaps because of the missing nightdress and the tales of a runaway Constance four years earlier, the inspector fixed his suspicions on the sixteen-year-old girl, but he also thought the nursemaid might be guilty. After questioning both, the nursemaid was let go and Constance was arrested and charged with the murder of her half brother.

She appeared before local magistrates on July 27 and Whicher's scant and circumstantial evidence was presented. Perhaps he hoped that under the pressure of a hearing she would confess to the crime, but she did not. She sat with her black-gloved hands folded and listened calmly to her school-friends testify that she had disliked her stepmother and had found her young half brother annoying.

Other witnesses pointed out that the day before the murder, Constance had been playing happily with Savile and that he was making a bead necklace for her, as she had painted a picture for him not long before.

I'll bet the locals felt sympathetic toward her, Elizabeth thought. A pretty sixteen-year-old whose stepmother mistreated her and whose father was a louse. The police probably came off looking like bullies. "And she didn't confess," Elizabeth said aloud. "Interesting."

The barrister hired by the Kents to defend Constance made short work of the prosecution's case. How could this frail girl carry a heavy child down the stairs and so far from the house? he demanded. Of the murder itself, he said: "Is it likely that the weak hand of this young girl . . . can have inflicted this dreadful blow? Is it likely that hers was the arm which nearly severed the head from the body? It is perfectly incredible."

"I don't know," said Elizabeth. "Lizzie Borden was a nice young gentlewoman and she committed two ax murders. Still, I wonder why Constance waited five years to confess. Why did she confess at all?"

Someone tapped her on the shoulder. Elizabeth looked up to see a nervous-looking librarian, apparently uneasy about approaching this patron who kept muttering to herself. "I'm sorry, but we're about to close for the day."

Elizabeth gathered up her photocopies, and thanked him for his help. I suppose I'll have to find another source of information farther along on the tour, she thought. So far she hadn't found anything to convince her that Constance Kent was innocent, but the lack of motive troubled her. So did the girl's winsome smile. Had Constance been a poisoner, Elizabeth wouldn't have questioned her guilt, but butchering a child? The savagery of the crime seemed beyond the emotional range of that shy young girl who had no other history of violence. But if not Constance, then who? And why?

◆　◆　◆

THAT EVENING IN the bar of the Francis Hotel, the tour members gathered around for an evening of beer and storytelling. Emma and Miriam were still absent from the group. Susan and Rowan argued for an hour over the guilt of Richard III in the murder of the little princes in the tower. Susan, citing Josephine Tey's *Daughter of Time* and Elizabeth Peters' The Murders of Richard III, argued the king's innocence. Rowan quoted a few historians of the era and insisted that Richard was guilty. Neither succeeded in convincing the other.

Finally, Elizabeth MacPherson managed to divert the conversation to her own pet case. "Did you find out whether Road Hill House is still standing?" she asked.

"I asked another crime expert, Kenneth O'Connor, and he assures me that it is," Rowan told her. "Unfortunately for our purposes, he also assures me that the road is too narrow for our coach. After the King

Harry Ferry incident, I am loath to ask Bernard to make risky excursions to unscheduled places."

"I did some more reading on the case this afternoon," said Elizabeth. "And I'm still not convinced of Constance's innocence. How do you explain the bloodstained nightdress?"

Rowan cleared his throat and glanced at the rest of the group. "Perhaps the way Lizzie Borden explained it in her case," he said.

"Oh," said Elizabeth blushing. "Menstrual blood."

At this point Charles Warren stood up, yawned, and said that it was past his bedtime.

Rowan glanced at his watch. "Perhaps we all ought to turn in," he said. "We have a long day tomorrow. We're off to Wales. I am sorry to say that Emma and Miriam won't be joining us. In view of Emma's illness, they have decided to fly home."

"Is she very ill?" asked Frances Coles.

"The doctor thinks not," Rowan said truthfully. "But she isn't up to the rigors of the tour. She'd be better off at home in bed."

"What are we seeing tomorrow?" asked

Kate Conway. She had been making sheep's eyes at him all evening, he noticed uncomfortably. Rowan had immersed himself in double Scotches and ignored her overtures.

"In the morning, Hereford Cathedral," he said, avoiding her eyes. "But I think the real treat for some of you will be our lunch stop at the Welsh village of Hay-on-Wye."

"Herbert Rowse Armstrong!" cried Elizabeth, in a tone of voice usually heard in connection with rock stars' names.

"Yes, Hay-on-Wye does have its local poisoner," the guide conceded. "He's the lawyer I told you about, who kept inviting a rival attorney over for tea. The fellow noticed that tea with Mr. Armstrong invariably made him ill. He was canny enough to save a bit of it and have it tested. Lawyers are a suspicious lot, aren't they? He was right, of course. His tea was poisoned and Armstrong went to the gallows. Actually, though, I was thinking of Hay-on-Wye's other claim to fame. The village is known for its large assortment of used bookstores."

"Make it a long lunch stop," said Susan with shining eyes. "You may be able to find some more books on Constance Kent," Rowan told Elizabeth.

"She didn't write an autobiography, did she?" asked Elizabeth suspiciously. "What ever happened to her anyway?"

"Let us leave that chapter for our next fireside chat," Rowan said. "I have had enough double Scotches this evening."

CHAPTER 13

"Excuse fingers."
Herbert Rowse Armstrong,
offering an arsenic-laden scone to a rival
solicitor

HAY-ON-WYE

SUSAN COHEN WOULD forever think of Hereford Cathedral as an obstacle on the way to the used book mecca at Hay-on-Wye. She trotted through the morning tour of the Gothic cathedral with ill-concealed impatience, barely glancing at the cathedral's pride and joy, the Mappa Mundi, a thirteenth-century map of the world. So great was her disdain that she did not even bother to liken the church or its exhibits to any comparable wonder in Minnesota. She fidgeted through the tour of the sanctuary and had to be nudged to remind her to stop tapping her foot while the guide was speaking.

Elizabeth MacPherson, unable to discover any murders, witch-burnings, ghosts, or other sensational items connected with the stately old church, shared Susan's restlessness. The lunch stop, Hay-on-Wye, had both a famous murderer and used bookshops.

At last, the serious-minded members of the group finished inspecting the Mappa Mundi, the ancient books chained to benches in the library, and the carved choir seats. Rowan, for once, had little to add to the information supplied by the cathedral guide, and the tourists hurriedly resumed their places in the coach and headed for the green hills of Wales.

The A4338, a pleasant road with sweeping views of meadows, forests, and picturesque farms, took them out of Hereford and Worcester—and into the Welsh province of Powys. Only Bernard's announcement, "Coming into Wales now!" indicated the change of country.

"How very odd," said Elizabeth, studying the landscape. "Since England and Wales fought bitterly for centuries, I expected some sort of major barrier between the two. A great river, perhaps, or a forbidding chain of mountains. I come from Appalachia, where the customs and the accent are different from the rest of the South, because the mountains kept the cultures separate. But here there seems to be no geographic barrier. How did the Welsh maintain their separate customs and language, and why did they feel so different from the English?"

"I don't know," said Rowan. "They were Celts, of course, rather than being Angles, Saxons, Normans, and so forth, but I see what you mean. One would think that they'd have been intermarried out of existence years ago. Emma might have a theory. It's a great pity she isn't here." *For more reasons than one,* he thought sadly.

"Of course, the different regions of Britain do have their individual characteristics," Elizabeth mused. "Cameron and I have a tea towel at home that says: *There were the Scots, who kept the Sabbath and everything else they could get their hands on. Then there were the Welsh, who prayed on their knees and their neighbors. Thirdly there were the Irish who never knew what they wanted but were willing to fight for it anyway. Lastly, there were the English, who considered themselves a self made nation, thus relieving the Almighty of a dreadful responsibility.*"

Rowan smiled. "A generalization, of course, but arguably accurate. What about Cornishmen?"

"Much like the Welsh, I expect, judging

from the tales you tell of smugglers and wreckers."

Susan Cohen yawned and looked at her watch. "How long until we get to Hay-on-Wye? Welsh people speak English, don't they? And the money's the same?"

Rowan suppressed a sigh of exasperation. "Wales has been part of Great Britain for considerably longer than Minnesota has been a state," he told her. "You may recall that the Prince of Wales is a close relative of the Queen."

Susan blinked. "Charles? Is that what that means? I thought him having Wales in his title was just a coincidence; you know, like Mars candy bars and the planet Mars."

Deciding that a dose of remedial history was in order, the guide turned on his microphone and said, "Perhaps I ought to explain the origin of the royal title. In the late thirteenth century, King Edward the First defeated the Welsh prince Llewellyn and made Wales part of his kingdom. Legend has it that the Welsh demanded a Welsh-born ruler, who spoke no English, to be their prince, and Edward promised them such a prince. At Caernarvon Castle he brought out his own infant son, who met the conditions of the request: he had been born in Wales, and he didn't speak English—or anything else yet. Since that time, the heir-apparent to the throne has always held the title of Prince or Princess of Wales."

"Typical of the English," said Maud. "Phony islands, carbonated lemonade, and now royal impostors."

"We'll be coming into Hay-on-Wye soon, Rowan," said Bernard, making a turn off the main road. "There is a tourist welcome center just south of the village, with a proper car park beside it. It's the best place to leave the coach if you don't mind a quarter-mile walk or so into town."

"Will we be able to see Mayfield?" asked Elizabeth MacPherson eagerly.

"Is that Herbert Armstrong's house?" asked Rowan. "I don't know. Would you recognize it if you saw it?"

"I doubt it," Elizabeth admitted. "I suppose it would be uncouth to ask at the tourist center?"

Alice MacKenzie laughed. "The Chamber of Commerce won't want to promote their local murderer, I'm sure."

"How long ago did he live here?" asked Frances Coles with a little shiver. She preferred her murderers to be fictional.

"About 1920," said Rowan. "Armstrong was a major in World War I. He moved here to become junior partner to the local solicitor, who conveniently died as soon as Armstrong learned his way about the firm."

"Armstrong was such a stick!" said Elizabeth. "In the picture I've seen of him, he looks like a horse with rimless glasses and a mustache."

"His wife was rather fiercely plain as well," said Rowan. "Of course, she had money. And he did have a girlfriend, so perhaps he didn't mind. He wrote cagey letters to his ladylove, hinting that should his wife pass away, he would be in the market for a new missus."

"I suppose he killed his wife?" asked Alice with a disapproving frown.

"Oh, yes. Arsenic in the champagne. He might have got away with that one, but then he tried to poison the other local solicitor, and he was found out. The man noticed that every time he went to tea with Major Armstrong, he became ill. Armstrong was actually carrying a packet of arsenic when they arrested him."

"How did he explain that?"

"He said he used it to kill dandelions on his lawn."

Nancy Warren laughed. "I wonder if I should try arsenic on our dandelions, Charles?"

Her husband shook his head. "I don't think it would work on them, dear."

"No," Rowan agreed. "But it did put Mrs. Armstrong under the dandelions, so to speak. She was a tiresome woman, by all accounts. She banned another solicitor from local society because he came to one of her parties wearing flannel trousers. Despite this great provocation, her husband was hanged for doing her in, of course."

"Why are murderers so stupid?" sighed Maud Marsh.

"I rather think that most of them aren't," said Rowan, trying not to take the question personally. "Crime experts will tell you that only a small percentage of killers are ever caught. Most murders are passed off as accidents or natural causes. The trick is to stop with one. When lots of acquaintances begin to die, people tend to ask questions."

"Do you think murder is habit-forming?" asked Elizabeth. She was looking at him thoughtfully.

"For madmen it is," said Rowan, turning pale as the question hit home. "But I suspect that scores of people commit one prudent little murder and live happily ever after."

"Surely their conscience torments them terribly," said Frances Coles.

"Yes, of course," said Rowan. He thought nothing of the sort, but to say so would be unwise.

"Hay-on-Wye," Bernard announced, swinging open the doors of the coach. "Two hours for lunch. And don't get so caught up in shopping that you forget to eat. It's a long way to Ruthin Castle!"

◆ ◆ ◆

TWO HOURS LATER, the tourists returned to the coach, laden with souvenirs emblazoned with the red dragon of Wales, carved wooden courting spoons, and paper bags of old books. Rowan and Bernard, impervious to the commercial lure of the village, had spent the two-hour lunch break in the local pub, enjoying ploughmen's lunches and a pack of cigarettes between them.

Susan Cohen arrived at the coach with such a stack of books that Bernard had to open the luggage compartment to allow her to stash them away.

"How will you ever get these back to the States?" he asked, shaking his head.

"Ship them," she replied. "I'll get back before they do. They had some pretty good stores. Of course, we have better ones in Minneapolis, but ours are more spread out."

Elizabeth MacPherson boarded the bus waving a battered green volume from one of the bookstores. "Look what I found!" she called out to Rowan. "A book on the Constance Kent case."

"Oh, good," said Rowan. "Is it Iseult Bridges' *Saint With Red Hands?*"

"No. The bookseller mentioned that one, but he didn't have a copy. This is an anthology of nineteenth-century murder cases."

As the coach rumbled down the country lane and onto the main highway, the tourists settled back in their seats to enjoy the pastoral scenery or to read their newly purchased books. Susan took her usual afternoon nap. With a smile of amusement, Rowan Rover watched Elizabeth Mac-Pherson poring over her crime volume. "Reading about Constance again?" he asked.

She nodded without looking up from her reading.

"Well? Did she or didn't she?"

Elizabeth looked puzzled. "She con-

331

fessed. Her nightdress was missing. She was admittedly jealous of her stepbrother. It seems very clear-cut and yet it doesn't sound right somehow. The throat-cutting bothers me. Women poison; they may even strangle; but throat-cutting is very rare indeed. And a helpless baby whom she knew!"

"She didn't confess at the time," Rowan reminded her. "Four years later she said she did it."

"Conscience?"

"Perhaps," said Rowan. "Or she may have felt that suspicion was hanging over the family. And she offered herself as a scapegoat to remove suspicion from the rest of the household."

"If she didn't do it, who did?"

"Let's leave that for a bit," said Rowan. "Did you read the newspaper accounts of the initial police investigation?"

"Yes. The police were allowed to search the servants, but not the family."

"There's more to it than that. When the officers first arrived at Road Hill House, Mr. Kent offered them something to eat. He showed them into the kitchen and gave them plates of food."

Elizabeth stared. "Victorian hospitality?

Not even my aunt Amanda would be that gracious with a murder in the immediate family. I speak from experience," she added.

"There's more. When the Trowbridge policemen had finished their meals, they got up to continue the investigation, and found that the kitchen door was *locked*. No one let them out for two hours."

"Good God!" said Elizabeth. "That wasn't Constance's doing. No one would let a teenage girl get away with that if they really wanted the murder solved."

"Well put," said Rowan carefully. "If they really wanted the murder solved. Indeed."

She considered the implications. "They were hiding something. Then it couldn't have been one of the neighbors or a marauding tramp, could it?"

"I think not."

"One of the family, then. And you think Constance was protecting the killer?"

"Or the family was protecting Constance," Rowan suggested. "Let us be open-minded for now."

Elizabeth was silent for a few moments while she digested this information. Then she began to reason it out, speaking slowly and ticking off the suspects on her fingers.

"Not the stepmother. There was no love lost between her and Constance. Not the nursemaid. Why should Constance bother to help a servant? One of her sisters perhaps?"

"I doubt it," said Rowan. "Constance had the most spunk of any of them. Besides, all that you said about teenage girls not being able to lock up policemen applies equally to them."

"Daddy!" whispered Elizabeth. "She'd have confessed to save Daddy!"

"Most daughters would. And Samuel Kent certainly ruled the roost at Road Hill House. If he locked the constables in the kitchen, no one would have dared to let them out."

"But he wouldn't kill his own baby son," Elizabeth protested. "It was such a violent murder."

Rowan raised his eyebrows. "Well?" he drawled. "Was it?"

She flipped through her notes. "Oh, wait. The throat-cutting was done postmortem, wasn't it? For effect. And the child was actually smothered in his bed. We know that because the impressions were still there on the mattress."

"Yes," said Rowan, nodding approvingly.

"So Constance might have gone in during the night and smothered the sleeping child, but that would be a risky sort of murder, wouldn't it? The nurse was sleeping nearby, of course. Why not take the child out for a walk one afternoon and drown it in the river when no one was around? Much safer."

"Yes. Why didn't she do that? Why would anybody kill a child in a nursery with two other children and the nursemaid present? Why would Mr. Kent do it?"

The guide contrived to look innocent. "Why would he be there in the first place?" he said casually.

Elizabeth narrowed her eyes. "Well, he fooled around with the first nursemaid, didn't he? We know he did, because he took her for carriage rides while the first Mrs. Kent languished in her bedroom. And when his first wife died, he married the nursemaid! Mary Pratt, who was baby Savile's mother. So you think he was up to his old tricks again?"

"I can see how it might be habit forming," said Rowan, thinking of various escapades on his boat.

"Okay." Elizabeth nodded, following the sequence now. "Mary Pratt Kent is asleep.

335

Samuel gets up and goes into the nursery to fool around with the new nursemaid Elizabeth Gough. Baby Savile wakes up and sees them. Perhaps he starts to cry, which might wake the household—and then their little tryst will be discovered." She was staring off into an expanse of blue sky, picturing the scene in the dark nursery at Road Hill House. "Samuel Kent just wants the child to shut up. He tries to make him stop crying, but he doesn't know anything about child care or he's too excited to be cautious, so he slams the baby's face into its mattress and holds it. A little too hard, a little too long."

"It wouldn't take much," Rowan pointed out. "Children are more fragile than adults. A minute. Not much more."

Elizabeth shuddered. "The child suddenly goes limp and he realizes he's killed it. Elizabeth Gough knows, though, doesn't she?"

"Yes, but what can she do? It's 1865. If she admits she was having it off with her employer, her character is ruined and she'll never get a husband or another job. She might even be charged as an accessory to the murder."

"And instead of thinking about his poor

dead son, Samuel Kent worries about his own reputation. He wraps the child in the crib blanket and carries it out of the house." She flipped through her notes again. "Which is why the housemaid found the door ajar at five A.M.! And then to make it look like an outside killing, he cut the baby's throat."

"Murderers have done that sort of thing," Rowan remarked. "In the 1970s the Green Beret doctor Jeffrey MacDonald killed his wife in an argument, and then murdered his two toddlers to make it appear that a band of drug-crazed hippies had killed the family."

Momentarily distracted from the Road Hill murder, Elizabeth smiled. "Any band of hippies that would kill two babies and a pregnant woman, and then leave a husky Green Beret soldier with only a scratch, would have to be on a ton of drugs. I don't think there's that much stupidity in the world."

"No, but he nearly got away with it. It took ten years to get the civilian trial that convicted him. And Samuel Kent got away with it, too, didn't he? He was an upstanding man, well-to-do, and obviously sane. Although people did suspect him, they were finally persuaded to believe the confession of an unbalanced adolescent."

Rowan pointed to Elizabeth's newly purchased crime book. "Did you find a transcript of Constance's confession in there?"

"I remember seeing it," she said, leafing through the pages. "Here it is. Shall I read it? Okay, this is in 1865, after she's confessed to her half brother's murder, and everybody wants to know why she did it. Her lawyer, Mr. Coleridge, asks the court's permission to say two things on Constance's behalf:

"First, solemnly in the presence of Almighty God, she wishes me to say that the guilt is hers alone, and that her father and others who have so long suffered most unjust and cruel suspicion are wholly and absolutely innocent—"

With a thoughtful expression Elizabeth looked up from the book. "You think that's why she confessed, don't you? Because suspicion was still lingering over the household, perhaps damaging her father's career. The tension of continuing scandal was probably very hard for a young girl to bear. Maybe she thought she had the least to lose."

"And the second part of her statement?"

Elizabeth ran her finger down the page.

"Here it is. *Secondly, she was not driven to this act, as has been asserted, by unkind treatment at homed as she met with nothing there but tender and forbearing love* . . . What a crock! So she supposedly had no motive at all for killing her young half brother? Just a whim, huh?"

"So she would have us believe," said Rowan in a carefully neutral voice. "Let me see the book. I've been told by a fellow crime buff, a Mr. O'Connor, that we will find her explanation of the crime most informative." He skimmed the pages of the chapter on Constance Kent, paying special attention to the blocks of print in smaller typeface, denoting a quotation from court documents or other primary sources. "This must be it," he said. "Dr. John Charles Bucknill, the physician who examined Constance by order of the government to determine whether she was of sound mind, published an account of her confession in several newspapers, supposedly at the prisoner's request." Rowan considered. "Well, perhaps she did ask him to publish it. If her intention was to divert suspicion from the rest of the family, she would need to convince as many people as possible of her own guilt."

Elizabeth frowned. "Go on. How does she say she did it?"

Rowan adjusted his glasses and began to read in carefully measured tones. "A few days before the murder she obtained possession of a razor from the green case in her father's wardrobe, and secreted it. This was the sole instrument which she used. She also secreted a candle with matches, by placing them in the corner of the closet in the garden, where the murder was committed."

Elizabeth looked up sharply. "It was not!" she declared. "The police investigation said that the child was smothered in his own bed! The throat-cutting was post-mortem. Why should she lie about that?"

"Why indeed," murmured Rowan. "Let us continue. *On the night of the murder she undressed herself and went to bed, because she expected that her sisters would visit her room. She lay awake, watching, until she thought that the household were all asleep, and soon after midnight she left her bedroom and went downstairs and opened the drawing room door and the window shutters.*"

"How very premeditated!" said Elizabeth sarcastically. "Why, there's mafia hit men who are less thorough than that. And this is a sixteen-year-old planning to kill a baby for no particular reason. Sure!"

Without comment, Rowan resumed the narrative. *"She then went up into the nursery, withdrew the blanket from between the sheet and the counterpane, and placed it on the side of the cot. She then took the child from his bed and carried him downstairs through the drawing room."*

Elizabeth interrupted again. "What about the suffocation?"

"She seems unaware of that detail, doesn't she? Where was I?—*Having the child in one arm, she raised the drawing room window with the other hand, went round the house and into the closet, lighted the candle and placed it on the seat of the closet, the child being wrapped in the blanket and still sleeping, and while the child was in this position, she inflicted the wound in his throat. She says that she thought the blood would never come—"*

"It wouldn't if he was already dead," said Elizabeth. She looked thoughtful. "But she says nothing of having smothered him in his bed."

"No," Rowan agreed, "in fact, she says that the child was not killed, so she thrust the razor into its left side, and put the body, with the blanket round it, into the vault."

"What?" cried Elizabeth. "She claims that she stabbed Savile with the *razor?* I'd like to have seen her try that!"

"Yes, it is hard to stab someone with the blunt tip of a straight razor, isn't it? Slashing, yes. But puncture wound? No, I wouldn't have thought so."

"Well, this is rubbish," Elizabeth declared. "If I were going to confess to a crime, I believe I'd endeavor to know more about the circumstances than this poor girl did."

"Perhaps she was doing her best," Rowan pointed out. "Some of it may even be true. If the child had been killed in the nursery, she could have carried him down as she described and inflicted the postmortem injuries to divert suspicion from the household. And I suppose that such an act might prey on her young mind as much as an actual murder."

Elizabeth was silent for a few minutes, contemplating the evidence. "She had no reason to lie," she said at last. "If she was admitting to murder, she might as well tell how it really happened. Since she got it wrong, we can assume that it was because she didn't *know* what actually occurred on the night of the murder. She was taking the blame for somebody else." She sighed. "You're right, Rowan. Your version is the only one that makes sense. Daddy is fooling around with the nursemaid, when the child wakes up and starts to cry. In trying to hush the boy, Mr. Kent accidentally smothers him, and then—perhaps with Constance's help—he takes the child to the privy and cuts its throat to make the killing look like an outside job. Constance may be guilty as an accessory after the fact, but she didn't kill the child. Why didn't the authorities realize it at the time?"

"It was an unsolved case of four years' standing," Rowan reminded her. "I don't suppose they wanted to look a gift horse in the mouth. I myself think that there was a certain amount of religious hysteria involved in her confession. Since the crime, Constance had been living at Brighton in a religious institution, and it was to the minister in charge that she first confessed. Why not? The crime had blighted her life anyway. What marriage prospects would she have with her family under perpetual suspicion of butchery? And what else could she hope for in that era? Not a job as a governess, surely?" He smiled at the absurdity of it.

Elizabeth took back the crime book and turned to the end of the chapter. "What happened to Constance? It says here that at her trial she was condemned to death, but that sentence was commuted to life imprisonment. I wonder how Mr. Kent felt about that."

"A regrettable but necessary sacrifice," said Rowan, in his best imitation of a Victorian patriarch.

"She served twenty years, then was released from prison. Oh, damn! This book says that no one is certain what became of her after that. That's not fair! I want to know." She looked suspiciously at the guide. "You know, don't you?"

Rowan shook his head. "No, but I suspect that the answer is known these days. Scholars of Victorian crimes are like bloodhounds, and that's just the sort of puzzle that would send them off baying through the courthouses on three continents."

"I don't have time to do that," said Elizabeth, frowning. "Here," said Rowan. "Give me one of those mawkish postcards you're always buying. Yes, that one of Glastonbury will do." He pulled out his fountain pen and wrote on the back in his nearly legible scrawl: *Please send information on final whereabouts of Constance Kent to Dr. Eliza-beth MacPherson, c/o Mountbatten Hotel, Seven Dials, London.* He addressed the card to Kenneth O'Connor in Yorkshire. "There," he said cheerfully. "That will give you something to look forward to at journey's end. Kenneth will know the answer to this, if anyone does."

CHAPTER 14

"Last night as sad I chanced to stray,
The village death-bell smote my ear,
Thy winking aside and seemed to say
'Countess, prepare—thy end is near.' "
Traditional English Ballad
on the death of Amy Robsart

OXFORD

THE GROUP SPENT one night at Ruthin Castle in North Wales, where they attended the regular Friday night medieval banquet, learning to eat soup with their fingers and gaining a new appreciation for the beauty of Welsh singing. Since they had to leave at ten the next morning ("Before the shops even opened!"), they were unable to form much of an opinion of Wales. Frances noted that bad carpeting seemed to be endemic among the ancient castles of Britain, but otherwise the company found it a pleasant and picturesque place. It did not have the aura of a thirteenth-century castle, though. Centuries of renovations probably accounted for that. It seemed no older nor more impressive than Moretonhampstead, nine hundred years its junior.

Rowan Rover, who was not well-versed in Welsh law, decided to refrain from any questionable activity until the party again crossed the border into England.

Another long drive on Saturday took them south again, with a stop to tour Powys Castle, and finally to the Shropshire town of Shrewsbury, where Frances would at last walk in the footsteps of the fictional Brother Cadfael. Rowan Rover had the weekend off, as was his custom, and he bade them farewell at the train station, promising to see them Monday morning for the journey to Oxford.

They checked into the Lion Hotel, an old coaching inn on the summit of the town's old street, Wyle Cop. Former guests at the seven-hundred-year-old establishment had included Charles Dickens, and Jenny Lind, the Swedish Nightingale. Such real celebrities, however, paled beside Shrewsbury's true celebrity: Brother Cadfael, who never existed at all. In his way, though, he was as much a local dignitary as was Jack the Ripper in the East End. The bookstores and curio shops sold Brother Cadfael dolls and hand-drawn maps, and the Abbey Church of Saint Peter and Saint Paul, his erstwhile home, featured an entire rack of Brother Cadfael paperbacks in the back of the sanctuary itself.

Susan was extremely amused by that. "That's great!" she said with a laugh. "Ellis Peters has become a local industry. Boy, I'll bet Joan Hess wishes they'd sell her books in the Baptist Church in Fayetteville, Arkansas! Wait till I tell the fans back home."

Elizabeth, whose interest in fictional crime was minimal, had to have all this explained to her twice, but she went along uncomplainingly on the one-hour Cadfael walk, provided Sunday morning by a knowledgeable city guide. (The shops were all closed, of course.) Susan, who had read all of Ellis Peters' work several times, was being her usual tiresome self, embellishing all the guide's remarks with plot summaries of each of the books. At one point Alice MacKenzie was heard to murmur that a reenactment of a Brother Cadfael murder wouldn't come amiss. She was looking pointedly in Susan's direction at the time.

That afternoon, many of the group took walks of their own along the Meole Brooke (now called the Rea Brook) or up to the castle overlooking the River Severn. The weather was still more warm and fair than anyone had a right to expect in an English autumn. By now they were quite spoiled by their good fortune and were taking it for granted.

Elizabeth spent the afternoon writing more letters and examining her map to see what real murder sites lay on tomorrow's route. She had found Shrewsbury disappointingly peaceful and law-abiding. As she looked over the names on the map, one quite near Oxford struck a familiar chord: Cumnor.

"Amy Robsart!" whispered Elizabeth. In addition to her true crime addiction, she had taken to reading the novels of Sir Walter Scott, as an homage to her newly adopted homeland. In *Kenilworth* she had discovered a sixteenth-century mystery that seemed to implicate Queen Elizabeth herself. Her latter-day namesake took her collection of crime books out of her suitcase and began to search for an account of the mysterious death at Cumnor Place. In the third book she found an article on it, and soon she was happily engrossed in real medieval intrigue.

Amy Robsart, the only heir of the Duke

of Norfolk, fell in love with Robert Dudley, third son of the Earl of Leicester, and in 1550, at the age of eighteen, she married him in a grand wedding attended by the boy king Edward VI. *"The Prince and the Pauper,"* muttered Elizabeth, whose knowledge of history was heavily reinforced by popular fiction.

The young couple lived together in the country, seemingly happy, and certainly wealthy. At the death of Amy's father, she inherited his considerable fortune. There was trouble for them, when Dudley was imprisoned for taking part in the Lynn Rebellion, but by and by he was released and they went home to the country once more.

In 1558 Queen Elizabeth ascended the throne, and Robert Dudley was summoned to court. First he was made Master of the Horse, and then a Knight of the Garter. He was constantly in the company of the queen. Amy stayed at home in the country. Soon it was common gossip in the court that the queen was *familiar* with Dudley, and people began to speculate on whether he would divorce his wife to marry the Virgin Queen. Ambassadors reported home that England would soon have a King Consort.

On September 4, 1560 the queen remarked that Lord Robert's wife was exceedingly ill, and perhaps already dead. In fact, twenty-eight-year-old Amy was in perfect health at Cumnor Hall—but four days later she lay dead at the foot of the main staircase with a broken neck.

"The queen was an accessory before the fact," murmured Elizabeth. "I wonder what Rowan will say about that?"

♦ ♦ ♦

ROWAN, WHO WAS somewhat tired from his morning train ride, and even more preoccupied with more current intrigues, looked completely horrified at his seatmate's suggestion that Queen Elizabeth was an accessory to murder. "Nonsense! I don't believe a word of it."

"But how do you explain the fact that she knew Amy Robsart was going to die four days in advance?"

"Amy Rob—oh!" Rowan reddened. "*That* Queen Elizabeth. I thought you meant the Queen Mum. Sorry, I must have drifted off for a moment."

It was a clear day, with a chill wind making it cooler than usual, as the coach sped eastward out of Shropshire and back toward Oxford, which even in Amy Robsart's time was considered within commuting distance of London.

"Well?" said Elizabeth. "Was she murdered?"

With considerable effort the guide turned his attention to the conversation. "Who? Oh, Amy Robsart? Yes, of course she was murdered. Wives never fling themselves down staircases just because one has one's eye on a new bird." He spoke with heartfelt sincerity. "At least mine never do."

"I thought her death was rather convenient. Wealthy little Amy dies, leaving her husband with a fortune and with the freedom to marry his sovereign, untainted by the divorce courts."

"He wasn't home at the time," Rowan pointed out. Elizabeth snorted. "Would you be?"

"No. I suspect that his henchman-in-residence, Forster, did the deed, and that it was all hushed up at the inquest, which Dudley stage-managed personally. All the documents concerning the inquiry into Amy Robsart's death were destroyed, you know, so we can't very well second-guess the case from this century. But perhaps the most damaging writing about the case was an anonymous bit of libel called *Leicester's Commonwealth.* Copies of it went round England like a naughty chain letter. That book called Lord Robert an adulterer, a murderer, an atheist, a coward. Just about every bit of invective imaginable. And even before that book appeared, people were scandalized by Amy's convenient death, so the queen had to give up her intention of marrying him—if indeed she had ever meant to. She was very sharp in public relations, was Gloriana."

"Can we go and see Cumnor Place?" asked Elizabeth. "It's just outside Oxford."

"I'm sorry," said Rowan. "You are several hundred years too late. Not even the ruins remain, and I have no idea where the hall itself actually stood. It's probably a street of bungalows these days. But Amy herself is buried in St. Mary's Church on the high street in Oxford, if you'd like to pay your respects."

"Thank you," said Elizabeth. "I will."

♦ ♦ ♦

THEY HAD A cold afternoon's walk at another medieval ruin, Minster Lovell Hall, a roofless stone shell on the banks of the River Windrush. The stately ruins lay in pastoral solitude in an expanse of meadow, bordered by the little country Church of St. Kenelm, resting place of the manor's builder. As they walked about the site, chivvied by the wind, Rowan told them Minster Lovell's romantic tale: the discovery in 1708 of the body of the last Lord Lovell, hidden away in a secret room.

"That was silly!" Susan Cohen declared. "Did they forget where they put him? It was the English Civil War, wasn't it? I know about priests' holes from *The Gyrth Chalice Mystery* by Margery Allingham—"

"No," said Rowan hastily. "Francis, Viscount Lovell, was somewhat ahead of his time on that score. He supported an impostor named Lambert Simnel, who attempted to depose Henry VII. You remember Henry VII?"

"Fiberglass statue in Exeter," said Alice MacKenzie.

"People have been remembered for less," said Rowan without missing a beat. "Anyhow, Simnel was defeated, and the viscount conveniently disappeared. Otherwise, he'd have been executed. Apparently, he was concealed in a secret room here at Minster Lovell, but unluckily for him, the one servant who knew his whereabouts died suddenly, and Viscount Francis was never found. His bones were finally discovered two hundred years later."

"And after he meets the Gyrth's heir in the book, Albert Campion has to protect this gold cup that has been hidden in the house since ancient times—"

Rowan stopped and looked at her. "What did you say?"

Susan repeated her summary of the Margery Allingham plot, in which the Gyrth family must retain and display an ancient golden cup of mystic significance in order to keep their lands.

When she had wound down, the guide smiled. "Well, Susan," he said, "at last I am able to contribute something in your area of interest. Apparently your mystery author based her tale on the tradition of a house called Nanteos, near Capel Seion in Wales. Until recently its owners displayed an ancient wooden cup, said to possess miraculous healing powers. Now do be quiet."

Susan opened her mouth and shut it again.

"What happened to the viscount of Minster Lovell?" asked Frances Coles quickly.

"I'm afraid he starved to death in his hiding place."

"And where is the secret room?" asked Charles, fingering his camera lens.

"I've no idea," Rowan replied. "There isn't enough left of the building to tell us, either."

"Too bad," said Elizabeth, eyeing the still-prattling Susan. "Yes, isn't it?" said Rowan.

◆ ◆ ◆

As THEY DROVE through Cumnor that afternoon, Elizabeth scoured the landscape for a sign of stately ruins—an old gatepost, perhaps, or a lone chimney—but Amy Robsart's residence had apparently been swallowed up by modern developments, and she could find no trace of the scene of the crime. Her disappointment was short-lived, however, for twenty minutes later Bernard announced, somewhat unnecessarily, that they had arrived in Oxford.

He navigated the busy streets, clogged with rush hour traffic, and set them down in Beaumont Street, at the door of the Randolph Hotel. Susan was rattling on about Colin Dexter and someone called Inspector Morse, but everyone contrived to ignore her. Rowan drowned her out, explaining that the neo-Gothic hotel was built in 1864 and was named after Dr. Francis Randolph, a principal of Merton College. "In the Spires Restaurant, you will find the coats of arms of all the colleges," he told them. "After I check you in, you are at liberty until tomorrow morning. I'll take you on a formal tour tomorrow, but do go out exploring on your own this afternoon. The shops are open," he added wickedly.

Twenty minutes later, as he pretended to study the notice board in the hall next to the lobby, Rowan saw most of the tour group troop out of the hotel, chattering among themselves. Only the Warrens had not departed, which did not affect his plan in the least. Their whereabouts did not concern him. The important consideration was that Susan was gone, and with only four days left until the end of the tour, he could not afford to tarry any longer.

When the group disappeared from sight, Rowan strolled up to the registration desk and intoned in an impeccable Oxonian drawl, "I say, I wonder if you remember me from a quarter of an hour ago? Guide on the tour that checked in? One of the young ladies left her purse in the coach, and I'd like to put it in her room, if I may. I know you have bellmen who generally fetch and carry, but in this case I'd rather do it personally. The purse contains the young lady's passport, you know, and a bit of cash. They *will* do it, these tourists. So careless. If I could just have the passkey to Miss Cohen's room, I'll pop right in with it and bring the key straight back." His smile was dazzling. "Thank you *so* much."

Fortunately the timid young thing at the desk did not notice that the guide was not carrying the aforementioned purse as he dashed off upstairs with the key to Room 307. He was, instead, carrying a screwdriver and a pair of needle-nosed pliers, but they were concealed in the pocket of his tweed jacket, well out of sight. Rowan had spent the weekend at home devising alternate, ever-more bizarre and risky schemes for dispensing with Susan Cohen. He had returned to the tour, armed with various devices to implement those schemes—and a renewed determination to finish the task once and for all. A newly arrived stack of demands for payment and invective from yet another ex-wife had fueled this latest resolve to complete the contract—and thus to extricate himself from financial ruin.

As he hurried upstairs, he scarcely noticed the church-like windows and the ornate ceiling designs above the Randolph's main staircase. His mind was focused on the task at hand. *God knows it will need concentration,* he thought. *Electronics is hardly my forte.*

He stopped in front of Room 307 and looked up and down the hall to make sure that no one else was lingering. Satisfied that he was unobserved, he slipped the key into the lock and let himself into the room. It was a small, nondescript single room with a view of an alley. The private bath was nearly half the size of the room itself. Barely glancing at the luggage still piled in the corner, Rowan took out his tools and headed for the bathroom. *The light fixture over the sink,* he decided. *It's the only thing she'll be sure to touch.*

Carefully, he reached up and unscrewed the protective cover over the light. After several minutes' tinkering with the wires, he was satisfied that he had made the correct modifications. Hurriedly he replaced the metal cover, wiped his fingerprints off everything with a hand towel, and left the room. Once downstairs, he waited until the clerk was talking on the telephone, with her back to him, before he strode over and placed the key on the counter. He was gone before she turned around. Perhaps she wouldn't remember him at all, he thought—with more hope than conviction. Sighing in relief to have it over with, Rowan Rover wandered away in search of Chapters Cocktail Bar, where he would await further developments in a haze of cigarette smoke and double Scotches.

It was nearly six o'clock before the light faded and the shops closed, driving all the stragglers back to the safety of the hotel to plan their evening's entertainment. Elizabeth MacPherson had met Kate Conway on Broad Street, in a gift shop specializing in Oxford sweatshirts, and they walked back to the hotel together.

"Maud went to Evensong with Alice MacKenzie and Frances Coles," Kate told her. "Martha is seeing a friend from Oxford this evening, and Susan is still shopping." She giggled. "You know that beautiful navy-blue coat of Martha's? I saw Susan buying one just like it at Laura Ashley. She'll probably wear it, too. I wonder what Martha will think of that."

"Plenty, but she's too well-bred to say anything," said Elizabeth. "Dinner is out of our own pocket tonight, I suppose?"

Kate nodded. "Do you think Rowan would like to join us?"

"We could ask him. What time are you planning to go out?"

"In about an hour," said Kate, glancing at her watch. "Shall I come and get you when we're ready to leave?"

"Yes, do. I'm in Room 307." She made a face. "Susan, being her usual impossible self, insisted that we change rooms because there's a light outside her window that she was sure would disturb her sleep."

Kate wrote the number on the back of the sweatshirt bag. "Okay, 307. Got it. I'll see you around seven. Where do you suppose Rowan is?"

Elizabeth paused at the foot of the stairs. "Try the bar."

◆ ◆ ◆

AFTER DIALING THE guide's room and surveying the lounge where cream teas were served, Kate did indeed extend her search to the downstairs bar, where she found Rowan Rover seated at a tiny wooden table, blowing smoking rings like the Wonderland caterpillar.

"Hello, there!" said Kate, blushing a little

361

at the memory of their last solitary encounter. "Mind if I join you?"

"Not at all," he said graciously, glad for any distraction from the scenario in his mind.

"We were wondering if you'd like to go out to dinner with us in about an hour."

Rowan raised his eyebrows. "We?"

"Yes, Maud and I. And Elizabeth. We thought you might be able to recommend a good restaurant. We thought we'd treat you to dinner."

This enabled Rowan to recollect any amount of acceptable restaurants in the vicinity of Oxford. He spent several cigarettes detailing the virtues of each establishment and recounting stories of escapades at many of them during his student days. Kate listened with a wide-eyed expression of awe that he found almost as gratifying as the Scotch. Perhaps, he thought, if the Susan problem resolves itself neatly, I can forego my vow to Mrs. Thatcher after all.

As he finished his recital of restaurants, Kate glanced at her watch. "Golly!" she said. "It's twenty to seven and I still have to change. Would you mind going up to get Elizabeth? I promised her we'd stop by, but I'm running late."

"Certainly," said Rowan, mellowed by the pleasant interlude with his favorite sedatives. "What is her room number?"

Kate's lovely face went blank. "I forget. But I wrote it down somewhere." She picked up her packages and began to examine them for pencil marks. "Let's see . . . I met her in the sweatshirt shop. Here it is! Room 307."

"Right. I'll go and get her," said Rowan, striding briskly away, as he wondered why that number sounded vaguely familiar. Finally, recognition overtook him and he stood for one frozen moment to let the calamity sink in. An instant later he was running down the hall toward the stairs, trying frantically to remember the first-aid treatment for electrocution. And what should he do if he knocked on her door and received no answer? It would look awfully suspicious to panic on so little provocation. He couldn't ask for the pass-key again.

"Hello. Rowan! Yoo-hoo!"

With a sigh of exasperation the guide turned around. "Not now," he began. "I'm in a hurry."

"All right," said Elizabeth, waving him on.

Rowan stared. "It's you!" To cover his

gaffe, he said the next thing that came into his head. "You look ghastly."

"So would you if you'd just been zapped by a light switch," she murmured. She was about three shades paler than usual. She looked as if she might fall down at any second. "I came down to report it to the desk clerk."

"Go and sit down," said Rowan. "I'll see to it."

Later that evening at dinner, Elizabeth told the story of the vicious light switch to her table partners with considerably more aplomb and self-deprecation than she had felt at the time. "And to top it all off, it wasn't even my room!" she concluded with a laugh. "It was Susan's, but she made me swap with her because she didn't like the view. Just my luck!"

No, thought Rowan with a heavy heart. Just *mine*.

◆ ◆ ◆

THE NEXT MORNING, Rowan endeavored to be cheerful during breakfast, but his thoughts were elsewhere. His face was beginning to show the strain of too much planning and too little success. He had got very little sleep, and he made only a perfunctory show of paying attention to the conversation of his breakfast partners, the Warrens. Fortunately, since they were pontificating about their children, his long lapses into silence went unnoticed.

At ten o'clock he downed his coffee and signaled for the last of the stragglers to finish their meals and prepare to depart. "You will need coats today," he warned them. "It's rather windy."

"I'll just be a minute," said Frances Coles, scooping up the uneaten pastries from beside her plate.

Eyeing Frances' slender figure, Nancy Warren sighed. "Where does she put it all?"

"In her bag," snapped Rowan.

A short time later the troop marched down the front steps of the Randolph and set off to see the dreaming spires of Oxford. To everyone's quiet amusement, Susan had appeared wearing her newly acquired navy coat, identical to Martha Tabram's. As predicted, however, Martha appeared oblivious to the occurrence, although she did manage not to walk in the vicinity of Susan.

Oxford really was a perfect town for a tour, Rowan reflected, as he led the procession: compact, picturesque, and with historical associations for every taste.

There were plenty of photo opportunities for Charles. Mystery readers like Susan could visit Balliol College, alma mater of Peter Wimsey, and scour the campus for scenes from the Edmund Crispin novels. Elizabeth MacPherson could see the cross in the street marking the place where the martyrs were burnt, and the church where Amy Robsart was buried. For Kate, the TV buff and moviegoer, he could offer vistas from *Brideshead Revisited* and *Dreamchild*. The intellectuals would enjoy the descriptions of the various colleges and a brief look at the Bodleian Library. And for the rest- the easiest tour of all: the Oxford of *Alice in Wonderland*.

The two-hour tour of the city that he conducted that morning was a skillful blend of all these, as he walked them from college to college, reeling off anecdotes dredged up from his prodigious memory. All the while his mind was busy on another track altogether.

He marched them out to Somerville College, which boasted Dorothy L. Sayers among its graduates. That venerable institution for women was not located in the cluster of other colleges, but was a good distance away from the city center—and scarcely worth the walk when supplemented by Susan's droning recital of the plot of *Gaudy Night* in meticulous detail.

"And it wasn't her best book to begin with," muttered Maud Marsh.

They admired the Radcliffe Camera and the Sheldonian Theatre, while Rowan fantasized about the possibility of throwing Susan out a window of either one. They walked through the Bodleian courtyard and into the churchyard of St. Mary the Virgin, where Elizabeth instituted a search for the final resting place of Amy Robsart. A clerk in the church gift shop told her that a small plaque in the chancel was the only trace of the ill-fated lady of Leicester.

Susan kept saying that she didn't see how students could get any studying done at Oxford, since all the colleges bordered on streets that hummed with incessant traffic. The others contrived to ignore her remarks.

"It isn't like the American university system," said Rowan. "Traditionally, tutors made assignments entirely on an individual basis."

"But suppose you don't want to learn anything?" asked Elizabeth.

"Then you don't," Rowan replied.

Elizabeth considered it. "What about graduate school? Did it take you two years to get your master's?"

The guide sighed. Trust her to ask. "At Oxford, a graduate is automatically awarded a master's degree upon graduation if he pays an additional fee."

"What?" howled Elizabeth. "You mean the only difference between a B.A. and an M.A. at Oxford is fifty bucks?"

"Less than that in my day, I believe," Rowan admitted.

"I am going to drown myself," Elizabeth declared. "Now you tell me! After I've spent umpteen months of my life writing term papers for that gang of pedants in Virginia! Honestly!"

"Typical," sniffed Maud Marsh. "Did I tell you about their so-called lemonade over here?"

The tour continued past Braesnose and looped back past a cordoned area of renovation work beside the library.

"And this is the back wall of Exeter College," Rowan was saying. "You see that it is quite high and without foot-holds. As I am too old to demonstrate, let me just tell you how undergrads used to sneak over the wall to get in after curfew . . ." *Exeter,* he thought. The very name of the college was urging him on. *Exit-her.*

Forty-five minutes later their ramble had led them to the gardens of Christ Church, which is both college and cathedral. It was there, he told them, that Charles Dodgson—in literature Lewis Carroll—came as an undergraduate in 1851 and remained for the rest of his life. His literary inspiration, Alice, was the daughter of the Reverend Henry George Liddell, the dean of Christ Church, and many of the images in *Alice and Wonderland* are based on familiar objects in Oxford.

"Name one," said Maud Marsh, still resentful over the non-isle of Glastonbury and other misrepresentations.

Rowan was ready for her. He had done his homework on Oxford. "The brass firedogs in the Great Hall at Christ Church have the figure of a woman's head set on a long stalk of a neck. Remember when Alice drinks the potion and stretches out of shape? The Tenniel illustration greatly resembles those firedogs. And the illustration of Alice and the frog knocking at the door shows that they are standing at the Chapter House door. And the deer at Magdalen are featured—"

Susan Cohen interrupted. "What is that place across the street?"

"That was the shop kept by the sheep in *Through the Looking Glass*," said Rowan triumphantly. "Now it is called Alice's Shop and, appropriately enough, it specializes in *Alice in Wonderland* memorabilia." He called after the sudden stampede in the direction of the shop, "That's it for this morning, then! I shall see you all for tea at four! *Look out for the traffic, all!*"

♦ ♦ ♦

ROWAN SPENT THE remainder of the sunny afternoon in a solitary walking tour of the university town, reminiscing about his student days. He found a wonderful serenity in Oxford that somehow diminished all his financial problems—and the even more pressing moral one that confronted him at present. As he contemplated the graceful arch of the Bridge of Sighs in Hertford College, he found it easy to believe that he was nineteen again, with a glorious academic future in front of him and no ex-wives to haunt him like avenging Furies. He strolled through the South Park and wondered if life would have been simpler if, like the Reverend Dodgson, he had come to Oxford at nineteen and never left.

"Not bloody likely," he muttered in a moment of realism. "I'd probably be crazier than Lewis Carroll. I'd like to see him try to get away with his infatuation with little girls in this jaundiced century!"

Besides, there was no point in getting despondent about a few minor financial and professional setbacks. As soon as he performed his small service for Aaron Kosminski, all would be well. He could do whatever he liked. Fix the boat. Take a year off and write a book at his leisure. Vacation in the sunny Caribbean. Were such worldly luxuries really worth the life of the fair young Susan Cohen? he pondered, gazing up at the spire of St. Mary's. Oh, yes, he told himself. Cheap at twice the price.

When it was nearly time for the afternoon tea scheduled at the Randolph, Rowan wandered back along the high street, dismayed by the ceaseless blur of high-speed traffic along the road. Susan had a point about the modern-day disturbance of the academic peace. Perhaps the city ought to consider restricting some of the downtown streets to pedestrians only, as Winchester had done.

As he joined a clump of shoppers at Broad Street about to cross over to St. Giles, he noticed Susan Cohen a few yards in front of him. She was surrounded by a knot of people, still bundled up in her new navy wool coat, and she was chattering nineteen to the dozen, oblivious to her surroundings as usual. By the time Rowan saw that a red city bus was coming, he could measure his planning time in fractions of a second.

Resolutely he pushed his way through the package-laden pedestrians, head down like a charging bull. When he saw the back of the navy coat in front of him with no obstacles in between, he took a deep breath for courage, put out his hands, and pushed.

With a shout of alarm, she went down, inches from the front wheel of the oncoming bus, which somehow managed to swerve out of the way, horn blaring. There she lay face-down in the street, surrounded by horrified shoppers who were going off like air raid sirens.

"Gee, Martha," said Susan Cohen. "Are you okay?"

◆　◆　◆

BY THE TIME good Samaritans had helped Martha Tabram to her feet and dusted off

372

her soiled coat—no longer identical to Susan's—Rowan Rover had melted into the fringes of the crowd without anyone having seen him. He crossed the road and wandered into a shop, where he observed the drama in the street from the anonymous vantage point of a tie rack.

He saw that Martha was unable to walk unassisted. She had not been seriously injured, thanks to the bus driver's phenomenal reflexes, but apparently she had twisted her ankle in the fall. True to form, though, she was not displaying any obvious signs of distress. Her calm, dignified countenance was paler than usual, but it registered no emotion. She seemed to be ignoring the ministrations of Susan Cohen, who was hovering at her side like a small terrier attempting to chivvy a marble statue.

As the procession inched out of sight, Rowan slipped out the door of the department store and resorted to a circuitous series of back routes to find his way to the hotel.

When he arrived, the other members of the tour were already assembled in the parlor around a laden tea table, wolfing down pastries and discussing the latest stroke of misfortune to befall the group. Elizabeth

MacPherson looked somewhat distressed. He wondered if it was the lingering effects of the electric shock or philanthropic concern for a fellow traveler. Martha, he noted, was not present, but Susan was—reciting her version of the events through a mouthful of cucumber sandwich. Her eyes shone with self-importance. She was apparently oblivious to the real intent of the accident.

"It's the uneven pavement in these streets," she insisted. "Not that Martha could see where she was walking, of course, because the street was absolutely packed, and I expect she was paying pretty close attention to what I was telling her about that Colin Dexter novel."

Not bloody likely, thought Rowan. *If she'd been listening to you all afternoon, she might have dived under that bus on purpose.*

◆ ◆ ◆

LATER THAT EVENING, after too many pastries and cups of tea had robbed her appetite for dinner, Elizabeth MacPherson retired to her room—and finally wrote more than a two-line postcard. Since her new husband was still incommunicado on the high seas, she reverted to her lifelong habit of confiding in her brother back in Virginia.

Dear Bill,

The ghouls on wheels, as you are pleased to call this very sedate mystery tour, have nearly finished their trek through the south of England. Since my last postcards we've seen Hereford, Ruthin in Wales, Shrewsbury, Minster Lovell, and now Oxford. You will be glad to know that I have taken very few photographs, so you will have no slide show to dread at future family gatherings.

Tomorrow we return to London for a few days' sightseeing, including the Jack the Ripper tour, which I am greatly looking forward to. That is one of Rowan's specialties. He's our guide, and he's marvelous on true crime. We've had several inquests *a few centuries after the fact.* Unfortunately for your struggling law practice, all the criminals we've studied are dead, and not in need of the services of a new law school graduate who works cheap. I hope you are managing to catch a few ambulances in Danville.

For a while tonight, though, I thought you might have to defend me on an assault and battery charge, but I managed to keep my temper and did not slug the *woman, much as she deserved it. No doubt you are not wondering what I am talking about, but I'll tell you anyway.*

I was sitting in the parlor of the Randolph Hotel, waiting for everyone else to turn up for tea, when this apparently friendly English lady came over and started chatting me up. This Mrs. Pope-Locksley lives in Oxford; she just comes to tea at the Randolph for fun, I suppose; or possibly to bait the Americans. I suspected nothing; she seemed nice enough. Ha!

So she asks me where I'm from, and I said Virginia, and she starts going on about Alexandria and Fairfax, and all the other bedrooms of D.C. No, I told her, I live in the Blue Ridge, close to Tennessee and eastern Kentucky. That set her off "Eeee-oow," she says in that little toffee voice, "Appa-lay-cha." And she goes on for what seemed like a week about the primitive people living there, and what gun-toting barbarians we all were. Apparently, the old bat mistook Deliverance *for a documentary!*

I wasted a lot of time protesting. You know, "I live in Appalachia, and I have a Ph.D. and my brother's an attorney."

And "Pearl Buck is from West Virginia, and she got the Nobel Prize for literature." And "Actually, the homicide rate in the mountains is quite low. It's Richmond that's dangerous, and it's on the coast, where the English settled." Waste of breath. I don't think she heard a word I said. She droned on and on about what a wild and savage place it was, and then she called a friend over, and they asked me if we had electricity and indoor plumbing at home!

Fortunately, the Warrens arrived just then and rescued me, but I was close to tears for half an hour. Oxford has been a great shock to me. All my life I've thought of it as a center of culture and learning, and in one day I discover that they sell master's degrees like a matchbook diploma mill, and that people in Oxford can be just as ignorant and rude as people from anywhere else.

Aside from the boorish Mrs. Pope-Locksley, the rest of the tour has been delightful, although somewhat restrictive on shopping opportunities. And fraught with bad luck. We seem to have had more than our share of accidents. First, our guide almost falls off a sixty-foot precipice *in Cornwall, and then a lovely woman from Colorado becomes ill and has to fly home. Yesterday and today we had two mishaps! I tried to turn on the light switch in the bathroom and got a severe electric shock. If I'd tried it with wet hands, I might be dead. And then, Martha Tabram, the Canadian surgeon's wife, fell in the street and was almost hit by a bus. She has turned her ankle so badly that she has to leave the tour as well.*

Unfortunately, the one member of the group that we could really spare—the interminable Susan—is impervious to harm and impossible to shut up. With all these accidents going on, I do wish one of them would zero in on her. She really is a pain. Hey, wouldn't it be funny if somebody were trying to kill Susan, and kept missing?

Before Elizabeth completed the letter to her brother, she stared at that last sentence for a long time, lost in thought.

CHAPTER 15

"Funny little fellow,
Crippen was his name,
See him for a sixpence
In the hall of fame."
—*"Belle—or the ballad of Dr.*
Crippen"

LONDON

AS OXFORD IS only thirty miles from London, the last day's coach journey was a brief one. Before Rowan had finished elaborating on the gruesome details of Francis Dashwood's Hellfire Club in the caves at West Wycombe, Bernard announced that they were coming into the city. "You think Cornwall's country lanes are bad," he added. "Wait till you see the asphalt bridle paths they call streets in Bloomsbury. We may have to orbit the hotel for an hour, before I figure out a way to get the coach in there. Thank God it's not rush hour."

"No hurry, Bernard," Rowan assured him. "It's just on eleven now."

The coach had one less passenger for the trip to London. An Oxford physician recommended that Martha Tabram stay on a few days to rest her injured ankle. After that, she would be meeting her daughter in London. The group had signed a get-well card and sent it up to her room before they left. Undaunted by this latest patch of misfortune, the remaining tour members spent the ride to London making plans to see shows and discussing the London phase of the tour. Only Elizabeth MacPherson was quieter than usual. She kept looking over at the sleeping Susan Cohen, with a thoughtful expression on her face.

That afternoon, armed with daily passes to the Underground, the tour members assembled in the Baker Street station for their visit to Madame Tussaud's famous wax museum. After Charles Warren posed them for photographs with the wax effigies of the royal family in the Grand Hall (Elizabeth, Kate, and Nancy Warren), and with Agatha Christie in the Conservatory (Alice and Frances), Rowan led them hurriedly past the rock stars and the politicians, down the stairs to the Chamber of Horrors.

While everyone else maintained a polite interest in the realistic atmosphere of the

Victorian street scene and the sinister wax images lurking about the dimly lit tableaux, Elizabeth and Rowan rushed from one display to another, greeting the killers like old friends.

"People from home!" giggled Elizabeth, pointing to two men carrying a body in a wooden tea chest.

Rowan nodded. "Ay, yes, Burke and Hare, the Edinburgh bodysnatchers. The gallows over there is authentic, by the way. The museum got it from the Hertford Gaol in 1878."

"Why don't they label these things?" grumbled Alice MacKenzie. "Some of these people could be politicians, for all I know." She pointed to a prosperous-looking wax gentleman in a vintage brown suit.

"That fellow is John George Haigh," Rowan told her. "He's famous for luring a wealthy old lady to his so-called factory in Sussex, where he murdered her and dissolved the body in an acid bath. He's wearing his own suit, by the way. He donated it to Madame Tussaud's on the eve of his execution. Over here is John Christie, of Ten Rillington Place, who entombed his victims behind the walls of his house. Imagine the surprise of the next tenant when he began to redecorate!"

"I don't think we have any weird killers in Minnesota," said Susan. "They're all from Wisconsin."

"Who is the couple in the dock?" asked Maud Marsh, pointing to a small bespectacled man and the pretty dark-haired girl beside him. "She looks rather sweet."

Rowan motioned the group over to the exhibit. "That charming couple is Harvey Hawley Crippen and the lovely Ethel LeNeve," he told them. "Poor old sod. He killed his shrew of a wife and buried her in the basement. If he'd done it today, the case would barely have made the papers and he'd have been out in ten years. But in 1910 people called him a monster, and he was hanged for it."

"That's his girlfriend, I suppose?" said Alice, pointing to the young girl's statue.

"Yes, that's his motive for murdering his wife, who was much less charming. Ethel may not have known about the murder. She was acquitted at the trial anyhow. Although I think she might have suspected something when he asked her to dress as a boy and flee the country with him on a steamship. Over there is the actual telegram that was dispatched by the ship's captain to alert Scotland Yard to their presence on his ship."

"*The False Inspector Dew!*" cried Susan, at last able to make a connection between the exhibit and her addiction to crime novels.

Rowan ignored the interruption. "The captain spotted them immediately. Apparently our Ethel wasn't a very convincing boy. Crippen loved her, though. He pleaded guilty at once and insisted that she knew nothing about the crime. At his execution, he asked that a photograph of her be buried with him."

"I take a very dim view of burying wives in the basement," said Alice.

"So did I a couple of marriages ago," said Rowan. "But I've mellowed."

Meanwhile Kate Conway had found the Whitechapel setting dedicated to Jack the Ripper. She was staring in horror at the blood-caked body of a woman in Victorian dress, sprawled behind an iron railing. "She looks familiar somehow," Kate murmured. "They never caught the Ripper, did they?"

"No," said Elizabeth. "But he'd be about a hundred and thirty by now, so I shouldn't worry. It's only wax, you know."

"Who is this?" asked Frances Coles, tapping Elizabeth on the shoulder. "Over here in this little alcove decorated like a bedroom. I wish they'd label these things."

"I'll see if I can figure it out," said Elizabeth. "Show me."

Frances led her to a dark doorway opening into a tiny candlelit bedroom. There in the shadows, a small child in a white nightshirt sat up in bed, staring wide-eyed at the doorway where the viewers stood. The simple furnishings of the room seemed to date from the previous century. The child was alone in the tableau.

"There aren't any clues," murmured Kate, who had followed them over. "I suppose that's the victim, poor kid. We can't see the killer, and we don't even know how it's going to be killed."

Elizabeth stood for a long time, as motionless as the wax statue, staring into the eyes of the frightened, dark-haired child. "Smothered," she whispered, turning away.

"You recognize it?" asked Frances.

She nodded. "Yes. Oh, yes. I see him in my nightmares. It's Francis Savile Kent of Road Hill House, looking up at Daddy."

The tour ended a little before five and

Rowan sent them off for tea, after making sure that everyone knew when and where they would meet again: seven-thirty that evening, outside the Whitechapel tube station. Tonight they would be given their own private Jack the Ripper walk.

"There wasn't anything about the Charles Bravo case in Madame Tussaud's," Elizabeth complained as they went back into the Underground.

"That's because the lovely but lethal Florence was acquitted of poisoning him," Rowan reminded her. "There'll be no slander in the waxworks, madam. But if you want to pass up half a day of capitalism, I'll take you out to Balham and show you the Priory, where it happened. You don't want to run out there now, do you?"

Elizabeth hesitated. "No," she said at last. "I think there's something else I'd better attend to."

"Off you go, then. I'm going back to my boat just now, but I'll see you all at half past seven."

Once they boarded the train for the ride back to the hotel, Elizabeth sat down next to Susan Cohen, who had fished a paperback out of her purse and was reading with an intensity that suggested she might orbit the city for hours if no one made her get off at the right stop.

"What made you decide to take this tour?" Elizabeth asked, with a certain satisfaction at interrupting Susan for a change.

"Crime. England. Sounded good," said Susan, turning a page.

"So you didn't know Rowan before we started?" She gave a deprecating little laugh. "You're not his ex-wife or anything?"

When Susan looked up from her book, her face was a study in astonishment. "I'm not anybody's ex-wife. Why do you ask?"

"Oh, no reason." She tried a new tack. "Isn't it a shame that Martha was unable to continue the tour? It must have been a bad fall. I saw her when you helped her into the hotel. Were you with her when it happened?"

"Pretty close," said Susan. "I spoke to her as we started off the curb—and she said something and went on. I didn't see her fall, though. We were in a big crowd."

"Hmm. Was anybody else from the tour there?"

"I didn't see anybody. Why?"

Elizabeth smiled. "I just wondered. I was thinking about sending a get-well card to

Emma Smith and telling her what we've been up to since she left. If she has food poisoning, it's lucky that we all didn't come down with it. You haven't been feeling ill, have you?"

"I'm fine. I don't see how it could have been food poisoning. I was sitting right next to her at the dinner in St. Ives—and we ordered the same thing."

"Well," said Elizabeth, "you never know."

"Is anybody else sick?" She looked around the car for another seat to move to. "You aren't, are you?"

"I'm fine," Elizabeth assured her. "Except for that nasty shock I got from the light switch in my room." *Which should have been your room,* she finished silently.

Susan went back to reading her book and Elizabeth left her alone. As the train clattered on in the darkness, she stared up at the map of the Underground, lost in thought.

♦   ♦   ♦

WHEN ELIZABETH RETURNED to her hotel, the desk clerk hailed her and informed her that she had a letter. She seized it eagerly, hoping for a message from Cameron, but the stamps were British and the address an unfamiliar one in Yorkshire. When she reached her room, she read the message, at once remembering Rowan's promise that his friend would answer her question. It said:

Dear Madam:

An old reprobate of my acquaintance, Rowan Rover, has asked me to reply to your question on the fate of Constance Kent, not because he respects my superior skills in scholarship, but because he is too lazy to attend to it personally. However, a small matter of a burned cushion in his aquatic residence impels me to be generous, and I shall now set your mind at rest concerning the matter of the tragic young lady from Rode. I assume that if you have studied the case in enough detail to be concerned about her fate, you have surmised her innocence.

At her trial Constance Kent was condemned to death for her crime, but popular sympathy (perhaps people were not without their suspicions) persuaded Her Majesty's Government to commute the sentence to life imprisonment. Constance served twenty years of this sentence, which would still leave her just under forty, and by all accounts she was a model prisoner, serving first in the prison laundry and later in the infirmary. Interestingly enough, her father died in 1872 while she was still in prison, but still she did not recant her confession. In for a penny, in for a pound, I suppose. Or perhaps she doubted that anyone would believe her. Of course, he left no deathbed confession to free her, the selfish old trout!

For news of her whereabouts after her release from Fulham Prison in 1885, I rely on Bernard Taylor's account in his 1979 book Cruelly Murdered. *He maintains that Constance changed her name to Ruth Emilie Kaye (Emilie was her middle name) and emigrated to Australia. She served as a nurse from 1890 until 1932, later founding a nurses home. When she died in 1944, she was one hundred years old. I believe she is the only convicted murderer ever to receive the congratulatory birthday telegram from the monarch.*

I hope this has set your mind at rest. Please give my regards to R. R. and tell him that I am always happy to be of service in his little schemes, in return for a berth on his Love Boat. It is less painful than agreeing with his Ripper theories.

Yours sincerely,
Kenneth O'Connor

◆ ◆ ◆

AT TWENTY MINUTES past seven that evening, Rowan Rover was slouched in the doorway of a news agent's shop near the Whitechapel tube station, smoking his fifth cigarette. Any moment now the mystery tour members—what was left of them—would emerge from the tube station, jovial and ready for an evening of nostalgic mayhem.

"I am following in the footsteps of a man who killed five women and was never caught," he muttered. "Surely I can manage one!"

It was the perfect setting: a series of dark, somewhat dangerous streets in an area that he knew perfectly well, while none of the others had ever been there. Every advantage was his. Except for the fact that his heart was pounding like a ten-shilling pocket watch and his skin crawled with cold sweat. For the first time he wondered what it had felt like to be Jack the Ripper. He had always imagined the mad killer bristling with excitement, breathing heavily at the prospect of his evening's sport, sliding through the dark streets of Whitechapel with a song in his throat. Somehow Rowan had neglected to think of the victims in any way at all except as costumed clay pigeons, necessary to the game. Suddenly he was forced to picture them as real people, with personalities and families, and with a pathetic innocence of the evil that stalked them, denying their humanity. Perhaps the Ripper's indifference toward his victims came from the fact that they were strangers. Susan Cohen, as irritating as she was, had become all too real to her intended assassin. He even knew the names of her cats, for God's sake! He should have killed her early on, he thought, when she was just a face in the crowd. He fingered the metal cosh in his pocket, a gift from an old burglar acquaintance. Now he would probably need months of counseling or gallons of good Scotch to recover from the horrors of this evening's ordeal. Fortunately, he reflected, he would be able to afford them.

When the first members of the group emerged from the tube station, chattering and laughing, as unaware as lambs to the slaughter, he went to meet them with a heavy heart and a plaster smile.

"Good evening, ladies and Charles. Welcome to the Jack the Ripper tour. Shall we proceed?"

Alice MacKenzie was wearing her new wool shawl from Wales. Frances Coles was sticking to her side as if Alice could protect her from any spectral Ripper who might descend on them. Maud Marsh and Kate Conway looked brightly inquisitive about the evening walk, not quite belying their boredom with historical crime. The Warrens were fiddling with camera attachments and Elizabeth MacPherson was looking about her with narrowed eyes as if she thought there was a chance of catching the killer this evening. Susan Cohen, in her blasted navy coat, made her way to the front of the group, nattering about some bookshop she'd found in Bloomsbury. No one was listening. He wondered whether to keep her near him at the front of the group or let her fall back in order to divert suspicion when the accident occurred.

As he led them into the fetid alley where Bucks Row had once been, he issued his usual warning to refrain from touching the walls, but he felt a flicker of satisfaction when he saw Susan run her forefinger along the brickwork.

"Winos pee there!" he belatedly explained.

Her scowl held him personally responsible. "Not in Minneapolis they don't!"

When they emerged from the alley, where progress had been single file, Elizabeth MacPherson appeared at his side. "So this was Bucks Row," she remarked. "Polly Nicholls, right?"

Rowan gave her a fishy stare. He'd be damned if he was going through the Ripper walk with a Greek chorus, even if she did know her facts. With the barest of nods, he recited his piece about the discovery of Polly Nicholls' body, verbally sketching in the geography of the site at the time of her death.

"It doesn't look too scary now," said Susan Cohen, yawning.

"Thank the Luftwaffe," snapped Rowan. "A lot of London geography changed during the Blitz. Some of it for the better. They got Crippen's house up in Islington, too, by the way."

He led them down Durward Street, across Vallance Road, and along Hanbury, toward the site of the Annie Chapman murder. Susan, whose interest in Jack the Ripper seemed confined to his influence on crime fiction, was nattering on about *The Lodger* and *The Threepenny Opera*, with complete disregard for Rowan's scheduled lecture. "Actually," she was saying, "I thought the guy in *Psycho* was a lot scarier than Jack the Ripper. And has anybody read *Silence of*—"

They were about to cross Brick Lane at this point and Susan, with her usual self-absorption, was not paying attention to the guide or to her surroundings. Blithely wittering about her reading list, she stepped off the curb and into the path of an approaching car.

Rowan Rover was not sure what prompted his spontaneous reaction. Perhaps it was instinctive, or perhaps some part of him made an inevitable decision in that split second. He was never sure. He only knew that as the silly woman blundered out into the street, looking as usual in the wrong direction for English traffic, he lunged forward in an attempt to drag her back out of the path of the oncoming car. His fingers actually touched her coat. He nearly got a grip on it when he felt himself being shoved out of the way, back toward the curb, nearly falling with the force of the blow.

The speeding black car, which seemed to come in slow motion, looming ever larger in their path, like a locomotive in a Saturday matinee film, missed the guide and the rest of the party by inches, but Susan, who had stood squarely in its path while she looked the wrong way, was struck with a chilling thud. She went down in mid-sentence without so much as a whimper.

As he struggled to regain his balance, Rowan looked around to see who had prevented him from saving Susan Cohen. Standing nearest to him was Elizabeth MacPherson, regarding him with a frown of lofty disapproval. Her expression explained it all: she had been watching him, expecting an attempt on Susan's life, and she had—she thought—prevented him from pushing her in front of the car. The silly girl! Another second and he would have saved her! (So much for his aptitude as a murderer.)

By the time they reached Susan's crumpled body, some yards away near the other curb of Brick Lane, the driver had stopped his car and had joined the throng hovering over the victim. "I never meant to!" the man kept saying. "She walked straight in my path, she did!"

Charles Warren had run to the nearby pub to telephone for an ambulance. Kate Conway was kneeling over Susan, examining the body with medical precision. After a few minutes she looked up at the group of tourists and shook her head.

Rowan fumbled for his cigarettes, feeling at once appalled and frightened but also relieved that her death was not on his conscience. He had not done it. He gave a deep sigh of relief and uttered a silent prayer of thanks to whatever saint looks out for criminals. He was standing a few feet away from the group, watching the scene with a detachment born of shock.

A few moments later Elizabeth MacPherson appeared at his side. "I couldn't save her," she murmured.

No, you bloody fool, and you kept me from doing so as well, thought Rowan, but his numbness prevented him from venting his exasperation.

"By the time I figured out what was going on, it was too late to speak to you privately, but I thought that if I could just protect her tonight, you wouldn't get another chance."

Elizabeth sighed. "Why did you do it, Rowan?"

"I didn't!" said the guide with perfect sincerity. Even to himself it sounded hollow.

"I can't prove it," said Elizabeth in a low voice. "And perhaps what you said was right: really clever killers usually get away with their first murder. Frankly, I think you're a rather good fellow, and for all I know you might get acquitted anyhow."

"I didn't do it," Rowan said plaintively.

She fixed him with a meaningful stare. "But this must not happen again, do you hear? I shall say nothing to anyone, but if I ever hear of anyone else on your tours meeting with an accident, I shall go to the police at once. Do you understand?"

He sighed. "Yes. It shan't happen again. You have my word." There was no use arguing with her, he thought. Her mind had seized up like a frozen motor, holding this one thought against all suggestions to the contrary. There was nothing for it but to play the humble felon, and vow to sin no more. Then she would feel noble. He supposed it was better than telling her the truth: that if anyone had killed Susan Cohen, it was she.

Sometime later, after the police had investigated the incident and had sensibly deemed the matter a case of accidental death, Rowan had led the quiet gaggle of tourists to the Ten Bells, where he'd insisted on standing them drinks to counteract the shock. They had talked for some time in sorrowful tones about poor Susan and what a sad ending to the tour this was. No one wanted to finish the Ripper tour: they had seen death enough that evening.

As they left the pub to summon taxis to Bloomsbury, they each shook hands with Rowan Rover and wished him well. Elizabeth, the last to leave, regarded him more in sorrow than in anger. "It was like Leopold and Loeb, wasn't it? You thought you were smarter than the police. You had to prove you could get away with it just once?"

"I've often thought of that," Rowan admitted truthfully. He did not add that he had never been tempted to try it.

"It stops now," she said firmly, and walked away.

Rowan stayed in the Ten Bells for another hour, smoking a pack of cigarettes and thinking about murder. It was an art for which he was grateful to have no talent whatsoever.

SEVERAL DAYS AFTER the end of the tour, Rowan Rover had reflected further on the unfortunate matters of the past few weeks and he decided that greater penance was required. After much thought and even more Scotch, he wrote a carefully worded letter to Aaron Kosminski, telling him that his niece Susan had been killed in an unfortunate traffic mishap in Whitechapel. It was an accident, he wrote, underlining the phrase twice. He was not daft enough to spell out the murder-for-hire agreement in a letter, but he hoped that his explanation of his own innocence would be clear and that Kosminski would read between the lines and realize that his orders had not been carried out. The sacrifice of the money was a small price to pay for a clear conscience, Rowan decided. Well, not a small price, but he wasn't used to having any money anyway. With his lectures and his crime writing, he could continue to scrape by as he always had, living mouth to hand.

He had not expected to receive a reply to his ostensible letter of condolence, but in mid-October an airmail letter bearing

American astronaut stamps arrived at his London postal address. It was postmarked Minneapolis. With shaking hands, not entirely attributable to a hangover, Rowan Rover tore open the envelope and read the terse reply:

Dear Mr. Rover:

I remember with pleasure our meeting at your lecture in Whitechapel.

I know that my niece Susan enjoyed her travels on your mystery tour, and we are grateful for your expression of sympathy to the family. We want you to know that we do not blame you in any way for her death, which the London police assure us was a tragic accident.

Please accept the enclosed donation from her estate for the Ripper project that we spoke of at our dinner together. I wonder if you remember how I like my steak.

Yours sincerely,
Aaron Kosminski

♦ ♦ ♦

ENCLOSED IN THE letter was a check for fifteen thousand pounds, the remainder of the agreed-upon sum for the killing. For almost thirty seconds Rowan toyed with the

400

idea of destroying the check, but a recent spate of financial ultimatums dissuaded him. After all, he reasoned, Kosminski is guiltier than I am. Why should he receive all the ill-gotten loot? He decided to send a present to Emma Smith, who was recovering nicely in Colorado, and to give some of the money to charity in Cornwall. The rest would be distributed among his needy creditors. The wages of sin, he decided, were minimal, all things considered.

The final paragraph of the letter puzzled Rowan Rover for quite some time, since he clearly remembered that he and Kosminski had *not* dined together. Their only meeting had been over drinks in the Aldgate pub. Finally the reference to the steak enlightened him, and he was able to decipher Kosminski's own encoded comment: *well done*.

The employees of G.K. HALL hope you have enjoyed this Large Print book. All our Large Print titles are designed for easy reading, and all our books are made to last. Other G.K. Hall Large Print books are available at your library, through selected bookstores, or directly from us. For more information about current and upcoming titles, please call or mail your name and address to:

G.K. HALL
PO Box 159
Thorndike, Maine 04986
800/223-6121
207/948-2962